Bruce's Fables

Bruce's Fables

Bruce Saunders

Quartet Global Books

Dedication

This book of fables is dedicated to my daughter Kaiti and my wife Laura, without whom there would be no story. And I dedicate this book to the wonderful Southwest, which I regard as my homeland.

Acknowledgements

I'm grateful to Jack Remick for all his hard work bringing this book to print and for our 35 years of friendship, to Laura for saving my emails into Word files, and to Kaiti for suggesting I write a book of fables. Huge thanks also to Thom Laz for the splendid illustrations and Dana Gaskin Wenig for editing the work. Thanks also to all my friends who suggested ideas for fables.

BRUCE SAUNDERS

BRUCE'S FABLES

1. Up the Hill

Cowboy and Coyote went up the hill to fetch a pail of water.

The well was almost dry. They lifted mostly empty buckets, got tired, and wiped sweat from their eyes.

On his way down the hill Cowboy tripped and fell. The water spilled into a large puddle.

Coyote licked it up and said, "Let's go back up to the well."

"Thanks but no, I'd rather not, I'll drink some milk tonight. "

But when the sun went down, the rain began and Coyote had an idea: Put the water bucket under the ranch house's gutter drain and soon they could drink all night.

When the bucket was full, Cowboy poured a bowlful for Coyote.

With Cowboy's own mug filled, he and Coyote sat together and watched lightning flash and brighten the dark, cloudy sky.

"Wonderful storm," Cowboy said.

"I always like it when it rains," Coyote said.

"I bet this rain will put more water down the well," Cowboy said.

"Being together is good for both of us," Coyote said, licking Cowboy's hand.

2. Runaway Sheep

A small herd of sheep escaped from a farm near the Rio Grande River. They ran away from the dog who protected them because it was very cruel. Every day he bit one of them.

Several nights later the sheep were grazing near the mountains. One of them smelled and heard the nearly silent movements of a mountain lion sneaking toward them. She warned the others by 'Baaaaaaaaa-ing' very loudly.

The very frightened sheep nestled together into the tightest possible flock.

Coyote was out hunting. He happened to be standing on a rock nearby watching them. Quickly he crouched down and sneaked around the herd in a large half circle. Every few yards he stopped, stood up, and howled as loudly as he could.

The mountain lion stopped in her tracks. One coyote could not threaten me, she thought, but several here are too many. I had better hunt elsewhere to get meat for my cubs, she said to herself as she retreated quietly.

"Thank you, coyote," a sheep 'Baaaaaaed.' "You saved one of our lives."

"You will be safer under kind human care," Coyote answered. "Let me take you to my friend the Mexican Cowboy. He will feed and protect you."

"You are wonderful," all the sheep 'Baaaaaaa-ed.'

"Not true," Coyote replied. "If there had been only one sheep here, I would have eaten you."

3. **Coyote Protects His Meat**

With four pups to feed, Coyote had to spend hours hunting each night. Coyote worked hard to feed his children.

He carried each rabbit or grouse back to his den before going out to hunt again.

One night Coyote caught two rabbits only a minute apart. Coyote could not carry both in his mouth. So he hid one under a thorn bush, and took the biggest rabbit back to his den.

When he returned, buzzards were tearing apart the meal that Coyote thought was his. With his lips pulled back and teeth snapping, he growled and charged the birds. They jumped into the sky and flew overhead, looking down at him.

There wasn't much of his rabbit left, and he could not gather enough of the remains to carry back to his hungry pups.

"What should I learn from this?" Coyote asked himself. Then a bright idea occurred to him.

Very loudly he said, "If I hide myself in the thorn bush I will be able to capture a buzzard or two. My kids will love eating bigger birds."

Above him the frightened buzzards darted away.

"I scared them off," Coyote said, starting to hunt again. "They won't steal from me again."

4. **The Cowboy and the Flea**

Cowboy had been noticing flea bites all over his body ever since the little white dog Mazzie had moved into his house. His tiny, itchy wounds got red and grew as big as thumbnails because Cowboy couldn't stop scratching himself.

"What should I do?" Cowboy asked Coyote, one evening.

"Put up with it," was Coyote's answer. "That's what I have always done."

"I'm not you. I can't bear being bitten constantly by fleas."

"I'll have to help you then."

That evening Coyote took Cowboy outside, leaving the door open behind him. In the nearby dry arroyo bed, Cowboy took off his clothes. Coyote sniffed through all of the clothes, lapping up every flea he found. Then as Cowboy sat and turned, Coyote licked his body all over, and went through his hair.

"There. I got every one of them, "Coyote said. "They aren't my favorite meal."

"But I am theirs," Cowboy replied.

Back in his house little Mazzie's white fur was wet. She was sitting and not scratching, looking happier than Cowboy had seen her for a long time.

"While I was taking care of you many of my coyote friends came in to lick her clean," Coyote said. "They searched for fleas and their eggs everywhere in your house and swallowed all they found. You and Mazzie will be all right now."

"What can I do to repay you and your friends?" Cowboy asked.

"Put some food out every night. That's a good way to return the favor."

"Will your coyote friends eat tortillas, enchiladas, tacos and frijoles?"

"If they get hungry enough. They would probably prefer eating fleas instead."

5. Neglect is Hard on Others

Celesto's mother kept calling Cowboy because she wanted him to come over and see her. Cowboy, who always tried to please his friends, kept going—but he was growing tired of walking back and forth the three miles to her home.

So, he stopped answering his phone.

Which turned out to be a terrible mistake for him and for her. Celesto's mother had lifted a pot of boiling water off her stove. Her hands were slippery with oil she had been rubbing onto a chicken breast. She dropped the pot and burned both of her feet badly. She called Cowboy many times, desperate for him to come over and help her.

When he didn't answer the phone she made up her mind to never see him again.

Soon after she stopped phoning him, Cowboy started to miss her. As days went by he missed her more and more.

He began calling her.

He was very disappointed and then distressed when she never answered.

Ignoring others can be very bad for me too, he thought as he put down the phone.

6. The Race to Salerno Rock

Coyote was sitting on the Mexican Cowboy's porch telling him about something odd that had happened the night before.

"Another Coyote has a den close to mine. She and I sometimes hunt together. Last night she took the first rabbit and went running back to her den. She is very fast. But when I caught my prey and trotted back to my den, I got there before her. I am the speediest coyote on the planet."

"I can move pretty fast too," Cowboy said.

"But there's no way you can run faster than me," Coyote said.

"Sure I can," Cowboy answered.

"Prove it to me!" Coyote said confidently.

"All right. Let's have a long race tomorrow. Let's run from my barn to the big rock at the edge of Salerno Canyon and back. That will be just over nine miles."

"I will win the race before you get to the rock," Coyote says confidently.

"We'll see," Cowboy replied, with a glint in his eye.

Next morning at the barn's door, Coyote and Cowboy crouched down. Cowboy counted backwards, "Five, four, three, two, one, Go!" Coyote ran away so fast he was out of sight in a few moments.

Trotting after him a small distance, Cowboy turned around, returned to the barn, opened a stall door and saddled his beloved stallion Turco.

Five minutes later they galloped away toward the turnaround rock.

Less than an hour later, Cowboy was back in the barn, feeding Turco after unsaddling him. A panting Coyote limped in to the barn and collapsed onto the stable floor.

"I am exhausted," he said. "And I'm very angry at you for not trying to race me."

"Oh, I raced you all right. And I won. I rode Turco to the rock and back. It was a quick and easy ride for the two of us."

"You cheated!" Coyote said angrily. "I will never trust you again."

"Please don't do that. I didn't cheat. I would not have raced on Turco if you had asked me to try beating you on my own two feet. I used my imagination to beat you."

"Clever!" Coyote said marveling. "You are right. Good imagining can help competitors win any race."

7. Eating Different Foods Does Not Change Us

Cowboy had trouble figuring out how much of what types of food to put out every night for animals he was feeding. It bothered him too that some animals eat only during the day, and others eat only at night.

"Why can't they all get together and eat after I put out their food?" he asked Coyote.

"Because then many of them will eat each other," Coyote answered.

"But they don't need to eat each other if I keep feeding them." Cowboy said.

"I don't mean to be cruel, but eating each other tastes better and is better for us than the food you put out," Coyote said.

"Is there any way I can put out food that tastes better and is better for my hungry friends than eating each other?" Cowboy asked.

"You want to change our nature," Coyote said. "We all like being who we are. You have no right to make us into different creatures."

"So I shouldn't mess with God's designs?"

"Not unless it is in your nature," Coyote said grinning. "Now, please feed me."

8. Each to Her Own

When he was a young, inexperienced adult, Coyote sneaked incautiously into a nearby town early one evening to discover what he might find there to eat. Cars passed by on the street and the sidewalks were full of children playing. He tried to move invisibly from house to house, but there weren't very many bushes to hide in. In one front yard, the dogs indoors smelled him and barked loudly. They were disappointed that their owners made them be quiet because they couldn't smell the nearing coyote themselves.

"I'd better get away from here," Coyote thought. He was trying to sneak out of town when two men approached him from opposite sides, one holding a big net. Before he could dodge them they threw the net over his head and caught him. One of the men picked him up and carried him into an empty garage nearby. They pulled the garage door down and left him there. Coyote clawed his way out of the net and explored the garage for ten minutes. He felt frustrated that there was no way to escape.

Ten minutes later a door leading inside the house opened, and a woman came out carrying a big dish of dog food. "Don't feel bad," she said kindly. "This bowl of dog food is to keep you happy until later this evening. Then we'll take you away from our town and release you."

When she went back into the kitchen Coyote sniffed and began sampling the food he'd been given. It surprised him how tasty and filling it was. With his head inside the bowl, he gulped down the wonderful food. He was startled when a small, fuzzy white dog came into the garage through the open door and sat down in front of him.

"That's my bowl but I'm glad to share it with you," she said.

"I'll step back so you can eat," Coyote said.

"No, you finish it please. Do you like the food they buy for me?"

"I didn't expect I would, but I do like it very much," Coyote answered.

"Maybe then you should let my owners adopt you. They are very nice people."

"Thank you," Coyote said, lying down and burping. "But I need to live outdoors. Being inside would never work for me."

"Even if the food is better and you don't have to hunt for it?"

"You've got an excellent point, but I believe that the way we grow up is the way we want to live the rest of our lives."

"You are right!" the little white dog said excitedly. "I couldn't bear living outdoors by myself and having to always hunt for my next meal."

"Each to her own," Coyote said burping. "And if we meet up away from your town, I'll catch some game for you to try."

9. Accidents Can Turn Enemies Into Friends

One early spring day, mesa land next to the Cowboy's was sold to a nearby farmer. The farmer drove his tractor across Cowboy's property onto his land, lowered the curved blades behind the drive wheels, and began to plow his mesa.

When Cowboy returned from a ride on the magnificent mustang Turco, he saw the tractor's tracks in front of his house and heard the machine's unmuffled engine roaring. Cowboy was furious and rode Turco over to the new owner's property and made the tractor driver stop plowing. Cowboy got off Turco, the farmer climbed down from his tractor seat, and they began talking.

The farmer wanted to meet his new neighbor and become friends with him. But Cowboy was so furious about the farmer's presence and how he plowed up what Coyote had always taken to be his mesa that the farmer realized there was nothing he could say that would calm him.

Cowboy told him never to cross his property again, and never plow the mesa next to his property again either. The farmer nodded and tried to shake hands with Cowboy, but Cowboy turned his back on him and got on Turco to ride away.

Telling his wife about what had happened that evening, she said insistently to the farmer, "You should have ordered him off your property and never ride his horse onto it again." The farmer nodded, but wasn't sure he agreed.

He hired workers from Mexico to ready his property for planting. They used shovels and axes to clear the mesa and then used small gasoline plows to ready the field. Cowboy had a fence put up separating the two properties, but he enjoyed leaning over it and talking in Spanish with the workers from his homeland. While the Cowboy was out riding most days, the farmer used his big tractor to hurriedly plant the big cleared property with a mix of crops. The farmer had a well dug on the side of the new farm farthest from Cowboy's land, and his workers used giant sprinklers to water the growing crops.

One day before the crops were ready to pick, Cowboy was returning home and saw the farmer's tractor stopped in the middle of the dusty, red dirt road. There were tools lying beside the tractor but no sign of its operator. Riding further, ahead of him the road dipped out of sight into the tiny canyon of a usually dry arroyo. Coming over the hill top, Cowboy saw the farmer sitting on the small bank at the bottom, with one of his legs stretched out into the small stream caused by last night's heavy rain. He rode up to the man, leaned down over him, and said, "You are being lazy now, and you are contaminating my arroyo."

The farmer's face was flushed and the water flowing away from him was very red, Cowboy noticed, his anger vanishing. "Are you hurt?" he asked, getting off Turco.

"Yes. I cut my leg badly while I was trying to take apart the tractor's generator, which stopped working. It was greasy and my screwdriver slipped while I pressing down hard on a screw I was trying to turn."

Cowboy asked the farmer to show him the wound. It was a bad one, he could tell. Cowboy took off the bandana around his neck, folded it into a bandage, and tied it as tightly as he could over the farmer's bleeding wound. He helped the farmer stand up and, with a great deal of effort, managed to lift him onto Turco's saddle. Putting his left foot in the empty stirrup, he swung up behind his saddle, reached around for the reins, and set off at a fast trot into the nearby town.

Twenty minutes later he was helping the farmer off the horse in front of the town's only physician. A nurse inside had seen him ride up with the pale farmer leaning on the horse's neck before him. She came outside with a wheelchair. The two of them helped the farmer get off the horse. She took her patient indoors, who turned around and waved before he was pushed inside the clinic.

Two months later the field next to him was filled again with migrant workers harvesting crops. Next afternoon the farmer drove up in his truck and began unloading boxes of corn, strawberries, onions, potatoes, carrots, radishes and many other fresh crops onto Cowboy's porch.

"I know you feed local wild animals every night. These boxes are filled with food for you and them. I owe you more than I can every repay," the farmer said hesitantly, fearing Cowboy's answer.

But Cowboy went to him, shook the farmer's hand, and pulled him into a light hug. "You, my good friend, have taught me that we would all go hungry if were not for farmers and their workers. I'm glad to have you for a neighbor."

"And I am glad to be your friend," the farmer said, sitting down in a chair on the porch.

"Thank you for your gifts." "Now, coffee or soda pop?" Cowboy replied.

"Either, as long as I can have your company too," the farmer said. "Getting along with neighbors is essential in the farming business."

10. The Dandelions and the Flowers

Cowboy had a small patch of grass behind his house, which he cut regularly with a hand mower. Cece, a woman friend of his, who had moved to New Mexico from back east, loved the greenery of the tiny lawn and asked Cowboy for permission to plant and care for a bed a bed of flowers.

"Just blooming cactuses?" he asked.

"No, I want dahlias, tulips, roses, irises, and lilies. Not the asters or cactus flowers that grow wild on your mesa."

Cowboy allowed her to plant whatever she liked of course, and soon there was a lovely tiny garden next to his grass. When her flower plants began to blossom, she cut them and put vases of attractive flower mixes in the living and dining rooms.

Initially not liking these, after a week or two Cowboy got used to the attractive bouquets. But there was one thing he didn't like. He wanted to see a mesa flower or two in each vase. Next time before he mowed, Cowboy knelt down and snipped several dandelions, which he put on the flagstaff patio before cutting grass. When Cece was away, Cowboy slipped one or two dandelions into each bouquet. Now he enjoyed looking at the flowers even more.

That night however, Cece removed the dandelions from the vases and pitched them into the garbage. When he got up next morning and was eating breakfast Cowboy noticed that his flowers were missing from the vases. "Why did you throw them out?" he asked Cece.

"Because dandelions aren't attractive. I like beautiful flowers. Dandelions are just weeds you mow with the grass. I can't put weeds in my vases."

That afternoon Cowboy picked many more dandelions, brought them inside, and arranged them in two drinking glasses, half-filled with water. When Cece returned later she was astonished to see these sitting next to her vases.

"You look at yours and I will look at mine," Cowboy said smugly. "We can put a sheet of paper between them, if you like."

"No!" Cece said, hugging Cowboy. "You got used to my flowers. Now I must get used to yours."

11. Who is the Gift Giver Here?

Cowboy was riding Turco up Salerno Canyon when he heard yipping and chewing from around the bend ahead of him. Climbing out of the saddle and leading Turco, Cowboy stealthily approached the bend.

Dropping down on his hands and knees, he looked over a rock and saw a puma and Coyote eating a deer carcass together.

"Hello," Cowboy said softly, standing up with his hands open to show he wasn't armed. "How is your dinner going?"

"Fine," said Coyote after swallowing. "I saw a jeep hit this deer. The driver didn't stop. I disapprove of that."

"If he'd stopped he might have taken the deer away with him and we wouldn't have a meal to share," the puma said.

"So the driver left the dinner for you," Cowboy replied. "That was kind of him."

"He was frightened, not kind," the puma said back. "He didn't want to be arrested for hitting a deer."

"Either way it was good for both of you," the Cowboy said.

"Either way it was bad for the deer," Coyote said back.

"Could he have meant to give himself to you?" Cowboy asked.

"No one wants to give himself away to be eaten," Puma answered.

"Then who is the gift giver here?" Cowboy asked.

"The jeep," Coyote answered.

12. Sneaky Humans Can be Good for Snakes

There were always a number of rattlesnakes around the Mexican Cowboy's run-down place. One even lived under his porch. Cowboy trusted the snakes to go about their business, but never to bite him. Or any of his visitors.

Late one morning Coyote stopped by the Cowboy's to pass on some unwelcome news. "There are two snake hunters coming up the arroyo," he said. "They carrying bags filled with rattlers."

"If they come onto my property they are going to have a big problem," Cowboy replied, getting out of his rocking chair. Cowboy went inside to his kitchen and loaded a big plastic bag with soft drinks, potato chips, fritos, and candy bars.

Carrying the bag, Cowboy and Coyote walked down to the arroyo. Cowboy put the food down on a high bank toward the middle of his property. Then walked along along the arroyo until he came to the edge of his property.

In a few minutes the snake catchers had worked their way up to him. Cowboy introduced himself and said, "It is wonderful what you are doing. You'll keep me safer. But you guys look tired and hot. I have a bagful of drinks and snacks where I usually sit and munch. Want to join me?"

"Sure," one of the snake hunters. "Is it all right if we leave our bags here?"

"Of course, as long as they are tied up so the snakes can't escape," Cowboy said.

The snake hunters tied their bags tightly and followed the Cowboy to the bag of snacks on the high bank of the arroyo. They sat down with their legs over the bank, Cowboy passed the food and drinks around, and the three of them had a wonderful time talking. About an hour later the happy snackers got up.

"It's wonderful what you did for us," one of them said. "If we see any rattlers here we'll snatch them for you."

"Thanks," Cowboy answered. "I'm glad I had company with my lunch today." They shook hands, and the snake catchers departed to pick up their bags.

Cowboy was picking up empty bottles and bags and putting them into a sack when one of the snake catchers came running back, panting heavily. "Our bags of snakes have disappeared. Somebody must have taken them!"

"Oh, I'm so sorry. Any idea who might have done this?"

"Probably it was one of those stupid people who don't want us to catch and kill rattlers."

"Maybe if you hurry back to your car you can spot them and get your snakes back," Cowboy said.

"Good idea. We'll do it," the man said and hurried away.

Late that evening, when he was certain he was alone, Cowboy crawled under his porch and pulled out the bags of snakes Coyote had dragged there. Carrying them to the edge of his property he opened the bags and released the snakes.

Before they vanished they coiled, and without rattling, they seemed to bow in gratitude to him. "Take care, guys," Cowboy said as they slithered away. "And avoid humans if you can."

The departing snakes stopped, turned, and waved their heads at the Cowboy.

"Every species has lots of good guys," Cowboy said to himself, walking back to the porch.

13. **What is the Best Thing to Do?**

A bee was very proud of herself. "I can fly, I can visit hundreds of flowers every day and take pollen back to my hive, and I can defend myself by stinging. No insect is more perfect than bees," she said.

But one day while she was flying between flowers on a bush she was snared in a spider's web. She struggled endlessly but only entangled herself more. She was alarmed when the spider climbed to her side.

"Let me go please and I promise not to sting you," she pleaded.

"You may be my next meal," spider answered. "Why should I free you?"

"Because I am a bee, I can fly, I can carry pollen back to the hive, and I get along perfectly with my silent hive mates. You are alone, you stay in one place, you can't fly, and you don't work hard for your meals. Because I am superior to you I should be set free."

"I can weave giant, artistic, intricate webs," the spider said.

"And I can help make large, comfortable bee hives," the bee replied.

"When I was small I could fly in a light breeze, and I didn't need wings to do it," the spider said.

"I can defend myself by stinging," the bee said.

"And you die after doing this," said spider. "When I sting, only my victim dies."

"I can escape most attackers," the bee said.

"And I can defend myself better than you can."

"All right," the bee said. "I give up." Go ahead and eat me."

"No," said the spider, moving in to free her. "This has been the most interesting conversation I've ever had. You defended yourself by engaging me. Talking with someone is always better for me than being alone. Most of us can't survive long without friends."

"Thank you!" the bee said. "I'll come back and see you every day."

As the bee flew back to her hive she said to herself, "It would be best for me to spend more time talking with others. The spider made me more perfect in a way I did not expect."

14. **Two of Life's Big Rules**

Late one cloudy evening, animals were busy enjoying all the different kinds of meals Cowboy had put out for them. Each species of animal had its own mini-territory staked out and stayed inside it. It was safe for all, and meant the Mexican Cowboy was willing to continue feeding everyone at the same time.

This evening however a wolf had come to the night feed for the first time. Cowboy had spotted the wolf and gone into his kitchen to put together some food for her.

But the wolf thought a delicious meal was already before her. She ran through the mix of eating animals and grabbed a nibbling rabbit by his neck. She was about to swing him back and forth until he was dead when the bear beside her looked up and roared.

"You can't do that here," the bear said, moving to attack the wolf. "If one of us eats another here the Cowboy will stop serving us these meals. He is determined to protect defenseless animals."

Frightened, the wolf dropped the rabbit, who wasn't injured, and who hopped back to his friends and began nibbling again. The wolf wasn't sure whether to run away, stay and defend herself, or perhaps wait for another chance to eat some of the available prey.

"Be patient. Cowboy will feed you," the bear said. "Just sit and wait a few minutes."

"And I can't eat him either?" the wolf asked the bear.

"Me and my friends, the coyotes and the pumas, will kill you if you to try to hurt our Cowboy. We defend all the animals while we are here."

"Staying in one place and waiting to be fed hasn't been right for me since I was a pup."

"Doing the right thing at each new moment is best for each of us," the bear said. "Look over by the arroyo," he continued. "Cowboy's putting out a pan of food for you. If you do what's best for all of us, you will go eat it."

"Thank you," the wolf said before trotting away. "Learning what you just taught me will be better for me in the long run than even having Cowboy feed me."

"Learn and eat. Those are two of life's big rules," the bear replied.

15. Turco and His Rescuer

When Turco was a wild mustang and the leader of his herd, at night before falling asleep his horses would talk about many things. "One thing is critical for us," Turco said to them on a warm starlit evening, "and this is never to allow ourselves to be captured by humans. If this happens, we give up our freedom."

"I wouldn't want that," one of his mares said. "Humans often ride up to see us on their slave horses. These poor souls cannot even graze with those bits in their mouths when riders get off them."

"Sad and so true," another mare added.

Being free was wonderful, but dangerous also. Months later unhorsed humans came by a little after eleven p.m. and, using dogs, began trying to round up every horse in the herd. Turco fought the dogs and tried to attack the humans so members of his herd could escape by galloping away in different directions. Most of them got away. But he couldn't escape himself. Turco and three other horses were captured. The humans tied ropes around the horse's necks and pulled them into a truck with stalls inside and tied them to a rail.

With the humans in the cab of the truck, the vehicle pulled away and headed south. Heinaman's Packing Plant was written in large letters on the side of the truck, Three and half hours later and exhausted, the truck driver pulled off the freeway into the tiny town of Cordoba and parked in an empty church parking lot so he and fellow workers could get some sleep. Turco and his horses whinnied softly while they were snoring.

Several hours later, the horse snatchers, needing to pee badly, climbed out of the truck and went around to the back of the church. They heard the engine of their truck start and pull out of the parking lot. Zipping up their pants while they ran, they tried to catch whoever was stealing their loaded vehicle. But it was no use, they couldn't run fast enough and had to watch it head out of town.

Back at his ranch, Cowboy parked the truck and opened the back doors. He put down the ramp, went inside, untied each horse, and invited them to follow him outside. At first only Turco did. Looking around and seeing no signs of the humans who had kidnapped him, Turco whinnied commandingly. A moment later, the other three horses walked down the ramp looking around intently.

"You are all free," Cowboy said. "Go back where you came from, and avoid humans if you can."

Cowboy got back into the truck and drove it to a filling station close to his ranch. He left the keys in the ignition and he walked away. When he got back to his ranch only one horse was still there. "Why are you staying?" Cowboy asked.

"Because I wanted to thank you for rescuing us," Turco said in horse language.

"You are not my slave," Cowboy said. Stay as long as you want and go when you'd like."

"First, I might like to get to know you better," Turco said. "You are not a bad man."

"I don't know what you are saying, but if you stay I may want to ride you."

"We'll see about that when the time comes," Turco said. "For now, let's just try to get to know each other."

Cowboy led the horse down to his battered barn, opened the door and pointed to a stall. "Would you like to sleep here?"

"If you want me to," Turco said.

"I'll leave the barn and stall open tonight, so you can go outside and graze when you want to."

"Thank you. It has been a rough day for me. I'd like to stretch out and sleep now. Goodnight, savior," Turco whinnied.

"Good night friend," Cowboy said. "I'll buy some hay and oats for you tomorrow."

"This is one human who isn't going to take away my freedom," Turco said, lying down and closing his eyes. "I need to learn more about him before I go back to my herd. Maybe he can help wild horses stay free."

16. How to Win a State Election

It was New Mexico's brief bear hunting season. Cowboy told black bear Ursula that she could be shot by humans and asked her to hide in her cave den until the season ended.

"How will I eat then? You know bears must eat hugely before they hibernate for months."

"I'll bring food to you," Cowboy said, and started worrying how he would be able to carry the many pounds of bear food necessary up the steep trail to her den each day.

Next morning Cowboy loaded his saddlebags with bear foods, saddled his wild mustang Turco, and rode up Salerno Canyon. He dismounted where the trail began and with heavy bags over his shoulders, he struggled up the tricky climb to Ursula's den.

"Here you are," he said proudly. Ursula nuzzled Cowboy with her thanks and began eating furiously. Minutes later she looked up at Cowboy, hoping he had brought her more food. "I'm sorry," Cowboy said with open hands. "This is all I could carry."

Leaving Ursula, who was looking distressed, Cowboy carefully made his way back down the trail to Turco, who gladly carried the exhausted friend back to his cabin. The rest of the day Cowboy thought about different ways he might solve Ursula's problem.

Then a bright idea occurred to him. His sometimes friend, sometimes enemy, Mayor Howie, was a dedicated hunter. "I will tell him where Ursula is hiding if he promises to hire people to carry food up to her each day while the hunting season is taking place."

"Why would you expect me to agree to that?" Howie demanded when Cowboy phoned him that evening.

"Because we will phone reporters who will eagerly write stories about you protecting bears during hunting season."

"I'm a hunter, I won't do that."

"When TV stations follow you and your workers up the trail to feed Ursula, millions of viewers will watch. Fellow hunters will hate you, but all the non-hunters in the state will praise you and remember you. If you want to run for governor, this will get you elected."

"And if I just shoot Ursula in her den instead?"

"That will be a bigger story still! And you will never win another election after it."

"You are smarter than I thought, Cowboy. I will do it."

"And you are a craftier politician than I thought. You may turn out to be an excellent governor."

"Satisfying the public is what good politicians do after finding ways to win elections."

"Protecting animals is what I do," Cowboy said proudly.

17. Calli Wants a Bowl of Milk

In Cowboy's barn, Calli the cat was good at doing things. She could hide on beams and drop onto sparrows flying past to catch one for her dinner. Even in the driest time of year she could always find water to drink. But she had never figured out how to get herself a bowl of milk, a drink she always wanted to try.

Cowboy allowed Calli to come into his house whenever she wanted. She purred against his pants leg one day when he opened his refrigerator, looked up, but no milk bottle. She was frustrated.

But when the itinerant priest Father Gallapo began staying with Cowboy there was milk in the refrigerator because the priest wanted it in his coffee.

One morning when the Priest was at Cowboy's house he put down his half-filled cup on the porch. While the Priest was talking to Cowboy, Calli sneaked over, reached her tongue down into the cup, and tasted the coffee. She spat it back into the cup. "Milk with coffee is horrible for cats," she snorted. Then an idea came to her.

Every time Father Gallapo sat on the porch with his cup, Calli was with him, purring, being stroked, but always moving her head over his coffee cup and looking down into it. "Why is she doing this?" the priest asked Cowboy.

"Probably because she's a cat and cat's always want a bowl of milk," Cowboy answered.

"Let's see if you are right," Father Gallapo said getting up and going to the kitchen. He returned carrying a bowl filled with fresh milk and put it down on the porch next to his chair.

Calli watched him appreciatively and, when the priest was seated and sipping his coffee again, she strolled over to the bowl. Gently she put her tongue into the milk. It tasted wonderful to her. She lapped up most of the milk and then leaped onto the priest's legs to purr and thank him for doing this for her.

"See, it's what she wanted," Cowboy said.

"And it's what she made us do," the priest replied. "I'll keep giving her some."

As she jumped down to lap up the rest of her milk Calli thought to herself, invention can often be done best by manipulating others.

18. Becoming Cowboy's Supervisor

Mazzie, the small fuzzy white dog living with Cowboy, was enjoying her life. Her original owners had driven her out onto the mesa, led her out of the car, gotten back in, and driven away. She barked for them to return to get her, but they kept going.

Finding food on the mesa was very hard for Mazzie, who'd never had to hunt for her meals. She was starving when one of Cowboy's friends spotted her and brought her to live with him. Now Mazzie enjoyed spending hours in the barn with Turco and time with Cowboy was nice too. But she found herself missing being on the mesa and exploring. She wanted more in her life.

One day in the barn Mazzie asked Turco how he managed to get taken care of constantly, yet could still go everywhere with his friend Cowboy.

"Carrying him is work I do. He takes care of me and I go places with him."

"Could I do it too?" Mazzie asked back.

"You can't carry much," Turco said staring at the small white dog. "But see if you can think up a way to help him."

Mazzie pondered this problem for days until a thought occurred to her. "My nose is terrific. When I come to animal droppings I can sniff and tell if they have been getting enough to eat. Cowboy feeds all animals here. But he doesn't know if each is getting enough food."

That afternoon, instead of going to the stable, Mazzie slipped under the fenced pasture and began wandering the mesa, sniffing at animal droppings. That evening when Cowboy took pans of foods outside for animals he was feeding, Mazzie stayed outdoors afterwards and connected the foods in each pan to the animals eating these.

Next evening when Cowboy was putting food into each kind of animal's pans Mazzie barked when Cowboy filled the badger's pan only a third full. Cowboy looked at her to figure out why she was doing this. Mazzie put her head over the pan and backed away whining, then put her head over it again,and backed away yipping.

"You think I need to feed the badgers more?" Cowboy asked. Mazzie nodded her head up and down and tried to lick Cowboy's hand.

Checking badgers' dropping for the next week she saw they were doing much better. But the raccoons were now going hungry. Easily she persuaded Cowboy to put more food into their pan.

Next afternoon Mazzie was sitting on the porch with Cowboy. She was loving her life now. He reached over and patted her, saying, "Better go out onto the mesa again now and check on the animals' droppings."

As she trotted away Mazzie said to herself, "Now I'm his supervisor, and that got me onto the mesa again."

19. A Grouse Hen is Protected

Mazzie was getting to know Calli after she moved in with the Mexican Cowboy. There were many things they could not agree about, but surprisingly they often had the same opinions.

"I catch and eat birds and mice," Calli said.

"The Cowboy feeds me, but you have to feed yourself any way you can. I do feel sorry for the birds and mice you eat."

"Sometimes I do too," Calli replied, "but only after I am full."

One day a sage hen grouse appeared in the barn. She gathered some scattered straw on the stable floor and in an empty stall made herself a nest. Several weeks later she had three chicks in her nest.

Calli had been studying the sage hen for days, discovering oddly that she liked her. With hungry chicks to feed, the mother hen often had to leave her nest and go outside to collect food for them.

One day though Mazzie burst into the barn and warned Calli to keep the grouse from going outside. "There is a hungry coyote looking for game out there," Mazzie said. "If you let her go out she will be snatched and eaten."

"And her chicks would die too, because we couldn't feed them," Calli said. "All right. I'll keep her in here until you tell me it is safe to let her leave."

The sage hen was desperate to find food for her hungry chicks. She tried every way she could to get out of her stall. But Calli blocked her every time she tried. The sage hen was trapped and she knew it. She feared that Calli wanted only to eat her, and then her chicks.

"But then, why hasn't she attacked us?" the hen wondered.

An hour later Mazzie trotted into the barn with a smile on her face. "The coyote's gone. She couldn't find any game here and won't come back again."

"Thank you," Calli said back, moving away from the chicks and their mother. "Keeping this vigorous hen trapped inside the barn has been hard. I am hungry. And you don't like me to hunt either. Will you ask the Mexican Cowboy to feed me cat food instead?"

"I will find a way to get him to do it," Mazzie said, gratefully. "All animals living inside the barn should be protected."

20. Do Women Like Cats?

Calli the cat had a strong preference for men, in part because the Mexican Cowboy was the person who always fed her now. Other males often paid her some attention too. Once when she was walking by his legs, Turco stretched his head down and pressed his wet lips against her head. Calli took this as a horse's kiss. Whenever Cowboy's friend Father Gallapo came to the stable to pat Turco, he would sit down on a bench and lift her onto his lap. Even the male Coyote gently nuzzled her when she sat in Cowboy's lap on the porch.

But every time a female human came to Cowboy's ranch, Calli would reach out to her in one or another way cats have -- and be disappointed. Thelma always kept a Bible or purse in her lap and pushed Calli away if she tried to climb up. Another woman visitor was so intent on her own talking that she ignored Calli totally, even if Calli rubbed her crossed legs. Cowboy's dear friend Cece always focused on him, or on Mazzie, the dog she'd found and given to Cowboy.

"Women don't like cats," Calli said to herself. "And therefore I won't like women." She began avoiding women and hiding in the barn whenever a woman came to see Cowboy.

One night when Calli was keeping Turco company in the barn, Coyote passed along to Cowboy something she had recently told him. "Calli thinks that human women don't like cats and now will hide when they are here. I think she's very wrong about that. Can you think of something we can do to change her mind?"

Cowboy thought a few moments, then told Coyote his idea.

Two mornings later Cowboy went down to the barn with cat food in a picnic basket. After Calli had eaten he rudely picked her up, put her into the basket, and fastened both lids. He could feel her jouncing around inside the basket as he carried her back toward the house where a car was waiting. Cowboy opened the back door and put the basket onto the back seat.

Ten minutes later Calli felt someone lift her basket out of the car and carry it into a house. The basket lid opened and Calli looked out. What she saw made her duck down and hide inside again. Thelma and Cece and three other women were sitting around a dining table having a light lunch.

Thelma reached into the basket, gently lifted Calli out, and held and stroked her. Cece went to the kitchen and brought out a bowl of wonderful cat food. She put it on the table before Thelma and went back to her chair. The women talked for over an hour, looking often at Calli, petting her, and passing her from lap to lap.

Calli had never had a more wonderful experience. Finally one of the women, a very sweet young lady, gently lifted Calli back into the basket, and with a lid open so Calli could watch, carried her outside and drove her back to Cowboy's place. There she lifted the basket out of the car, carried it up to the porch, and lifted Calli out.

Cowboy, Coyote, and Father Gallapo were talking intently back and forth with one another. Cowboy merely nodded when the nice young lady put Calli back onto the porch. "I'm back!" she mewed happily.

The men ignored her.

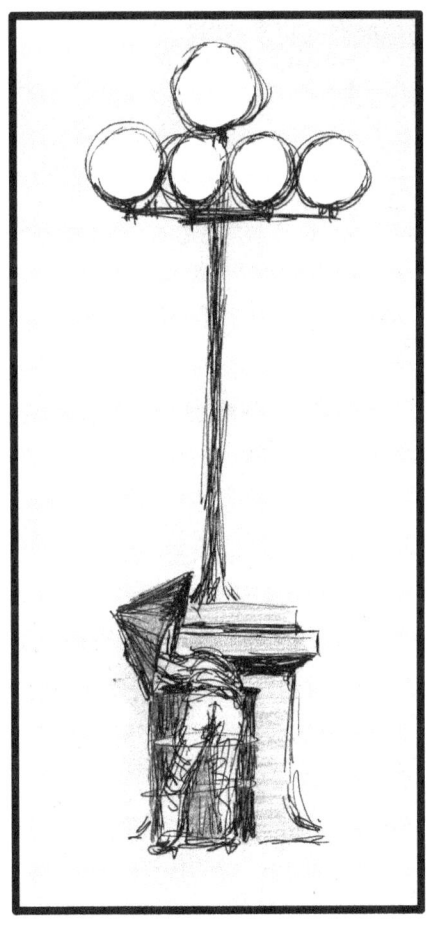

"You see," the woman who'd brought her said, picking her up again and ruffling the fur around her neck, "Men do their own thing too. Everyone's attention can be in different places when we see them again."

21. Taking Care of Others Helps Us and Them

Cowboy hadn't had a job for more than twenty years. He'd gotten by as animals do, by taking advantage of opportunities that pop up every day if we keep trying to fulfill our needs. But Cowboy was never able to focus just on himself. Taking care of others was his thing and he was proud of how many animals he'd been able to feed.

The Mexican Cowboy did help out humans as well, including the mayor of nearby Cordoba. But the two men didn't like or trust each other. Mayor Howie kept insisting that Cowboy should quit figuring out how to feed animals and instead find himself a job.

"Taking care of yourself is the only thing humans need to do," he insisted.

"I take care of myself by helping others," Cowboy insisted back. "And Cordoba will have a better mayor if you start doing more of the same thing."

22. **Quantity over Quality**

When he first started feeding wild animals on his property, Cowboy hunted for an affordable means of getting meaningful quantities of food for them. In Cordoba's tiny one room library, Cowboy read in an encyclopedia about foods that most animals living on the mesa around him preferred. He spent days struggling to come up with affordable ways to get these particular foods for his animal friends, but in most instances none existed.

So, Cowboy started going to Cordoba's garbage dump, where people threw away bags of garbage. The small town's one grocery store threw out all the vegetables and meats it could not sell by the date on the package. Early each evening he spotted and grabbed everything useful he could find.

He also collected sacks of garbage thrown away by the city's only restaurant, a crummy diner.

Back at his cabin in front of his porch, Cowboy dumped the contents of these bags on the ground and used a small shovel to sort food onto tin pans that he hoped would appeal to different kinds of animals. Or at least contents they would eat. The best meats he set apart for his friend Coyote.

Late one evening Coyote sat with Cowboy on the porch. Cowboy heard the many animals he was feeding making noises he couldn't understand. "Are they enjoying the foods I put out?" he asked Coyote.

"No. They are grunting about the crap you offer them," Coyote answered. "They want quality food like they are used to."

"If I had the money I'd buy the quality food they want," Cowboy said. "But for now, providing quantity over quality is my thing."

"For feeding so many hungry animals, putting quantity over quality is a great thing to be doing," Coyote answered.

23. **Giving Freedom to Others is Good for Us Too**

Cowboy fed and watered his magnificent wild mustang friend every day, and usually put him out in the meadow to exercise and graze. Occasionally though, the Mexican Cowboy had business to take care of that kept him away from his ratty cabin for hours at a time. Penned in his stall, Turco got restless. He paced, stomped, whinnied, and sometimes kicked noisily at the wallboards. The birds and other animals living in the barn with him found it distracting and annoying.

"Keep it down," Calli the cat said, when Turco's noisemaking kept her from focusing on hunting for birds and mice.

A raccoon who often nestled in Turco's hay and nibbled left-over goodies felt endangered by Turco's recklessness, and climbed up the barn wall to find a safer place to be. A pair of finches who enjoyed being on Turco's back and keeping him company were frightened also when Turco was so restless, and flew away from him.

"We have to find a way to solve this," Mazzie, the fuzzy little white dog said to Calli. "Turco deserves to be as free as we are."

Late one morning when Cowboy hadn't even come to feed him, Turco was constantly rearing and loudly whinnying in his stall.

"We've got to help him get outside," Mazzie said to Calli. "Let's see if we can open his stall door."

Mazzie stretched up on her hind legs and tried to lift and slide the latch to the right. It kept slipping out of her mouth. Calli walked across along the top of the narrow stall door and reached down with her left paw to try to lift and move the latch. She almost succeeded. Frustrated, she jumped down.

Then, with Turco watching expectantly, the biggest of his two finch friends, her wings flapping furiously, hovered above the latch. Tilting backward and gripping the latch with two of the three digits on her extended right foot, she managed to lift and slide the lift aside. Exhausted, she landed on Turco's back for a few moments' rest.

"It's unlocked. Push open your stall door," Mazzie barked.

Worrying whether Cowboy would approve, Turco lowered his head and shoved open his stall and came out. Climbing onto a nearby bench, Mazzie asked Turco to stand beside him and jumped onto the stallion's back.

"Let's go out to the meadow and play," Mazzie barked. Turco looked over his shoulder, gave a grateful neigh, and the two of them disappeared out the open barn door.

"Giving freedom to others can be good for us," Calli said, getting ready to hunt again.

"And my giving freedom to Turco stopped you from trying to capture us," the smaller of the two finches cheeped.

"Gifts of freedom won't last forever," hungry Calli replied, sticking out her tongue and licking her mouth.

24. **A Good Person Rescues an Evil Man**

One wintry afternoon, with snow flurries dusting the red caliche clay of the mesa, Cowboy rode Turco down from the mountains. When he saw Mayor Howie's well-preserved 1953 Cadillac parked at the edge of an unpaved road, the Mexican Cowboy debated with himself about what Howie was up to now. "I'd better ride over and see," he said to himself. "He's probably up to something I'll need to deal with."

Cordoba's squatty little Mayor watched Cowboy approaching, mentally kicking himself. "It's bad enough my Caddy crapped out on me," he said to himself. "Now I've got to put up with that mental jerk who calls himself a 'cowboy.' Every working cowboy I know always obeys top-down orders. But this so-called Cowboy only resists me."

"What's wrong with your polished junk-heap?" Cowboy shouted at the Mayor through the rolled up car window.

Mayor Howie opened the door but wouldn't get out of his car. "The engine stopped running. And the electric windows won't go up and down now. I forgot to bring my cell phone with me. All I can do now is wait for a car to come my way."

"Cars seldom use this road," the Cowboy said. "You won't get any out here when it is snowing."

"Then I'll either stay in my car or walk back to town."

"No you won't," Cowboy said. "Get out of your car and I'll take you back to Cordoba."

"I'm not getting onto your wild mustang!" the Mayor replied.

"And I'm not going to leave you out here in a snowstorm," Cowboy said back. "Get up on your car's bumper and we'll get you aboard Turco."

"No!" said the Mayor.

"Do I have to punch you and knock you out to carry you back to Cordoba?"

"I'll run away if you try that!"

"And I will chase you and dive off Turco and pin you to the ground."

"All right, I give up," said the Mayor, standing up and putting out his hands together as though he expected to be handcuffed. Ten minutes later Turco was trotting toward Cordoba with Mayor Howie bouncing up and down behind Cowboy.

"Hold onto me," Cowboy ordered.

"I don't want to ever touch you. You are grubby," the Mayor replied.

"Well then, keep falling off until you change you mind."

A minute or two later, after he almost bounced off once, Mayor Howie changed his mind. He took hold of the back of Cowboy's belt. Half an hour later they made it safely into the tiny city.

"Okay, get off here," the Cowboy said, reining Turco in in front of the Mayor's office. He grabbed the Mayor's arm and kept him from falling as he clumsily climbed off Turco. "I don't expect you will want to give Turco a hug for bringing you into town."

"Wouldn't think of it," Mayor Howie said, turning his back and marching away.

Next day Cordoba's only police car pulled into Cowboy's yard, and Frank Corso, the town's sole policeman got out and knocked on Cowboy's door.

"He's going to arrest me for rescuing the Mayor," Cowboy said to himself, opening the door.

"Hi Cowboy," Corso said. "Come with me to the car."

Angry as the dickens at himself for trying to help the evil Mayor, Cowboy followed Corso out to the squad car. Corso opened the back door and Cowboy was about to get in when he noticed the seat was filled with packages.

"What are those for?" Cowboy asked?

"They're presents for you and Turco that Mayor Howie wanted me to buy and deliver. "You rescued him yesterday and he wants to repay you."

"So," says Cowboy, "evil people buy gifts for good guys who try to help them."

"You got it," Corso said back. "Even the worst of evil guys cannot be evil all of the time."

"I bet doing kind things makes evil people hate themselves," the Cowboy said.

"That's one thing you got right," the policeman said back to him. "And remember, good people do evil things too occasionally."

25. **There are Different Ways of Joining People Up**

One day Cowboy did something unusual. He strapped on his 1953 Hamilton wristwatch before he went outside to water his recent plantings. At Coyote's suggestion, the Mexican Cowboy had planted a number of New Mexico native trees and plants on different parts of the mesa on his property. Coyote told him that doing this would attract a broader spectrum of native New Mexican animals, reptiles, birds, and insects and give him new thrills feeding living beings.

Cowboy had a hose several hundred yards long now, and he had wisely put his new plants and trees within reach of it. That morning the Mexican Cowboy spent more than an hour watering plants and trees within the wide half circle his hose could reach. Sitting in his rocker and sipping ice tea back on his porch, Cowboy was startled when he looked at his left wrist and found his gold wristwatch missing. "Darn, I'll have to go search for it," he said, getting up.

For an hour and a half Cowboy trekked over his partly replanted mesa, but could not spot his watch anywhere. "I need help searching," Cowboy said to himself. Fifteen minutes later he came out of the barn with the little matted white-haired dog Mazzie and slinking Calli cat behind him. The search began once more. Mazzie sniffed Cowboy's wrist where the watch had been, and then slowly moved wherever her furiously sniffing nose took her. Calli used her eyes to search for Cowboy's watch, but her motions were irregular and cat-like.

"There's no way those two are going to do a thorough search together," Cowboy said worrying. "Because they hunt in such different ways, they can't work together."

But then a crazy thought popped into Cowboy's mind. "What if I get a long leash and tie the two of them together. That should make their searching more systematic." Cowboy went back to his house, brought out a ten foot leash, called Mazzie and Calli over to him, and tied the two of them together.

He could tell instantly that each of them hated that. But still, he told them to put up with it and start searching together. For the rest of the afternoon the dog and cat kept trying to yank each other in different directions. But they did go over the property carefully enough to be fairly certain the missing watch wasn't there.

Disappointed, Cowboy untied the pair and invited them to follow him back to the porch to have the generous treats they'd earned. Cowboy was walking up the porch steps when he heard Mazzie barking and Calli mewing behind him. He turned around to see what was going on.

Each was pointing to something on the ground on the side of the porch steps he never used. It was his missing gold Hamilton watch!

"You both found it! You are wonderful searchers!" Cowboy said absolutely thrilled, reaching down to pat them.

That evening, alone in the barn again with Turco, Calli said to Mazzie, "We each spotted the watch separately. I saw it. You smelled it. We didn't need to search together at all."

"But Cowboy needed us to find his beloved wristwatch," Mazzie said. "If he hadn't come up with the idea of putting us together and then taking us back to his house for treats, he might never have gotten his watch back."

"You are right," Calli said back. "But just remember this: there are different ways of joining people up, and some are better than others."

26. **The Frog and the Beaver**

It was time again. Bobi the beaver had to rebuild the family's dam. Some years he had to do it every few months; once the dam lasted over two years,. Now an enormously heavy rainfall had swollen the Rio Grande and washed away many of its parts.

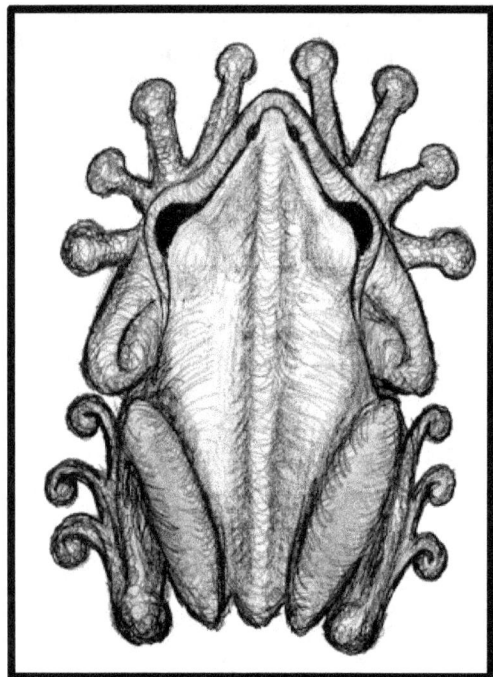

"At least no one was injured by the flood," Bobi said to himself, as he began hunting for young trees in the thriving Bosque on both sides of the river.

Alas, many of the fallen and younger trees had been washed away in the flood. Bobi hunted and hunted, but the poor beaver could not find or fell enough timber to rebuild his dam. "I'll have to move my family again," Bobi said, trying to make up his mind whether to paddle upstream or down.

That evening, very late, there was a continuous, annoying croaking of a frog from the east shore. Bobi's wife and children were being kept awake by the noise it was making. So to make it stop, Bobi dived through the hole at the bottom of his lodge and swam underwater to the shore. Silently he slipped his eyes out of the water to see what was going on.

A coyote was sitting on the bank, looking at him, and the frog was croaking loudly to summon Bobi to a meeting.

"I'm not here to eat you," the coyote said.

"I wouldn't let you eat me!" Bobi replied. "Why are you here?"

"Humans are rapidly repairing the damage the flood caused to their property."

"So?"

"I know one human who wants to help animals repair their property too."

"What can this person do for a beaver?"

"Bring you a truck load of downed trees."

"What's in it for him?" Bobi asked.

"Only joy in helping animals," Coyote said.

"All right. I doubt any human will help me but I won't move my family away for several more days."

"You won't regret this," Coyote said, vanishing into the dark.

Two afternoons later, a battered sand-colored Ford pickup pulling a trailer loaded with small washed-away trees pulled up on the bank alongside Bobi's ruined dam. The driver, an old human wearing a black collar, wasn't able to do much unloading. But a vigorous human wearing a yellow cowboy hat speedily spread out the small fallen trees up and down the bank, putting each in a place the beaver could easily access. With the driver looking grumpy, the man who did the unloading stood on the bank, took off his hat, and bowed toward the beaver in mid-river.

Bobi was overwhelmed with joy and gratitude. Four times he smacked his wide flat tail on the river's surface to make the loudest thanks possible for him.

The human on the bank bowed again, waved his hat once more, then got back into the truck and was driven away.

"That guy isn't so bad," Bobi said to himself. "And that coyote was pretty good too."

When he told her what had just happened Bobi's wife said to him, "Goodness is helping beavers. Don't forget the frog made this all possible for us."

27. Praying Keeps You Warmer

It was the coldest winter in Cowboy's memory. His shabby cabin leaked below-zero air so many nights that he piled every blanket onto his bed and climbed in with winter clothes and his overcoat on. He even wore sweaters for the first time in his life. The oddball thing was that Cowboy was worried more about the suffering of the animals he kept feeding than his own frosty breath.

"I need to come up with a way to get winter clothes for them," he said to himself. "Who could make these for me? And should I have shoes made for them too?"

Coyote wanted to stay in his warm den most nights, but he did need to eat and keep himself fed to survive the winter. Going hunting seemed to have little value, because so many hares, his favorite prey, were comfortable in their underground burrows.

Whenever he came over to eat, Cowboy invited Coyote inside and sat him next to the small electric heater, which was his only device for keeping the inside of the cabin above freezing. "Would you like me to make some warm clothes for you?" Cowboy asked the chomping Coyote the first night he visited after the clothes idea had popped in his mind.

"Sure. I prayed to my god to make me warmer and he told me to ask you."

"What would you like?"

"Anything you'd care to make for me. Just be sure that the clothes don't expose me to prey, don't keep me from running faster than hares, and are easy for me to take off and put on."

"Whoa, I can't come up with anything like that for you. Designing clothes you just asked for is far too technical for me."

"Do anything then."

Cowboy hunted through his bedroom drawers and found an old wool sweater he'd never used. Holding it against standing Coyote, he cut the sweater and taped it onto his friend. "This will keep you warm," he said. Coyote wriggled, took a few steps, and said, "Terrific! My god got it right."

"And so did I," Cowboy replied.

28. Celesto Thanks His Teachers

Nine-year-old Celesto's mother was cooking New Mexico style food for the Mexican Cowboy, herself, and her child. The kitchen was cluttered and when she wiped up a spill on the stove, the towel passed over the burner under a pot and burst into flames. Instantly Celesto's mother turned around and threw the towel toward the sink, expecting to douse it. But the burning towel landed on the wooden counter instead. With years of fat rubbed into it, the counter burst into flames too.

"Cowboy, come help. The kitchen's on fire!" Celesto's Mom shouted into the living room.

Cowboy and Celesto ran into the kitchen. Instantly Cowboy realized that pouring water on the fat-laden burning wood could not possibly put out the fire. Reaching under the sink, he grabbed the partially filled metal garbage can. "Come on!" Cowboy shouted to Celesto, as he ran out the back door. Celesto ran after him.

"They are abandoning me," Celesto's Mom thought, before going outside herself. Kneeling in the sand pile Celesto had played in when he was three and four, her son and Cowboy were scooping up sand with their hands and pouring it into the garbage can. A momentary wave of annoyance flashed through Celesto's Mom's mind when she saw all her kitchen garbage dumped on the ground outdoors.

"Hold the screen door open!" Cowboy shouted at her. Doubting, and afraid of choking on the smoke pouring from the kitchen, she opened the screen door.

"Stay here!" Cowboy ordered Celesto, and jumped out of the sand pile and ran into the kitchen. Holding his breath and fighting his way through the heavy smoke, he squinted at the rising flames and began sprinkling sand onto the burning towel and counter. It was almost impossible to keep from coughing, but Cowboy did it. Less than a minute later he ran out of the kitchen into clean air and began coughing and gulping deep breaths.

He was on his knees in the sand pit a moment later, heaping more sand into the garbage pail, when Celesto's mother shouted at him from the porch. "The fire is out, Cowboy! You saved my house." Her saying that didn't stop Cowboy and Celesto from carrying another pail of sand into the kitchen and spreading it over every warm surface.

"Now he's messing up my kitchen," Celesto's Mom said to herself. "But then it was me who messed up our dinner."

"Don't cry, Mama," Celesto said to her. "This has been the greatest adventure so far in my young life."

"It is a learning experience also," Cowboy said to Celesto. "Today you learned how to start a kitchen fire and how to put one out."

"Thank you, teachers," Celesto said to his Mom and Cowboy with an odd grin, before pulling the three of them together for a hug.

29. **Ursula and Coyote**

Ursula the bear had grown famous after she grabbed nine-year-old Celesto, who had crawled unaware into her den while she was hibernating, and wouldn't release him. She had thought he was her newborn bear cub and was trying to keep him safely with her.

Celesto's mother had asked Cowboy to find her missing child. The mustang stallion Turco, who Cowboy was riding, heard Celesto soft cries for help, and Cowboy and Coyote had rescued him from the mother bear.

Oddly, years later Celesto loved Ursula, and Ursula still loved her human cub. "Except for not letting me escape she was nicer than my mother," Celesto once said to a reporter. News had spread rapidly after this odd pairing, and tourists began stopping by Cowboy's ranch to see if he was feeding Ursula with the other animals. And he was, but only during the hardest weeks for Ursula when she and her new cubs couldn't find enough to eat.

Coyote could not help noticing however that on nights when tourists were parked in front of Cowboy's cabin, wandering around with flashlights looking closely for Ursula among the feeding animals, that many animals were frightened and kept away.

"Ursula, you are helping to keep a lot of animals hungry, just as you did young Celesto," Coyote said to Ursula, who was having a fine meal next to her cub.

"I'm eating here safely with my cub, so why won't your missing animals?" Ursula asked back.

"They don't trust human beings they don't know, that's why," Coyote replied.

"Let them go hungry then," Ursula said, putting her nose back into her giant bowl.

"You are adored by Celesto and the public, but you are a hypocrite," Coyote said angrily.

"You are just saying that because humans don't adore you," Ursula responded.

Overhearing the two quarreling, Cowboy came over to the pair and said gently, "Each of us is our own being and does our own thing. Let's try and respect one another, even if someone makes us angry."

"I adore you, Cowboy," Ursula said, lifting her head from the giant bowl.

"And I have learned a lot from you," Coyote said bitterly, turning around and walking away into the darkness.

"You don't have to agree with everything you learn from me," Cowboy shouted into the darkness.

30. **Marla's Study of Exotic River Fish**

It was fishing season along the slow twisty-channeled Rio Grande River that passed through Cordoba. The little town had a surprising number of residents who loved to cast flies or sit on the bank, legs in the muddy water, and let their bobs float down one of the slow moving channels. Older persons loved the joy of fishing for its own sake, but one high school biology major, Marla Colslaw, hoped merely to catch one each of the odd species of fish known to still inhabit the river humans had changed in so many places and ways. This was going to be Marla's senior biology project, one that might win her a school prize.

For the past two days, Marla had walked up and down both sides of the river, asking experienced fishermen what they had done to catch at least one of these species. "What fish are you talking about?" one older man had asked. Marla took a list from her backpack and handed it to him.

"Hmmm, you got river carpsucker, flathead catfish, red shiner, bluegill, mosquitofish, and smallmouth buffalo listed here. Sorry Hon, the only ones here I ever caught were carp and catfish." Marla jotted down everything the man said, thanked him, and moved on.

Marla walked through the marshes, jumped over irrigation ditches, and interviewed hundreds of fishermen. Filling three legal pads with interview notes, Marla was disappointed she still wasn't learning how to catch one fish from each of the species she wanted. Early that evening she sat disconsolately on a grassy bank, trying to figure out what to do now.

She watched birds skimming the water, and some splashing down onto it. Several hundred yards upstream she could make out a beaver dam creating a small lake behind it. "Should I give up being a biology major if I can't come up with a way to get a project done?" she asked herself.

Thumbing through her notes she found pages of descriptions of fishermen she'd met and detailed accounts about how each person fished. Suddenly a bright idea occurred to her. Biology is about humans as well as about fish. She would use her collected notes to write a biology paper about the desires and fishing mechanics of a large sample of Rio Grande humans.

Marla was very pleased when her thirty-five-page study won a prize for the best study in biology by her graduating class's seniors. Shaking hands with her teacher on stage, she said into the microphone, "Coming up with plans for a study **after** gathering data can be smarter than you might think." Her teacher winced when she said that, but seemed fascinated by the idea too.

31. **Where to Put a New Retirement Home**

Ursula the bear was proud of herself for going up into the mountains every night after eating meals provided by Cowboy. "I travel further than all of you animals here," she boasted one night before leaving.

A week later however a small herd of pronghorn antelopes appeared at the night's feeding. "Where have you come from?" a dining deer asked one of them.

"East of the mountains. We race around the mesas over there," an antelope answered.

"They've got you beat, Ursula," the deer said.

Several days later a pair of monarch butterflies were resting on flowers the Cowboy had planted. "That was a long hard flight we had from central Mexico," one of them said. "Let's stay here and rest for several days before flying on to Colorado."

"They've got your pronghorns beat," Ursula said to the deer eating beside her.

A robin hopping about and nabbing grubs and worms in the cabin's lone grassy patch flew over and landed between the grazing deer and bear. "I overheard your conversations about traveling long distances. I just flew here from Vancouver, Canada."

"You are our new champion!" Ursula said.

"Not for long," said a tiny squeaky voice. The deer, the bear, the butterflies and the robin turned and saw a very withered gray mouse sitting on a small pebble close to them. "When I was very young I was abducted and sold to a lab. They were doing space research and I was put into a rocket and shot into orbit. I was in the space station for two months and went around the earth hundreds of times in free fall, before being sent back and then freed."

"You are our champion!" the listeners cried, shouting for others to come and see the mesa's best traveler.

"I'd rather be back in space now," the old mouse said. "Free fall is much easier on old people than putting up with gravity."

Late that evening Coyote told the Mexican Cowboy about this conversation he'd overheard. "It's too bad we are not into building homes for old folks," Cowboy replied. "Putting retirement communities into space could make us richer than any earthbound builders."

"Living up there would make us mileage champions too," Coyote said with a grin. "But we'd miss your meals."

32. **Learning to Be a Better Student**

When he was ten, Celesto did well in school. He enjoyed attending, studied by himself at home, passed tests, and got good grades. But when he moved up to a junior high school for seventh grade, everything about school turned around for him. He had much further to walk each day, many new teachers and classmates to get to know, and his teachers were better at giving instructions than at helping their students learn. Celesto felt isolated and when he got his first report card, he worried that he could never be a good student again.

He kept trying however, looking for different ways to become a successful student once again, but he was enormously disappointed when he got his second report card and his grades were lower. "I'm a failure," he said to himself.

His mother was deeply worried about him, but she knew she couldn't be of much use to her only child in this situation. She had been a very poor student herself, and had dropped out of school in the ninth grade. Trying to figure a way to help Celesto, she spent an hour discussing the problem with Cece, a new friend she'd met when her car had broken down and Cece had given her a ride home on the back of a motorcycle, clinging tightly to her bag of groceries. Cece offered to help Celesto and his mother gratefully accepted.

Because both of them enjoyed hiking in the mountains, Cece took Celesto on a hike up a very steep and rough trail toward the top of a nearby mountain ridge. On the top they shared a light meal from Cece's backpack, talking back and forth to get to know one another.

They liked each other very much.

On the hike down the steep trail, Cece slipped, fell, and twisted her back. Celesto lifted her up, offered to go for help and, putting his small backpack into her heavy one, said he would do all the carrying down the hill. Cece was very grateful and, with her limping and stopping to rest often, the two of them made their way slowly back to Cece's car. Celesto even offered to drive it for her, though he admitted he'd never learned how.

Back at his house, Cece parked and talked with Celesto for several minutes more. "What saved me today," she said, "was making friends with you. And what will save you as a junior high school student is making friends there too."

Celesto said he would try her idea. In the next two months he worked harder at making friends with fellow students and even with the faculty. When his next report card came, he had jumped up two grade levels. And he had many friends to share this good news with.

"Cece was right," he said to himself. "But it was making friends with her that finally made me a better student."

33. **Who Really Loves Cowboy's Crappy Ranch House?**

"Your cabin is crappy," Mayor Howie said one day while visiting the Mexican Cowboy. "You ought to sell this junky place of yours and move into one of the new homes in Cordoba."

"I'll never do that!" Cowboy said back. But after the Mayor left he began looking at his home more critically. Boards on the porch were rotten. A step was broken and partly missing on the porch. The siding had cracks and small holes, there were shingles missing from the roof, and three of his windows were cracked. Inside, the kitchen sink and stove were filthy. The refrigerator was filled with scraps of food, many of them rotting. The bathtub was moldy and Cowboy had to pinch his nose when he sniffed the toilet.

"Mayor Howie's right. My cabin is crappy. I'd better start trying to clean and fix it up."

For many days Cowboy worked on his house, but even after putting in so many hours, a tremendous amount still needed doing. He was weary and frustrated.

"Guess I'd better take a look at a better place in Cordoba," Cowboy said, before phoning Mayor Howie.

Next afternoon Mayor Howie picked up Cowboy and his sleeping bag and took him to a brand new house on the edge of Cordoba. "Stay here overnight, and let me know what you think of it," Mayor Howie said after dropping off Cowboy and handing him a key.

"Shall do. Thanks," Cowboy said back. Walking around the little house he admired the yard and the home's construction. "Nifty place," Cowboy said, putting the key into the lock.

Cowboy enjoyed his afternoon there. The house was sparklingly clean inside and all the fixtures worked nicely. Early that evening Cowboy walked two miles into the heart of tiny Cordoba to buy a meal. It was tasty, but he was surprised how much he had to pay for it. Walking the long distance back, the sidewalk soon ended and he had to go along the edge of the road. It was Saturday night and cars filled with young people kept passing him, some honking at him to get out of the way. One car stopped beside him, a girl rolled down the window on the passenger side and shouted at him, "Get rid of that filthy old hat, Mister," before her boyfriend drove her away.

Back in the new house Cowboy unrolled his sleeping bag and tried to sleep. Cars kept rolling by outside and he could heard neighbors' televisions playing. A street light in front of the house kept him from seeing night sky rich with stars. What he missed most were the night cries of birds, bats and animals. This house was so tight he realized that he would never be able to hear wild animals in it, even if there were any in town. His potential neighbors may be nice people, but they aren't wild animals, Cowboy thought. "Do I want to live here? Absolutely not. This isn't my kind of place."

Next morning Mayor Howie picked up Cowboy, checked the house over to make sure Cowboy hadn't damaged it, and drove him back to his cabin. Mayor Howie's nose wrinkled with disgust as they parked in front of the porch. But Cowboy's eyes were lit with pleasure as he returned to the home he loved.

"So, are you getting out of here?" Mayor Howie asked him.

"I couldn't bear to do it," Cowboy answered. "You and I are different kinds of people. And we have different kinds of friends. You fit in Cordoba. I fit in here."

"So, do you want some helping fixing up your crummy cabin?"

"Thanks, but no. My animal friends really love this place just as it is. I do too."

"Nature is neater than your place. But if your animal friends love your crummy cabin they can have it, for all I care," Mayor Howie said, shoving Cowboy out the passenger door and driving away.

34. Controlling Vomiting in a Bee Hive

In a giant hive along the Rio Grande river in central New Mexico, every queen bee from hives as far as twenty miles away met to discuss, and try to find a solution to, a problem affecting every one of their colonies.

"In all your hives worker bees are taking longer to bring back the nectar they have sucked out of blossoms," the conference leader said at the conference's start. "We think we know what is behind this. For millions of queen bees before us, our honey bees have had to learn how to suck nectar from very few plants, mainly clover, dandelions, berry bushes and fruit trees. But now humans are living everywhere along the river and planting so many different kinds of flowers that our workers never learned how to suck nectar from the new ones they land on every day. But they spend hours trying. What should we do about this?"

For two days the conference continued as the queen bees debated different solutions being suggested. The conference leader threw out many of these saying things like: "No, I don't think we should sting all these humans to death. They might wipe us out instead." Or, "Yes, laying more eggs to produce more workers would be good for our hives, but most of us already laying as many eggs as we can."

The only proposal she stuck with through the end of the conference was the idea of better training for the hives' workers. "There is more nectar than ever before out there. If our workers are better trained before we send them out to collect, they will not have to spend so much of their time figuring out how to stick their long tongues into each new kind of flower."

Other queens could think of no more suggestions to offer, so they touched one another's antennas to say goodbye, and flew back to their own hives.

"How did the meeting go?" a worker asked Margaret, one of the queens, when she returned to her own hive.

"Poorly," the queen responded. "The conference leader decided we should school our workers longer."

"But our honey bees live for such a short time that training them for days will wind up bringing us even less nectar."

"That's right."

"What can we do then?"

"Someone suggested we should find a way to ask humans to make our workers live longer."

"That would change bee culture completely," the worker said. "So what do you want us to do?"

"I want each of our worker bees to suck nectar from no more than six kinds of flowers. Staying with the same kinds of flowers will make each of our workers more efficient."

"Good strategy! And it will keep so many of workers from getting sick after mixing so many different kinds of nectars in their honey stomachs."

"Right," the queen said back. "We'll have a lot less vomiting in our hive this year."

35. **Cowboy and Coyote Have a Contest**

"I don't like cats," Coyote said to Cowboy. "I know you've got one in your barn now. There's another reason for me to stay out of there."

"I understand," the Mexican Cowboy said back to Coyote. "You know that I'm trying to help people learn to get along with wild animals. What you may not have figured out yet is that I'm also trying to help animals get along with other animals too."

"I know, but you aren't ever going to be able to make me like cats," Coyote said defiantly.

"Let's make a contest out of this. You try to hold on to your hatred, and I'll try to change your feelings," Cowboy said.

"Okay, but you'll lose," Coyote replied.

A month later, on a very dark night, Coyote was trotting along his usual path to Cowboy's to get fed. At the edge of Cowboy's property the mesa in front of him had been dug up by someone. There were loose clods of dirt everywhere and several small mounds with tiny holes in them. "Looks like a mole has moved in here," Coyote said to himself. "If I can dig him out I'll eat him."

Coyote crept across the stirred earth and began sniffing down each hole. He couldn't smell a mole in any, and that puzzled him. At the third hole, he was sniffing for the last time before giving up, when the earth cratered suddenly beneath him. Coyote tried to leap to safety, but his back legs were pushing against empty air. He landed on the soft soil at the bottom of the pit.

For over an hour Coyote tried every way he could come up with to get out of the hole, but he could never quite do it. Very worried now, he sat at the bottom figuring out what he should do. "If I howl, Cowboy may come help me. But if the person who dug the pit wants to trap me, howling would tip him off. I'd better keep still and see if Cowboy comes looking for me," he decided.

Around two in the morning Coyote's anxiety was overwhelming him. He'd never been trapped before and fear was coursing through him. Coyote heard the soft footsteps of a small animal approaching. He wondered if it might be a skunk. A moment later there were two reflecting eyes close together on a head leaning over the pit's rim and looking down at him. Coyote took a deep sniff and could tell by its scent that a cat was up there. "Go away!" Coyote whispered. "I don't want whoever dug this trap to know he's captured me."

The cat mewed softly. "Go away, I said," Coyote snarled. "But if you can make Cowboy rescue me, I would be forever grateful to you."

The cat mewed softly again and vanished.

Ten minutes later Coyote heard a human running toward thepit. Fearing the worst, Coyote tried to make himself invisible by scratching loose dirt on top of him. With his head down and eyes closed he sensed a flashlight pointing down at him. "Coyote, are you down there?" his friend the Mexican Cowboy asked anxiously.

"It's me," Coyote said, standing up and shaking off the dirt. "Get me out of here."

"I can do that," Cowboy said. He lay down on his belly with his arms reaching down into the pit. "Jump up and I'll grab you," he said to his trapped friend.

Coyote jumped, Cowboy caught him and held onto him with one hand while he pushed himself away from the pit with his other. Coyote was saved.

"How did you know I was trapped?" Coyote asked his loyal friend.

"I was sitting on the porch and that darn cat Calli kept mewing and scratching my pants legs until I figured she might be trying to tell me something very important."

"She found me and I asked her to get you to rescue me," Coyote said.

"Well she did a good job of that," Cowboy said, sitting on the ground beside Coyote and rubbing his head and neck.

"I guess you were right when you said I should like cats," Coyote said.

"She did you a pretty big favor," Cowboy replied.

"You didn't dig the pit to win our bet did you?"

"Would I ever do such a bad thing to you?" Cowboy replied, with a tiny smile on his lips.

36. **The Best Human Error A Beaver's Seen**

About three miles down the river from Cordoba, Addy the Beaver was working to feed her family. It was late spring, the river was low and muddy, and Addy had to wade yards through water no higher than the top of her legs to get onto shore. There, she furiously chewed bark, branches she could reach, and fallen wood to fill her belly with food she could pass along to her kids.

Looking downstream toward her dam, the pond seemed lower than she could ever remember. "The river is drying up. It is going to be hard on beavers to find a new way to live if it goes away completely," she said to herself, peeling bark off a poplar tree.

That afternoon, her children happily full and napping, Addy dived into the slow-moving current and swam around the up-river side of her lodge. Then climbing onto it, she settled onto the comfortable place she liked to sit every afternoon. Resting and enjoying the late afternoon sunshine, she let her eyes wander. Many foraging birds flew back and forth overhead while several young fish bobbed up and down next to the dam, trying to find a way to go down river. "I love having so many different species around me," Addy said to herself.

Suddenly she was startled by a great deal of noise coming from the bank on the east side of the river. Addy turned and in a moment spotted a dozen or more young humans, giggling and speaking rapidly back and forth with one other, heading for the pond surrounding her lodge. "Uh oh," she said. "That could be dangerous for my family." She was about to dive into the river and disappear into her lodge when she noticed that the kids didn't appear to be carrying weapons. "These can't be hunters," Addy said, now doubting the youths had come to the river to hurt her.

While she watched, the youngsters peeled off their clothes, then adjusted and straightened the bathing suits each was wearing.

Oddly then, the kids turned around and walked almost ten yards away from the river. Now facing her pond again, the youths formed a wide line, and a girl in the middle counted down loudly, "Five! Four! Three! Two! One! **Go!**"

Each of the youngsters shot away, racing toward the river as fast as possible. Reaching the bank a few seconds later, every youth jumped or dove into the slow-flowing muddy water, hoping to be first to make an enormous splash.

Addy watched intently. Beavers, she knew, always slip into the water without making a sound. But these human youngsters made bigger splashes with more noise than Addy had ever heard. Water from some of the biggest splashes rained on her, yards away.

Several of the kids were laughing. But a few were crying. All of the splashers were either still flopped on their bellies or sitting up in water no deeper than eighteen inches. Addy spotted a child with blood dripping down one of her hands. Looking around she noticed that two other kids had drops of blood on their faces and legs.

"Shallow water hurt them," Addy said to herself. "But at least they landed on mud-softened rocks. This would have been a lot worse for them if the river weren't so muddy now."

The girl who'd given the countdown to the race stood up and said to the group, "We should have checked out the water's depth before we all dived in,"

"I agree," said one of the brightest of the kids, grinning with mud all over her face. "As I read not so long ago in one of *Aesop's Fables*, you should always look before you leap."

"I don't agree," Addy said to herself on top of her lodge. "If one of these youths had just put a hand into the water to find out how deep it was, I wouldn't have gotten to watch their incredible splashes. It's the best human error I've ever watched."

37. **The Worst and the Best Day in Mayor Howie's Life**

Cordoba's rising economy had pleased Mayor Howie, and he rightfully claimed credit he deserved for helping his small town to grow. But now there was a recession in New Mexico, and Cordoba was suffering more than other communities. Fearfully watching as money coming into the city's coffers shrank rapidly, Mayor Howie had to begin making cuts.

He spent several days thinking what city spending was best for Cordoba -- and for him! -- and which spending he valued least. Then Howie began making a list of necessary cuts. At the top of the list were the funds he spent buying so many different foods for Cowboy to feed to wild animals. "Humans come first. Wild animals come last," the Mayor said to himself, proud of his first decision.

It was fall, and hunting seasons were opening in New Mexico. With his revised budget now passed along to City Council members, Mayor Howie was yearning to go deer hunting. But alas, none of his friends were free to go with him. So, with no fears for his safety, Howie put on hunting gear, cleaned his rifle, and drove into the mountains. Other hunters were there, he knew, and he had to avoid them for safety reasons.

In a long valley branching off Salerno Canyon, Mayor Howie parked, picked up his gear, and began walking quietly into the woods. A mile and a half from his car he spotted a stag moving through brush and trees just yards from him. Crouching and aiming he was about to pull the trigger when a shot rang out from the canyon wall above him. The stag froze momentarily. Howie was about to shoot the stag himself when two more shots were fired from above. Both missed the stag. But one hit him!

Howie fell down, realized he had been shot in his left leg, and when he tried to stop the bleeding with a handkerchief, he passed out. Minutes later, the stag crept back to see the wounded human. Standing over Howie—and recognizing him!—the stag reflected on how important Cordoba's Mayor was to the deer population's winter-time feeding. This wounded hunter truly mattered to animals, the stag decided.

The stag began grunting loudly. More deer appeared and word spread rapidly, first among deer, then from species to species, that this shot human had to be kept alive. The stag had figured out how to do it.

Two hours later Cowboy, leading his stallion Turco and accompanied by two of Cordoba's policemen and a fireman, approached the prone Mayor. Coyote, who had steered them to the site, now sat worriedly watching the fireman treat the Mayor with the emergency goods he'd carried.

Awakened, and surprised at being rescued, Mayor Howie thanked the others for finding him.

"We didn't find you," the fireman said.

"We didn't even know you'd been shot," one of the officers said."

"I didn't either," Cowboy said. "Coyote told me about it and offered to lead us here."

"How did Coyote know what had happened to me?" the grateful mayor asked, as he was being lifted aboard Turco to be carried from the woods. "

"Beginning with the stag you wanted to shoot, a whole chain of wild animals rapidly passed the news along to each other and finally to Coyote and me," Cowboy said.

"Unbelievable!" said the fireman, grinning, as they hurried back through the woods.

"I thought wild animals wouldn't care if a hunter got shot," said a police officer.

"And you are going to stop feeding them," said the other police officer.

"Well I just learned what I thought mattered least to me, actually matters most to me," Mayor Howie said.

"You saved so many animals' lives by paying to feed them," Cowboy said. "The least they could do was return the favor."

"And they all did!" said Mayor Howie. "I promise I will always keep feeding them in the future."

Hundreds of hidden wild animals watching this felt satisfaction pouring through them. "We saved the Mayor and he will keep saving us," many of them were thinking.

"Turnabout can be fair play," the stag who'd saved Mayor Howie said to his deer herd.

38. A Downside to Calli's New Hunt

Though the Mexican Cowboy kept putting food out for her to eat, Calli the cat loved hunting for mice in Cowboy's barn. The problem she was discovering though was that she was pretty good at getting rid of all of them.

"How can I make more mice live here **and** keep being such a successful hunter?" she asked herself.

Then an idea occurred to her. "There must also be mice under Cowboy's house. I can start hunting those too!"

The first time she crawled under the Cowboy's shabby cabin Calli was surprised at the volume of smelly stuff there. "Garbage dumped under here by Cowboy?" she asked herself. "Or dead things carried in by animals living here? Or perhaps things blown in by the gusty wind?"

As she explored the darkened space, Calli quickly discovered where the smells were coming from. There were lots of dead and decaying small animals beneath Cowboy's home. "Who's killing them?" Calli asked, suddenly feeling scared and looking anxiously around.

Calli hurriedly left the horrible space. Several days later though she felt a strong urge to go back. "Even if there are rotting dead animals under Cowboy's place, there must be mice too. I'm still not finding any in the barn now. I guess I'll go back and take my chances."

That afternoon, under Cowboy's shabby cabin again, Calli began meticulously exploring, hunting for the mice she enjoyed catching and eating. Suddenly she saw a rattlesnake rear up in front of her. Startled and backing away, she watched the snake slithering toward the hole under the porch she'd entered through.

"It's blocking my way out!" the very frightened Calli said to herself. "It wants to kill and eat me."

Scared almost to death, Calli backed away into the darkest part of the space. But the snake ignored her and, making S-curves on the ground, exited through the hole under the steps. Calli waited half an hour but the snake didn't come back. "It must have been as frightened of me as I was of it," Calli said, cautiously exiting and hurrying back to the safety of the barn.

That evening she and Mazzie were talking about what had happened. "You are too big for the rattler to eat," Mazzie said, "and you are also too small to kill him. My guess is that the snake just ignored you."

"Perhaps that's true," Calli answered. "But I think the space I was in was both the snake's slaughterhouse and its kitchen. It was stupid of me to go back one more time. But you know, the desire to capture and eat mice is not mine alone."

"Agreed," Mazzie replied. "But the snake is keeping mice from living in Cowboy's house."

"That's good for him," Calli replied, "But it is bad for both me and the mice too."

39. Gus and Turco Go Camping Together

When Turco the stallion was first stabled with the donkey named Gus, he saw no reason to forge ties with him. While they were in the pasture together Turco studied Gus and kept finding new things he disliked about him. Gus could trot fast, but he never galloped. He was used as a pack animal and never carried a rider he loved. His braying was atrocious and painful. His ears were too large, his tail too small, and his tiny hooves reminded Turco of hooves he had seen on newborn foals. Also Gus would willingly eat more kinds of foods than Turco cared for. It bothered Turco too that his great friend the

Mexican Cowboy seemed to like having Gus around. So the stallion did his best to ignore Gus. And Gus didn't seem to notice or mind. Turco was looking forward to getting away from Gus on a camping trip Cowboy was planning to ride him on.

Several weeks after Gus moved into Turco's barn, the Cowboy began carrying camping gear into the stable and piling it up across from Turco's stall. The pile was enormous, much greater than the gear Turco had carried with Cowboy on previous trips. Turco groaned and said to himself, "This is going to be hard on me."

But on the morning Cowboy arrived dressed for their camping adventure, he saddled Turco but loaded all the heavy gear onto Gus. Gus didn't seem to mind and Turco could sense Gus was grateful he would be going along with the two.

As they left the stable and started across the mesa toward the mountains, Turco was exhilarated and wanted to gallop. He was angry when Cowboy reined him in so the burro trotting behind them could keep up.

At the mountains Cowboy started up the steepest trail he'd ever ridden on Turco. Turco stumbled and had trouble avoiding loose rocks or climbing over small boulders. But Gus was trotting uphill rapidly, almost bumping his nose into Turco's tail trying to get in front of him. This made Turco very angry.

When they came to a little stream, Cowboy rode Turco across and made him start climbing again. Turco looked back over his shoulder and saw Gus standing in the middle of the stream. "He gets to drink and I don't," the thirsty Turco said to himself. But a moment later Gus began braying more loudly than either Turco or the Cowboy had ever heard before. "We've got to go back and get him," Cowboy said, inching Turco around to go down the steep trail again.

At the stream Gus moved to the opposite bank, waiting. Cowboy started across on Turco and then thinking he may as well let the horse have a drink, he dropped the reins. In the middle of the stream, with cooling water flowing over his ankles, Turco put his head down and drank and drank. Gus walked across the stream past them, started up the steep trail, and stopped and waited for them. "He wanted you to have a drink and figured out how to get me to do it," the Cowboy said to his stallion pal.

Starting up the steep trail once again, Turco watched where Gus put his hooves and was surprised that stepping in the same places made the climb safer and easier for him and his rider. Gus was smaller, but with his taller ears he was almost as tall as Turco. Gus dodged or worked his way around overhead limbs that could hurt Turco or his rider. Turco followed him precisely and was never struck by an overhead limb.

Late that afternoon when they reached a small meadow, Cowboy was unloading Gus while Turco grazed. He spat out his first mouthful. Something was wrong with the grass here, the stallion realized, saying to himself "I may have to go hungry tonight."

When Gus was stripped of the huge load he'd been carrying he walked past Turco over to the side of the meadow and began eating something behind a large bush. Curious, Turco walked over slowly to Gus and looked down at the plants he was eating. He'd never seen them before, but they looked tasty. With Gus nodded at him, he picked up a mouthful and chewed for tasting. He liked the flavor! He swallowed his first mouthful and it went down smoothly. Soon, side by side, he and Gus were eating their fill.

That night Gus and Turco stood beside each other while Cowboy unrolled his sleeping bag. "You two seem to be getting along better," Cowboy said with a smile. "That makes me happy."

Turco put his mouth onto Gus's neck and rubbed him up and down. Gus seemed to be smiling with pleasure over his acceptance. As Cowboy crawled in and closed his eyes, Turco said to himself, "Bad things in another can turn out to be good things for me."

40. Cowboy and Mazzie Go Riding on Turco

Yesterday the Mexican Cowboy told Turco and Mazzie that he wanted to take them for a long ride over the blooming mesa next afternoon. Now Cowboy had eaten lunch, put on his ancient leather chaps, and with his faded yellow cowboy hat on was ready to walk down to the barn. But first he had to find Mazzie.

Usually Mazzie came inside through the dog door at mealtime and sat beside Cowboy, who couldn't make himself stop giving her small handfuls to gulp down. But today she wasn't by him while he was eating. Cowboy hunted through the house but Mazzie was nowhere to be found. Worried, Cowboy went outdoors and searched for his very smart small white dog. She wasn't on the porch. Or on the patio behind the kitchen door. Cowboy even leaned over the hole going under the house beneath the porch steps and called her name. There was a 'hiss' from under the house. Cowboy understood it was the rattler saying she wasn't down there either.

Something must have happened to her.

Very worried now, Cowboy stood on the porch shouting Mazzie's name. Usually when he did this she would yip a reply, and race from wherever she'd been to him. "Maybe she's still in the barn, though she always comes when I yell for her," Cowboy thought, walking determinedly toward the barn.

Standing in the barn door now he called for Mazzie several times. There was no sound from her. With his eyes focusing on the ground he searched the empty stalls, the saddle room, the room where tools were kept, and the huge space at the front of the barn filled with food for Turco and Gus the donkey.

Sitting on a bench at the back of the barn now Cowboy was on the verge of tears. "Something terrible must have happened to her or I wouldn't have this trouble finding her. I'd better go tell Turco now that we aren't going for a ride today. He'll be disappointed."

Walking toward Turco's stall Cowboy was trying still to decide whether to let Turco know that his best dog friend had disappeared. He had a carrot in his back pocket he'd brought from the house for Turco. Coming to Turco's stall, with the mustang stallion head's sticking out, Cowboy plucked out the carrot and offered it to his dear friend.

Reaching forward to pat the back of his stallion's neck he saw Mazzie stretched out on Turco's back.

"Mazzie! What are you doing up there? I've been searching everywhere for you!"

"And I have been waiting patiently for you while you were doing your thing," Mazzie barked with her answer.

"You looked everywhere but in the right place," Turco neighed at Cowboy.

Cowboy laughed, saying, "We can all be ready to go and still not be able to figure out how to meet up."

"Let's go riding!" Turco neighed.

"I'm ready!" Mazzie barked back, as Cowboy put her on the stable floor and began saddling Turco.

41. Humans Get in Wild Animals' Way

The badger and the raccoon had been neighbors for years in a tiny valley branching off Salerno Canyon. Each was envious of the other. The raccoon admired the badger's steadiness, his firmness of mind, and the determination that he brought to every task. The badger admired the raccoon's lightness of heart, his large family of friends, and the speediness with which he could climb trees and bounce over the ground. The badger thought of himself as a bully--which he hated being. The raccoon thought of himself as a

clown--which he didn't like being either. The badger admired the raccoon's useful hands, which resembled those of the able-fingered humans he watched doing different things, from a hiding place under the bush. The raccoon admired the badger's ease at finding food. He dug for earthworms, ate frogs, small mammals, ground nesting birds, roots and fruit. The raccoon ate many of the same things, but he wasn't as good at digging, stealing up on, or hiding and waiting for prey to come his way.

The badger and raccoon had spent so much time watching each other that they became friends. The two of them decided to work together and learn from each other, both hoping their existing ways of being would be improved with this collaboration.

A month later Hermana Montoya, a Mexican photographer who was working for *The National Geographic* magazine, was exploring the Manzano Mountains. She'd gotten away from the busy world of humans to have a peaceful while to muse and come up with a story she could offer to the editors of her magazine. By coincidence she happened to be camping overnight on the territory where the badger and raccoon were working together to learn each other's ways. Sitting by a fast-running stream at dusk, Hermana was listening to frogs begin night croaking, when she spotted a raccoon trying to catch a frog. She began snapping pictures.

This raccoon was plainly an inept hunter, and the frog was certain he could escape if she tried to nab him. The raccoon sat and scratched itself, inched toward the frog again, broke off, put its hands into the stream, and began slapping water onto its face, then inched again toward the frog. Nearing the frog, the raccoon paused to go to the bathroom. The frog kept an eye on the raccoon, but wanted to focus mainly on croaking. The frog noticed that the raccoon was inching between him and the stream. That didn't matter to him, because he could jump over it, or jump away sideways if the raccoon decided to attack. Between the frog and the water now, the raccoon was once more using its hands to splash water all over its face. The frog studied this odd behavior.

"Strangest thing I've ever seen," the frog thought. The raccoon then began making grunting noises the frog had never heard before. The frog was beginning to think he might be safer someplace else, when the badger, who had been sneaking up behind him, grabbed the frog, bit him, and killed him.

Instantly the 'inept' raccoon reverted to its normal self, whirled, jumped toward the badger, sat in front of him, and the two began dividing and sharing the frog meat.

"I've never seen anything like this before!" Hermana thought as she kept snapping pictures. "Those two were working together! Now there's a story idea for me."

For the next three weeks she followed the pair, taking pictures of the raccoon and badger coming up with new ways to gather food. Seven months later the pictures and accompanying story appeared in the *National Geographic.* The magazine's cover photograph was Hermana's close-up shot of the raccoon stretching up and pulling down a berry-filled blackberry vine for the ground-hugging badger. "Never have we seen before a pair of animals working this well together," the editor wrote on the magazine's introductory page about the cover story.

Back in the Manzanos, the raccoon and badger were still teaming up. One night, after they'd gotten all they wanted to eat, the pair was relaxing near the stream where they were first photographed by Hermana.

"Glad that human went away, aren't you?" the badger said.

"Right. That human got in our way every time we tried to get food," the raccoon said back.

"We should have gotten between her and the food she was taking out of her backpack," the badger replied.

"Humans don't seem ever to realize when they are getting in animals' way," the raccoon said back.

42. **Cowboy Advises a Friend Who Gets Lots Done**

Celesto's mother was living a very hard life. She couldn't find a steady job and had to make her living cleaning people's homes in the small town of Cordoba. She had a young son to raise, a house to take care of, bills to pay, and only by persistently working day after day could she keep their lives together. Oddly though, she was a happy woman who enjoyed the hard life she was coping with.

Her friend the Mexican Cowboy always suspected she was hiding her true feelings from him. When he was with her he could become a bully. He was always coming up with things she should be doing to earn more money. "Keep looking for a regular job," he said every time they were together, reading work ads to her from the local newspaper. While she was cooking a New Mexican meal for them, including his favorites, enchiladas with red and green chilé sauce, tamales, tacos, frijoles, Spanish rice and beer, he always kept coming up with suggestions. "You need to get out and meet more people. And you should get more education, you only completed ninth grade. Could you become a gardener? Or a nurse? You need to keep circulating a resume."

Celesto's mother thanked him for each of his suggestions, but he knew she would ignore them. Thinking about his own accomplishments, Cowboy recalled the many times he had pushed people or animals into doing something he wanted. "I'm good at pushing others around!" he said to himself. "That's the way I get so much done."

That spring a series of terrific wind storms blew into New Mexico from Arizona. Clouds of dust were whirling everywhere in miniature tornados. One afternoon Mayor Howie phoned and warned Cowboy to take the stallion Turco out of his crummy barn because a horrible windstorm was heading right at Cordoba. For once Cowboy believed the Mayor, saddled Turco, and rode him away from the barn.

They were up on the mesa near Celesto's mother's place when they stopped and watched a mile-high dust funnel heading straight toward his run-down barn. The storm funnel hit the barn squarely. Cowboy could see boards and bales of straw flying out of the tornado in every direction. And when the storm passed on, the barn was clearly down.

Cowboy found another stable to put Turco into, but when he phoned Mayor Howie and asked for money and help to replace his barn, Howie said, "Not on your life! You are a pushy guy. Take care of this yourself."

Disappointed, Cowboy had dinner again with Celesto and his mother that evening. She knew what had happened to his barn and told him how sorry she was. "But I can help you rebuild the barn if you'd like," she said.

When she said this, Cowboy realized suddenly that he had never helped this wonderful woman do anything. "I am just a pushy guy," he said to himself. "And I think being pushy is equivalent to actually getting work done. But she's the person who actually is getting tremendous amounts of work accomplished. She should be the bully here."

Celesto's mom put a hand on Cowboy's shoulder and said softly, "I can teach you how to get a lot of work done, good friend."

43. **Is Bad More Interesting than Good**?

Father Gallapo, the itinerant priest who had moved in with the Mexican Cowboy, was thinking about how things were going for his parishioners, and even for all of humanity. Persons who attended his small church in Cordoba appeared to be doing well enough, but listening to things they had to say about others convinced him that human life was worsening at an accelerating pace. Listening to news on his truck radio while he was driving only reinforced this belief.

"Nonsense," Cowboy said, when the priest shared this opinion with him. "The main thing people want to talk about is bad things that are happening. Newspapers, magazines, and TV programs are full of this. Hearing about good things is boring... unless a miraculously good thing happens to a person. And hearing about that can quickly become boring too."

"If you are right, why should this be?" Father Gallapo asked.

"That's for you to decide, Father," the Mexican Cowboy answered. "Why don't you ask God next time you pray to tell you why He wants humans to pay more attention to evil than to good."

"That question blows me away," Father Gallapo said.

"And God's answer may pull you back. Or blow you away further," the Mexican Cowboy replied. "You won't accept this, but I believe focusing on evil may be the main reason why there is so much boring good in our lives now. We are wired to find and control evil."

"That's certainly true for me," Father Gallapo said back to his friend, with a lightening soul.

44. Cowboy Was Always A Cheap Kisser

The Mexican Cowboy was still seeing his friend, Celesto's mother. Mostly they got along terrifically, but one thing kept troubling Cowboy: the clothes she was always wearing. These were Anglo clothes Celesto's mom picked up at Goodwill. Though she was Hispanic in origins, she wanted to wear clothes that made her blend in with all the Anglos making up ninety-five percent of Cordoba's population.

"They know I'm different," she once said to Cowboy, "but I don't want to remind them of this every time they look at me. And after all, I was born in America."

The Mexican Cowboy, however, was born in Puerto Palomas, a tiny community just across the border from Columbus, New Mexico. His parents, one Mexican, one American, had sneaked him over the border to Columbus and registered his birth there, but he still thought of himself as Mexican. When he was growing up, Cowboy loved to cross over to his grandfather's ranch outside Palomas where he learned to ride and herd cattle. With Celesto's mom, he hoped he would one day see her dressed in the Mexican clothes his grandmother wore constantly. But every time he asked she refused, pointing out that she didn't have those kinds of clothes and couldn't afford to buy any.

Celesto's mom knew Cece, a woman Cowboy had helped rescue from a nursing home where she was being held by a court order after crimes she had 'committed' -- 'crimes' which actually were fabricated by her children, who wanted to get their mom locked away so they could spend her money. Learning about Cowboy's pressuring, Cece came up a suggestion, which Celesto's mom adored.

Two weeks later Cowboy was putting on the vaquero costume he had worn when he led a famous parade in Socorro. Coyote asked why he was wearing these clothes again, and Cowboy explained he'd been invited to Cece's place for a memorial party for parade participants. Everyone attending was suppose to dress up in parade costumes.

"I should come too," Coyote said. "You know I was riding on the top of the giant Red Rock float and howling from up there. The parade made me famous. But there is no costume I should wear."

"Do come!" Cowboy said. "Everybody likes to see you."

That evening at Cece's there were about twenty people at the party, each wearing costumes they'd worn in the parade. Coyote and Cowboy were welcomed with huge applause. Each person was having a great time half an hour later when Cece stood up and asked everyone to raise his or her glass.

"Are you having a toast for me?" Cowboy asked.

"Nope," Cece said back, this is something much bigger than that." After checking to see everyone's glass was in the air, Cece said loudly, "We are ready for you."

The bedroom door opened and Celesto's mom walked slowly out, wearing the exact same clothes Cowboy's grandmother had.

"Toast her, guys!" Cece ordered.

With glasses clinking and drinks going down throats, Cowboy's lady friend walked majestically over to him, stood before him, and waited. Cowboy looked the clothes she was wearing up and down. A mix of joy and loss over his grandmother's death swept through him. He pulled her to him, hugged her tightly, and when she put her face up toward him, he kissed her. A huge wave of applause crashed through Cece's apartment.

Sitting next to each other at dinner, Cowboy asked Celesto's mother where she had found the clothes.

"Cece looked through the book of photos you loaned me and found a black and white picture of you standing with your grandparents," she replied. "Then Cece went online, hunted for hours, and found clothes that matched the picture in every way except possibly colors."

"The colors are exactly right," Cowboy said, leaning over to kiss her again.

At the end of the table, Cece watched this with a big smile on her face. Cowboy turned and blew a kiss of thanks toward her.

"Doing something I never thought of doing before earned me a kiss from you," Cece said with a huge smile. "And you ought to know this, your kiss was cheap because these clothes weren't very expensive."

"I've always been a cheap kisser," Cowboy replied, his arm around Celesto's mother.

45. **Solving The Problem Is Better Than Protesting**

Mayor Howie was frustrated and furious. A drunk driver, on the dirt road east of the Mexican Cowboy's ranch, had slammed into two deer crossing in front of him and killed them. It happened at night and the drunk was driving without his lights on, enjoying steering by moonlight. Coyote had been crossing the mesa also and ducked down and hid himself as the car approached. The driver stopped, staggered out, and pulled the dying deer aside, got back into his car and swerved away. Coyote memorized his license plate.

Word spread swiftly and soon crowds of animal lovers were protesting every way they could. In order to protect the animals that Cowboy fed nightly, the protesters insisted that Cordoba's police department put up barricades to check on motorists before allowing them to drive over the mesa.

"That's absurd!" Mayor Howie said to his secretary. "We don't have enough police to do that, and we need them to keep our citizens safe rather than to protect wild animals."

Protesters were angry over the Mayor's refusal. From Cowboy, who passed on the license number of the drunk driver, they speedily learned his name and even traced him to the bar in Cordoba where he'd gotten drunk. He was a nice young man, a graduate student at the university in Socorro, and he met with them gladly and apologized for being drunk and killing the deer.

"I'm not a regular heavy drinker," he said to five who were meeting with him on campus. "And I love wild animals as much as you."

"That's true," a fellow student said. "We took him for dinner and drinks only because he'd just won a prize for his completed thesis."

"And a number of times I've gone with him into the mountains to watch wild animals," another student said.

"I didn't want him to get drunk," his girlfriend said. "But the others kept buying him more drinks.

"Why didn't you drive him home?" one of the protesters asked.

"Because I don't know how to drive. But I wouldn't ride with him either. It wouldn't be safe."

"So, you are not a drinker and didn't mean to hurt wild animals," one of the protesters said. "Are you willing to help us protect them?"

"Of course," said the deer killer. "I'm very remorseful. I love wild animals. And I have an idea what we can do!"

That night three cars with headlights on were parked on the mesa road facing oncoming traffic. A wooden barricade was blocking the road. The few cars that came on this Saturday night stopped, chatted with animal guardians, had their breath smelled, and were told to drive carefully as they passed through animals returning from their nightly feed.

"Thanks for protecting them!" one driver said back.

"We like seeing all those animals," another driver said.

"The Mexican Cowboy's made our lives more interesting," said a third driver.

Back in his office, and after learning about the citizens' protective road blocks from his police, Mayor Howie said to his secretary, "See! Rather than protesting, those guys figured out what to do. Solving a problem is always better than protesting."

"And cheaper for us too," his secretary said back.

46. Millie and Calli Save Each Other

Millie the mouse, who lived in the Mexican Cowboy's barn, was proud of herself for always being able to avoid Calli the cat, her predator. Keeping an eye on the stealthy Calli, Millie tried to keep herself as far away from Calli as she could. If Calli was in the rafters, Millie would be looking for food under the straw. If Calli was in Turco's stall, Millie would stay above her in the rafters. Always having to keep track of the cat was frustrating, but Millie wanted to be safe above everything else. Then, one day something bad happened for both Calli and her rodent prey.

The Mexican Cowboy began placing mouse- and rattraps around the barn, always in the same places. Rodents in the barn learned about these contraptions the hard way and now were successful at ignoring them. Frustrated over no longer trapping mice and rats, the Mexican Cowboy began sneakily placing the traps in new places. One morning, using a very tall ladder, he even put one onto an overhead beam.

Millie watched him do this from a pile of straw in an empty stall. "I won't go on that beam ever again," she promised herself. Then a thought occurred to her. Perhaps she should go onto the beam and squeak and rustle until Calli the cat caught sight of her and sneaked up onto the beam to trap her. But if she were on the opposite side and Calli stepped onto the rat trip when she ran to snatch her, that would be the end of Calli.

Millie was proud of herself for coming up with this plan. Next day she was on the beam close to the roof with the trap on the other side of her. Millie squeaked as loudly as she could, waved her tail back and forth on both sides of the beam and scratched the beam with her front toes, making as much sound as possible.

Several minutes later she was tiring but thrilled, and scared also, when she spotted

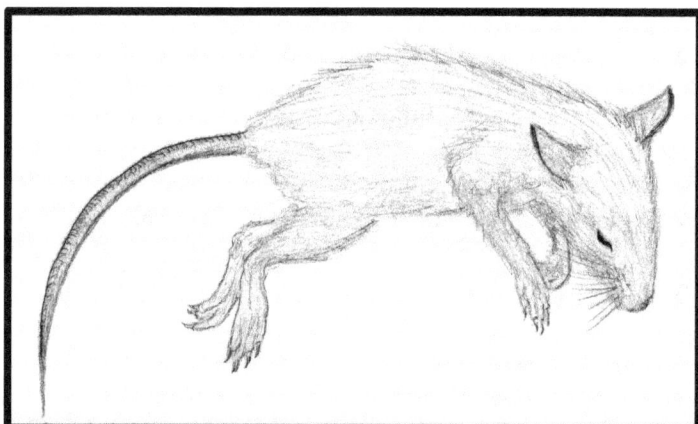

Calli edging over the center beam to trap her against the wall. Just seconds later Calli went racing across the beam toward Millie.

Oddly, Millie moved toward the trap and stood as idle as only a suicide planner might. Calli leaped to grab her and, at the same instant, Millie jumped off the beam. She was tumbling toward the straw pile in the empty stall when she heard the SNAP! of the rat trap.

On the ground now looking up, she could see parts of Calli struggling to free one of her back legs from the trap. And then Calli the cat fell off the beam and tumbled into the straw beside Millie. Calli was crying, and when she landed in the straw she mewed pleadingly for help.

Millie was about the strut proudly away from her wounded predator when a different feeling swept through her. In a crazy way Calli was both her neighbor and companion. Calli had shaped Millie's life, and by being easy to observe Calli had kept Millie from being eaten. "I'd better try to rescue her," Millie said.

Millie mewed "I'll save you!" to Calli, and climbed over the wall into Turco's stall. Eating, with his head down near the ground, Millie jumped onto his face and climbed up to Turco's ears. She bit an ear as savagely as a little mouse could.

Turco whinnied sharply.

She bit him again, switched ears, and bit him twice more. Turco rubbed his head against the stall door, and when that didn't get her off, he jerked his head in every possible direction. Millie hung onto his ear with her sharp little teeth, and kept biting.

Turco was whinnying continuously now.

Millie was putting up with a deafening volume of noise when the Mexican Cowboy came running into the barn. Seeing him opening the stall door, Millie jumped onto the straw laden floor and burrowed out of sight. Shivering, she felt Turco being led out of his stall.

Cowboy was examining Turco's pained ears when Calli began crying loudly in the next stall. Cowboy opened the stall door to see what had happened to her, saw she her back leg pinned by the trap, picked her up, carried her to the bench, sat down, opened the trap and threw it into a nearby garbage can, and began feeling her leg. It was bruised he could tell, but her leg wasn't bleeding and the bone didn't appear to be broken.

"Thank you for rescuing me," Calli mewed to Cowboy.

Not understanding her mewing, Cowboy petted her for several minutes, then put her down, stood up and went over to Turco. "Thank you for calling me to come here," he said to his beloved stallion. She might have died because of where I'd hidden the trap," Cowboy confessed.

"I wasn't neighing to save her," Turco whinnied. "I had a mouse gnawing on my ear."

Cowboy couldn't understand that either, but he rubbed some salve onto Turco's sore ears and put the stallion back into his stall. An hour later Millie was still under the straw in Turco's stall when Calli jumped over the wall, landed on top of her, and dug the straw away from her.

"She's got me," Millie said giving up, blaming herself for what she had done and Calli had been able to do finally. But Calli just lay down beside Millie and licked her, holding her gently with a paw.

"You saved me," Calli mewed, and I will never try to eat you again. "Let's be friends from now on."

"Gosh, my enemy is my savior," Millie said to herself. "And she wouldn't have become my savior if I hadn't been hers. I'm glad to have learned this. My mother never taught me the potential benefits of helping your enemies."

47. Mayor Howie Stops Funding Cowboy

The City Council of tiny Cordoba called an emergency meeting. Economies were collapsing around the world and Cordoba's was no exception.

"We need to rein in our spending," the City Council leader said to Mayor Howie. "But it will be up to you to decide what to cut."

"Just don't take away our salaries," another Councilman said.

"Or mine," Mayor Howie replied.

Back in his office with two assistants, Mayor Howie was going over the city's current budget, looking for big spending he could get away with eliminating. A clerk was reading aloud a list of the city's biggest recipients.

"Schools?"

"No," said the Mayor.

"Police and fire department?"

"No, of course not."

"Water company."

"No!"

"Garbage pickup?"

"Probably not."

"Street maintenance?"

"Probably yes."

"City staff?"

"Certainly."

"And here's an odd thing on the list," the assistant said with a frown. "You are giving a lot of money to the Mexican Cowboy to feed wild animals." "

"Well doing so keeps bringing lots of tourists to Cordoba," the Mayor said.

"But if you keep spending on him, but cut things we are providing to Cordoba's citizens, you are going to lose the next election."

"You're right. That worries me."

"Could you get him a job and let him earn enough to pay for the wild animal feeding?" an assistant asked.

"No, he's never liked to work, " the Mayor said.

"Well, if he won't work, why should we pay him?"

"Good point," the Mayor said. "We conservatives believe those who will not work deserve to starve."

"There's the basis for cutting off the money he's getting!" said the clerk.

Next day Cowboy was floored when he heard the terrible news that funding for feeding animals is being stopped. "They'll starve!" he said to Coyote.

"No, they won't starve, but they will have to work harder to find food for themselves."

"I don't doubt that, but I want their lives to keep being as easy as ours are. And millions of Americans agree with me."

"Why don't you ask them to contribute food payments then?"

"Good suggestion. Now I've got to figure out how to do it."

Cowboy's friend Bill, a bioengineer who had founded a big-earning company nearby, was great at figuring how to make tons of money. Hoping Bill could come up with a way to help, Cowboy rode over to Bill's house and spent an hour with him. Bill wanted a great deal of background information from Cowboy before he came up with a solution. When Cowboy passed along everything that he knew, Bill decided a mix of fundraising web sites would be the way to go.

"You'll have to hire good people to put these together for you, but I'll pay for them for a while. Go home and feed your wild animals the best you can until we get money rolling in."

"Thanks, Bill!" Cowboy said. "I have hundreds of reasons to admire and respect you."

"I can't say the same thing for Mayor Howie," Bill replied. "He told me he was cutting you back because you don't work and deserve to starve."

"He's right," the Cowboy replied. "I don't work and probably do deserve to starve."

"He's wrong!" Bill said. "You work more hours than any of us. And accomplish more than most workers, and get paid less. Feeding all the animals you do by yourself is heroic work. I'm going to see you get plenty of money to keep doing it."

"I wouldn't mind starving myself," Cowboy replied. "But I'll never let this happen to wild animals."

"You are the most noble worker I've ever met," Bill said, showing Cowboy out of his house.

48. Mayor Howie Is Cursed With Doing Good

The Mexican Cowboy's retinas were beginning to have cataracts. Working outdoors at night for so long, he'd never had trouble seeing threatening obstacles, even when the sky was moonless. But one early spring evening he tripped, fell, and skinned his hands—because he hadn't seen the small sagebrush his foot got caught in.

"I'm aging," Cowboy said. "I'd better start laying small fires along my night route so I can see my way."

Cowboy had lots of piled dried firewood, which he used in his cabin's fireplace. Now he began making small teepee-like stacks of wood, with newspapers stuffed in each of them, along his night route. One match would ignite each pile and it would burn brightly enough to enable him to see his way—and burn out soon after.

Late in the following summer though, after an unusually dry spring, there were fires all over New Mexico. Cowboy frankly didn't care if one of his small burning piles set the mesa on fire. "The mesa will only be fresher and greener in the spring next year," he said to himself.

And, on one very gusty, windy night at the end of July, burning embers from several of his lighting piles in fact did cause the mesa to catch fire and burn. He and the animals he was feeding watched the fire racing over the mesa toward the nearby mountains. And then suddenly it died out.

Animals crossing the burned mesa returning to their territories were not harmed in any way. The fire didn't seem to bother them.

Next afternoon Mayor Howie came by with his police chief. "You are to blame for starting this fire," Mayor Howie said.

"And we can arrest you for doing it," his police chief added.

"We won't do anything if you promise never to light these night fires again. Will you?" the Mayor said.

"Possibly, but if I do I'll hurt myself doing so much work outdoors at night. The mesa will speedily repair itself and be better than ever. But if I'm hurt I may not be able to keep feeding animals."

"That doesn't matter to us. The law says you have to quit lighting those fires," said the Mayor.

"Tell you what," the police chief said with surprising sympathy, "why don't I come out and string a power line over your route with small ground lights to keep you safe."

"That would be wonderful! Thank you. But why would you do this for me?"

"Because, to be honest, I really want to keep you safe. Feeding wild animals is one of my things too."

"You are my new hero," the Mexican Cowboy said back. "And Mayor Howie, because you've chosen this kind person as your chief, I'm going to vote for you next time too."

"You're always one of my biggest pains, Cowboy, but hard as I try, I haven't been able to stop helping you."

"I know. You are cursed with doing good," Cowboy said back, sympathetically.

49. **A Spider Makes a Human Befriend A Mouse**

The Mexican Cowboy loved wild animals, but he had mixed feelings about domesticated ones. When his friend Cece had made the little, fuzzy, runaway white dog Mazzie stay with him, he'd wished her owners would have kept her. But Mazzie loved him, and several important things she did for him made Cowboy love her back.

When Calli the cat showed up in his barn one day, Cowboy was pleased to have her there, helping to keep the rodent population down. He didn't like her eating wild birds she often snatched though. When Calli and Mazzie became friends, the cat began visiting her dog friend late at night in Cowboy's crummy house. Mazzie taught her to use the dog door to come in and out. Cowboy put up with the cat being there, but hated it—until Calli did several wonderful things in the barn that forced him to appreciate and love her.

But then Mazzie and Calli started bringing the mouse Millie into the house with them, Millie riding on one of their backs and ducking down when her carrier went through the dog door. Cowboy didn't know about Millie's visits for a long while, but one night she was quietly eating food crumbs off the floor in Cowboy's unswept bedroom when he got up to go to the bathroom. He almost stepped on her. She squealed and ran under the bed.

Cowboy was shocked to have a mouse in his house again, the first he'd seen since the rattlers living beneath it became excellent at swallowing the house's rodents for their prey. He looked under the bed, couldn't find her, and hoped she'd found a broken floorboard, dived under the house, and that a rattler had eaten her.

But Millie actually was hiding in the springs under Cowboy's bed. Realizing he was a threat to her, she avoided being seen by Cowboy from then on. Unfortunately one night she had a terrible decision to make. In the living room she watched as a brown spider, an inch in diameter and filled with potentially life-threatening venom, crawled into one of Cowboy's boots. All night she watched the boot to see if the spider left it, but it was still there in the morning when barefoot Cowboy came from the kitchen into the living room to put his boots on.

Without expecting she would do this, Millie ran out from under the couch, leaped onto Cowboy's foot, and began nibbling his little toe. Cowboy was furious. He pushed her away, grabbed his boot, and tried to smash her with it. Mille dodged the hammering boot, jumped onto his other foot and licked his middle toe there. She got away before Cowboy could smash her with a new blow. Standing in the middle of the living room floor, Cowboy threw the boot at her. She dodged and ran to the dog door going out onto the porch. Just before Cowboy accurately threw the boot at her, she pushed the door open and went outside. The boot slid through the dog door.

More furious than ever, barefoot cowboy opened the front door, picked up his boot again, and looked for Millie. There she was, standing on the side of the porch. Cowboy threw the boot at her and it sailed under the porch rail as Millie jumped sideways. Then she leaped off the porch and vanished.

Disappointed that he couldn't smash the annoying mouse with his boot, the fuming Cowboy walked barefoot down the steps and around the porch to pick up his boot. As he bent over to grab it he saw a stunned brown spider tremulously crawling out of it. "Good Lord! There was a deadly spider in my boot. And that mouse must have known it and was trying to save my life."

That night when Millie dared to come back into Cowboy's unkempt house, she found a trail of cheese crumbs leading into the kitchen. Following these she came upon a tiny bowl on the kitchen floor filled with crumbled bits of cheese, and several more things mice are known to enjoy.

Fearing that this was just a trap Cowboy had set for her, Millie avoided the bowl until Callie mewed to go ahead and eat from it. "You saved his life," the cat said. "He wants to make your life as good and as long as he possibly can."

As the grateful mouse began happily eating her marvelous dinner, she said to herself, "I never knew that a poisonous spider could make a human be friends with a mouse."

50. Birds, Bees, and a Pear Tree

The Mexican Cowboy planted a pear tree in his yard, watered and fertilized it carefully, and watched it grow into a beautiful tree. It was not large enough to provide shade in summer months, but it blossomed nicely in springtime and attracted a mix of birds. There were robins and sparrows of course, but Cowboy hung bird feeders in his pear tree and attracted goldfinches, Steller's jays, towhees, and even cactus wrens and woodpeckers. He was a mammaler at heart, and he had to struggle with himself to develop the desire and understanding necessary to become a good birder as well. He was proud of himself for making progress there.

Late one spring a queen bee and her first workers flew around Cowboy's crummy house looking for a place to build their new hive. A worker spotted the pear tree and led the queen back to it. Delighted with the tree site, she and her workers began building a hive to lay eggs in to produce hundreds of more bees. Day by day the hive grew bigger and, because the bees were building it next to the feeders, visiting birds became scarcer. This frustrated the Mexican Cowboy and he debated whether he should put up with this until the bees moved on. "Or will they?" he wondered.

He asked Coyote for his opinion, and Coyote told him that once bees build a hive somewhere, they are likely to stay there for generations. Cowboy could plant more trees of course, but Coyote said this might also attract more bees.

"What shall I do then?" the Mexican Cowboy asked his friend.

"You could put the hive into a plastic sack and stick in onto a rafter in your barn."

"No! If f I put bees into the barn some of them might sting Turco," the Cowboy said back.

"Well, why don't you just take your bird feeders out of the pear tree and put them onto poles in your yard?"

"I don't like that idea either," Cowboy said. "That's the kind of thing birders always do. I want my world to be as natural as possible. Also, I'm principally a mammaler."

"I think you're becoming a birder also," Coyote replied. "Suppose you just move the feeders in the pear tree as far away from the hive as you can?" Coyote asked.

"Now that's a good idea," the Mexican Cowboy said back. With Coyote watching, he got out his big ladder, unhooked the feeders one by one, and put them as far away as he could from the busy little bee hive. "It will be harder for me to keep filling these now," Cowboy said, attaching the last one.

"But you'll keep seeing the birds you love," Coyote said.

"Maybe, but the tree's only to get bigger and higher, which will make it even harder for me to keep filling the bird feeders," Cowboy said.

"Then you can move the feeders lower down, and still keep the birds away from the bees."

"Speaking of bees," Cowboy said, "these bees didn't attack and sting me while I was up in the pear tree close to their hive."

"They like and respect you for the way you dealt with this problem," Coyote said.

"But I wasn't trying to help bees; I just wanted to keep visiting birds from getting stung."

"Then you should have just poured gasoline onto the hive and set fire to it.

"I would never do that!"

"No, I agree, you would never do that. And partly because I believe you are becoming an *insecter* too."

"You could be right. But I'll let myself become an insecter only if insects are easy to feed," Cowboy said with a wide grin.

51. **Is The Cowboy A Saint?**

It was early May in the Bosque on the east side of the Rio Grande. A young crow, hatched recently and now learning about the world, was in a leafy cottonwood near the river when an exhausted barn swallow landed on a nearby branch. Looking her up and down, the crow could see she was breathing hard and so tired she had trouble clamping onto her branch.

"You are beaten down. What happened to you?" the young crow asked her neighbor.

"Life is hard for swallows," the older, neighboring bird replied. "We are in the air constantly. Last fall I migrated from northern Washington State all the way to South America. Only a few months later I had to turn around and fly north. Last week I was in Central America. Day before yesterday I left Mexico, crossed into Texas, and flew up the Rio Grande. I made it here today. You are right. I'm beat."

"Is there anything I can do to help you?" the young crow asked.

"Nothing, thanks, unless you can capture flying insects and stick them down my throat."

"That's beyond me, but I'll ask my parents what we can do."

Early that evening a plump human wearing an old, yellow cowboy hat, carried a ladder over to the cottonwood tree, and began climbing up. "Don't be frightened of him," the crow said to the shivering swallow. "He's helped us for years and he is on your side too."

Doubting this, the swallow flew to the topmost branch of the leafy cottonwood. On a branch next to the one the swallow preferred, the Cowboy was taping a small flashlight. Carefully positioning it upward, and making sure the flashlight was secure, Cowboy turned on the light, and then climbed down. He waved to the swallow and crow together in the top of the tree and carried the ladder away.

"What is this about?" the swallow asked her crow friend.

"When it gets dark, go back to your branch and you'll find out," the crow said with a smile on her bill.

An hour later the crow flew down to the branch the swallow preferred. "You'll be safe here, I promise. We crows will drive any predators away," she said.

Landing on the branch next to her the swallow replied, "I can't stay here. I have to fly all night to catch insects."

"Just try staying here for a few minutes, please," the crow said back. Hopping several branches away, the young crow watched her exhausted new friend.

Suddenly the swallow began snapping insects hovering over the small flashlight. Mosquitos and moths were attracted by the light, and couldn't avoid the swallow. An hour later the swallow burped and said happily, "Thank you, I'm full. But tell me, why did you crows take such good care of a worn-down swallow?"

"Humans are getting better at taking care of so many species," the crow said. "We think birds ought to be learning to help each too. That is one of the first things my parents taught me."

"I'll have to think about this. We swallows focus only on ourselves. Tell me, why did that Cowboy go to so much trouble just to feed me?"

"He's trying to change the world. He wants to make all species of animals and birds get better at taking care of one another."

"Your cowboy friend sounds more like a saint than a human," the swallow said, before nabbing and swallowing a giant moth.

52. **Coyote's A Genius**

Ducks are hard to catch, that's what her parents had taught Smoaki, the eagle, advising her to go after easier prey. But in the early spring and late fall, the sky was filled with flocks of mallards flying in V-shape formations, and Smoaki's desire to catch and eat one rose every time she saw them. At first she tried to catch a duck in the air. She swooped down like a fighter plane on a passing flock and with her claws extended, swung her legs from front to back as she passed tightly over the rearmost mallard. She flew away with just feathers from the duck's back pinned to her feet. Back in her roost, it took ten minutes to remove these and let them flutter to the ground.

A few days later Smoaki dived on swimming mallards close to the shore's reeds. Her target duck spotted Smoaki when she began her pass and, half flying and half paddling furiously, raced and beat the eagle into the thick and tangled jungle of shoreline vegetation. Smoaki's legs and feet were battered as her extended, forward-bending legs smacked into the mini aqua-forest just over the hiding mallard's head. It took Smoaki three days to recover.

Desperate now, Smoaki circled high over the mesa one evening, looking downward to try and spot her friend, the Coyote. Coyote's reputation for willingly helping every creature had become widespread. Coyote was just emerging from his den when he saw an eagle gently descending on a trajectory that would land her near him. He recognized it was Smoaki and guessed she had something to ask him.

Standing next to him now, Smoaki said, "My parents told me not to chase mallards. But I can't stop trying, and each time I hurt myself. Can you help me?"

"Sure," Coyote said. "Don't go after the grown-ups. Go after the mallards' chicks. They can't defend themselves."

Smoaki thanked Coyote and flew back to her roost. Mallards she knew were nesting and in a week or two there would be chicks to grab and eat.

Quakki, one of the nesting mallards, kept an eye on the eagle, realizing that she intended to prey on her chicks after they hatched. One day, with her husband sitting on the eggs, Quakki flew over the mesa hoping to find the sage Coyote. He wore a pink dog collar, she'd been told, and it wasn't long before she spotted him. Descending, she avoided cacti and thorn bushes and landed within earshot of him. Quacking vehemently, she called out to Coyote, and he trotted over to see what she wanted.

"We've never had to defend our hatchlings from eagles before," she said, "but now an eagle is poised and waiting to grab them. Can you tell me how I can protect my chicks?"

"Sure," Coyote said back, "keep your chicks in the reeds where the eagle can't get to them. Feed them there, and when they get ready to swim keep them just a short dash away from the reeds."

"That will work!" Quakki said, thanking Coyote before flying away. And his advice did work! But just for a short while.

Flying overhead Smoaki was disappointed now the mallard chicks were being reared in the reeds. "The mallards have figured out something new to do to keep me away from their young," Smoaki said. "I'd better go consult Coyote again."

Coyote told her to hide in the reeds and snatch the chicks when they were led there by their mothers to keep the eagle from nabbing them in the river. Smoaki thanked her sage friend, flew back to the Bosque, and began sneaking her way into the reeds.

A day later, spotting the eagle hiding in the reeds now, the mallard flew back to ask Coyote for more help. "Easy," he said, "just swim down the river ten of fifteen yards. You'll be safe until the eagle decides to hide where you are now. Then you go back upstream again."

As days passed, both Smoaki and Quakki kept taking turns seeing Coyote, each asking for more of his excellent advice. Three months passed, the chicks were grown and now could dodge the eagle on their own.

"Coyote saved you!" Quakki told her grown darlings.

The eagle was disappointed when the chicks had grown without her being able to eat even one of them. But her spirits lifted once more when she listened to Coyote's last piece of advice. "Smoaki, you should find a mate and raise chicks of your own. If there are more of you, you'll have no trouble catching mallards," Coyote said with a smile on his face. And Smoaki did find a mate and was thrilled to soon become a parent.

Several nights later Coyote was dining with the Mexican Cowboy and telling him about how he had helped both the eagle and the mallard. "When you give good advice, make sure you truly want to solve the others' problems. But keep your private views in mind as well. I wanted to save the mallard's ducklings, so the advice I gave to each of them both kept the chicks safe, and the mallard and the eagle still trusting me."

"A tricky thing to pull off, friend," Cowboy replied. "Has anyone ever told you that you are a genius?"

"Yes," Coyote replied. "I just made you say that."

53. New Forms of 'Thank You' Appeal To Many Of Us

The Mexican Cowboy was proud of how his efforts were bettering the lives of animals and birds he was helping—and dramatically increasing their numbers. But one evening

Coyote was next to Cowboy sitting in his green rocker on the beat-up porch, and telling him about how badly fish in the Rio Grande were doing.

"My friend the beaver says many species have vanished. Now bullhead minnows, chubs, and red shiners are endangered. And even species humans keep pouring into the river aren't doing so well."

"I've thought about this," Cowboy replied earnestly. "I've heard the Rio Grande is one of the ten most endangered rivers in the world. And this is because humans suck so much water from it and keep altering the river with dams, irrigation channels, farming, and many other things. So, what can I do to help?"

"I'm not sure," Coyote said back. "We need to talk with the fish to find out their most pressing needs, and I have no idea how we can do this."

"Does your friend the beaver understand fish talk?" Cowboy asked.

"Just tiny bits of it, I think."

"Well, let's go down there tomorrow and see if he can be our interpreter."

Next morning Cowboy walked along the river in the Bosque gathering sticks and twigs to give to the beaver. Shortly after noon he was sitting on the bank, his boots off and his dirty feet cooling in the slowly flowing muddy water, when there was a splash in front of him, and the beaver popped his head out.

"Brought you some food," Cowboy said, pointing to the large pile of sticks.

"Thanks," the beaver said in beaver talk, splashing his tail gently so Cowboy could understand what he'd said.

The beaver was taking loads of twigs over to his lodge when Coyote appeared and sat down next to Cowboy. Then all afternoon, and each afternoon the rest of the week, Cowboy would put a question to Coyote, who passed it along to the beaver, who then dived into the water, found one of the right fishes, tried to ask it and stumbled to understand its answer, then returned and passed the information up to Cowboy.

It was a slow and laborious process. But by the end of the week Cowboy had learned what he could do to help.

For the next three weeks he waded into the muddy river and, with beaver's help, constructed a small three-sided dam in the middle of the river. When fish breeding season began, he helped mothers deposit their eggs in the new safest place in the river. When beaver reported the eggs hatched, he brought the right foods for each of the baby fish species.

Underwater, the beaver guarded the infant fish and drove away catfish, sunfish, yellow bullheads, and largemouth rainbow trout who tried to eat them. Coyote kept several land animals from going after them also.

It wasn't long before this part of the Rio Grande had far more numbers of surviving native species than it had in years. Cowboy brought a truckload of wood for the beaver and Coyote passed on his friend's thanks.

"You guys did everything you promised," the beaver said gratefully.

"Your help was essential also," Cowboy said back.

Cowboy and Coyote were about to leave when the water before them churned with native, fully grown, Rio Grande and bullhead minnows, common carps, chubs, and red shiner fish, who were thrashing to express their appreciation to the beaver, and to the Cowboy and Coyote on shore.

"It's an odd thank you," Cowboy said to Coyote, "but one I kind of enjoy."

"New forms of thank you can appeal to many of us," Coyote replied.

54. Doing Lots For Others Can Be Good For Us Too

One spring afternoon the Mexican Cowboy was sitting in his green rocker on his rundown porch eating lunch, when he heard the sound of a helicopter overhead. He didn't pay attention to it because helicopters often fly up and down the Rio Grade Valley in central New Mexico. But this helicopter halted abruptly in the air, then slowly began making passes over the mesa between Cowboy's ranch and the Manzano mountains. Cowboy could see a man leaning out an open door taking pictures with a video camera.

"Someone's spying on me," Cowboy said with a groan. "Or maybe they are mapping the mesa out there to build a factory. That would be the worst thing that ever happened to me."

Ten minutes later the helicopter turned and flew away. Passing over his cabin a man

reached out of the cockpit and waved to Cowboy as the helicopter vanished overhead. Cowboy spent a while puzzling what this had been all about, but by bedtime he'd forgotten the whole thing.

A week later Mayor Howie drove into Cowboy's yard in his snazzy 1953 Cadillac. Without waving hello, the Mayor left his car and marched onto Cowboy's porch, carrying a laptop computer. The Mayor walked past Cowboy in his rocker, opened the house door and went inside.

"He's even more belligerent than usual," Cowboy said to himself, getting up slowly and going inside himself.

Mayor Howie was sitting at his table, after pushing aside piles of dirty dishes Cowboy hadn't bothered to take into the kitchen.

"Somehow you've managed to get your house even messier," Howie said. "If messiness was a sport, you'd be the world champion."

"So, give me a medal. And then tell me why you're here, Mayor," the Cowboy replied. "Did you come to just beat on me? I know that's your thing."

"No. I came to show you something and ask you a question."

"Show away, then, said Cowboy, clearing off a chair and sitting down beside the Mayor.

Mayor Howie opened his laptop and in a few moments was showing Cowboy videos taken from the helicopter going back and forth over the mesa last week.

"So, you guys are spying on me now?"

"No! We're not. You are not smart enough to keep secrets from me."

"So what's this about then?"

"Look carefully at the mesa video. What do you see?"

"A mesa that looks like every other one. It's the one between my place and the mountains."

"Are you sure?"

"I think so."

"Okay," Howie said, "here's a video of the mesa south of here." Cowboy stared at the screen and was startled to see how brown and dried the mesa on the screen now was.

"What happened down there? Is that what you want me to find out?"

"No! It's what happening between your place and the mountains that makes your mesa so green and vital."

"That's easy to tell you," Cowboy said with a grin. "Because I feed so many animals every night, when they get full and leave many of them poop on their way back to their territories. Feeding animals fertilizes the mesa and makes it green up."

"None of us every thought of that before! Feeding wild animals *does* green up our mesas, then," Mayor Howie said, rubbing one hand with the other. "So if I want to beautify the area around my small city of Cordoba, all I have to do is feed more animals?"

"You've got it, Mr. Mayor," Cowboy said. "Doing a lot for others can often do a lot for ourselves."

"You just taught me something I never thought about before," the Mayor said rising to leave. "Now I've got to figure out how to get you to work harder for me. Without paying you more."

"I'll teach you to feed wild animals at no cost to you," the Mexican Cowboy said back. "And you might want to start dumping your poop onto the mesa too."

55. Danger Does Spread in Opposite Directions

The Mexican Cowboy's friend Cece loved to hike in the mountains and take beautiful photographs of flowers, many very rare and exotic. She was hoping to assemble a book she could market to help thousands realize the beauty of central New Mexico.

Late one spring she was deep in the Manzano mountains stretched out on her tummy taking a close-up of a purplish red and green dichelostemma, when she heard bushes rustling behind her. Putting her camera down and turning her head around she saw a puma lying on its belly watching her. This frightened her.

"How can I save myself?" Cece asked. She thought about taking her cell phone out and calling for help, but she was miles from anybody. "Should I just stay here? Keep on taking pictures? Stand up and shout at the puma? Pick up some rocks and throw them at it?" Her mind raced with ideas, but she didn't trust any of these. She became more frightened.

The puma had now rolled on its side and was watching her intently, with a concerned look on its face. Pushing her pack before her in small jerks, Cece began crawling away from the mountain lion. It took her ten minutes to put enough distance between the two of them that she began feeling safe again.

She was sitting on a rock resting before moving further away when a thought occurred to her. There were attractive flowers in the bushes around the big cat. She could use the telephoto lens on her camera to zoom in on them. "This might be a picture everyone will love!" Cece said to herself.

On her knees now, with the camera resting on the rock she'd been sitting on, Cece focused on the flowers and puma. What she saw on her camera's screen amazed her. The puma was on its side nursing two youngsters.

"Now I get it," Cece said to herself, snapping picture after picture. "The mother was afraid of me and was hiding to protect her cubs!" Danger in settings can spread in opposite ways, she suddenly realized.

Getting up, putting her pack on her shoulder before walking away, she turned around and waved with an open hand, saying "Lovely kids you have there, Lady Lion."

Now feeling safe again herself, the puma purred gratefully back.

56. A Sheep Herd Is One Giant Being

One night a pack of hungry dogs attacked a herd of sheep grazing two ranches away from Cowboy's. The sheep tried to stay bunched, and the dogs kept trying to separate them. At last the dogs worked their way into the herd and the sheep had no choice but to separate into several smaller herds.

One of the sheep, an old ram, couldn't get himself into any of the smaller herds, because individual wild dogs were barking and snapping between him and the herds. As herd members moved away from the old ram, he witnessed the dogs surrounding a young ewe. Fearing for his life, the ram turned and ran, bleating in fear. Worse, the ram was filled with anguish over his powerful desire to hook up with his herd again.

Next morning the Mexican Cowboy was leading his magnificent stallion Turco, and the untied burro Gus, to their pasture when he noticed an old ram grazing in there. Recognizing the color markings on the ram's ears, Cowboy led Turco and Gus into their pasture, closed and locked the gate, and went back to his house to call the sheep's owner.

Grazing, Turco ignored the older ram, but Gus went over to have a chat with him. "Did you run away from your herd?" he asked him. "I thought sheep would never do this."

"I did, and it was the wrong thing for me to do. But a pack of wild dogs attacked us last night and succeeded in splitting us apart. Because of where I had to be to dodge the dogs, it was impossible for me to link up with my herd again."

"You sheep never want to be alone," Gus said.

"That's very true. Unlike so many other kinds of animals, being part of a herd is our thing."

"Your only thing."

"Right! And losing our herd is worse for a sheep than losing his life."

"Well, don't be afraid. Our friend the Mexican Cowboy will find your owner and get you back safely."

"I hope so. I'm very mentally troubled being here by myself."

"You are not alone. We'll be your herd while you are waiting."

"You can't be my herd. Neither of you are sheep."

"True, but if you are here for a while with us, you may get used to herding with other animals."

"If I'd been able to do that," the ram said despondently, "I would have joined the pack of wild dogs wanting to eat me."

"I agree," Gus said. "Not all herds are the same. You've got to be careful when you pick out which to join."

"Never, if we are talking about sheep herds here," the nervous ram replied. "Any herd is a good one."

"That's because your sheep herds aren't made up of individuals. You are all one giant being," Gus said.

"Right! That's exactly what a sheep herd is: one giant being!"

"We'll I'd better shut up. Let's graze. I'll try to be part of your herd's one giant being with you."

The ram nestled near the donkey and put his head down to graze. Try as he might, though, the donkey couldn't turn himself into a sheep. And no good feelings coursed through the ram as he grazed next to gracious Gus.

57. **Each to Her Own**

The Mexican Cowboy's lady friend Cece was one of the strongest, most determined women he'd every met. Facing problems he knew he couldn't deal with, the Cowboy would back away, making others suspect he was a coward. Cece though never doubted her ability to solve any problem she was confronted with. Backing away was not in her makeup.

One warm afternoon Cece and her friend the Cowboy were walking along the banks of the Rio Grande. Cece was enjoying taking pictures of flowers blooming in the Bosque, adding to the photo collection she hoped to publish soon. Cowboy kept spotting hidden birds and animals that Cece missed. Between them they were seeing lots of living things.

Wanting to sit down together and relax now, Cece spotted a comfortable bank under a leafy cottonwood tree. Cowboy sat down with his back against the tree, while Cece sat on the bank, took her shoes off, and began dabbling her toes in the slow-flowing muddy waters.

"I'd keep my shoes on, if I were you," the Cowboy said to his friend.

"Why should I not do this?" Cece said, swirling her feet around in the river.

"This is the season when snapping turtles do their most attacking," Cowboy replied. "One of them might mistake your toes for a meal."

"Don't worry, Cowboy. I can keep any turtles off me."

"Your choice," Cowboy said, pulling his faded yellow hat cowboy hat down over his eyes, and stretching out to nap for a few minutes.

Cowboy was deep asleep and having an exciting dream when Cece began screaming. "Let go, you damned thing!" she was shouting. Opening his eyes he saw her stretching over the water trying to get something off her exposed foot.

"Have you caught a turtle?" Cowboy asked with a touch of sarcasm.

"Shut up. Come and help me get rid of this thing."

Cowboy stood up, picked up his backpack, and sat down beside Cece. Flailing, Cece pushed herself away from the river and tried to pry her big toe out the big turtle's beak. When it wouldn't let go, Cece grabbed one of shoes and began thumping the turtle on its head. The turtle pulled its head inside its shell, dragging her big toe with it. In great pain now, Cece began banging her shoe on the turtle's shell as hard as she could. The turtle pulled its legs into its shell and wouldn't let go of her toe. Cowboy watched all this with a disappointed look on his face. "Do something!" she demanded, crying.

Cowboy gently pushed Cece over backwards, making her lie down. He sat down next to her feet, put both into his lap, and said, "Be quiet and don't move for a few moments. I want the turtle to put its head out again." Crying, Cece tried to do what he said. She couldn't stop her leg from jerking though.

Cowboy reached into his pack and brought out a plastic bag with sandwich makings in it. Stretching over the bank, he poured handfuls of river water over the turtle's shell. Several minutes later the turtle's head came out of its shell, its bill still clamped on Cece's big toe. Cowboy poured several more handfuls of water over the turtle's head. The turtle seemed to relax. Cowboy then opened the bag with sandwich makings, pinched a small wad of cheese and held it close to the turtle's nose. The turtle hung on to Cece's toe. Cowboy tried small bits of every kind of food in his bag. He hoped tiny shreds of lunchmeat might appeal to the turtle, but these didn't.

The only food left was a few marvelous chocolate chip cookies, sold by a baker named Kaiti in nearby Cordoba. Holding a large piece of the cookie over the turtle's face, he was surprised when the turtle shook its head, suddenly let go of Cece's toe, and began crawling off Cowboy's lap toward the river.

Cece sat up and began rubbing her pained big toe. "How'd you get rid of it?" she asked Cowboy.

"You clobbered the turtle with your shoe. I merely offered it gifts."

"You offered gifts to a turtle who was biting me! That was cowardly. The turtle was committing a crime. You should have punished it."

"The turtle was hungry."

"So, did the criminal turtle eat any of your food gifts?" Cece asked, looking at the bits of food scraps scattered on the ground around Cowboy.

"No, but I think it thanked me by letting go of you."

"I would have pulled the turtle's head out of its shell and cut it off with your knife," Cece said.

"You could have tried that, but it didn't occur to me," Cowboy said back. "But we both know my way worked."

"Doesn't mean that my way wasn't more efficient—and an act of justice too!" strong-minded Cece insisted.

"Each to her own," Cowboy replied. "And that goes for turtles as well. What works for me may not work for you. Or for turtles. Incidentally, turtles have their own views of what justice is about."

With a hard look on her face, Cece kept rubbing her sore toe.

58. Teaching Can Go In Opposite Directions Simultaneously

Ursula warned her cubs time after time to stay hidden and avoid humans during the brief fall hunting system. Her children were fast learners and none had ever been hurt—or even shot at. But now her newest cub, a youngster only months old, was turning out to be hard to train. He was a curious cub; a cub who liked to explore and learn about the world. Learning, and not self-protection, seemed to be his thing. Trying to bring him up correctly was making Ursula very frustrated. Yes, he was a good student. He listened attentively, asked questions back, experimented with her teachings, and then tried doing novel things, many of which were risky for him.

When she asked Cowboy for help one night when he was feeding her, he pondered for a moment, then replied, "Your new cub sounds like a very bright kid. He may turn out to be an explorer, or even one of the first bear scientists."

"That's well and good," Ursula said back, "but I need to know how to keep my cub alive. I don't trust him to look after himself."

"I agree, dealing with a cub like yours could be a huge problem. Give me a day or two to think about this and I'll get back to you."

"Okay," Ursula said, "but don't let this go on too long."

"I'll try not to," Cowboy said, putting down a giant pan of food for Ursula to eat.

Next day the Mexican Cowboy asked every one of his close friends if they had ideas about how to protect Ursula's cub.

"Beat him until he learns to obey," was Cece's suggestion.

"Get Mayor Howie to ban bear hunting," was Coyote's.

"Let me guard him!" the little white dog Mazzie said, jumping up and down.

"I'll ask my parishioners to put him into their prayers," Father Gallapo said.

Celesto, a former Marine, offered to guard the cub but warned, "Legally I can't shoot back if someone aims at him."

Thelma, Father Gallapo's church warden, suggested the Mexican Cowboy go talk to the superb bioengineer Bill. "He can figure this out for you, I'm sure of that," she said, giving the Cowboy a hug.

Next day Cowboy saddled Turco and rode over to Bill's house, on the very edge of the mountains. Bill was busy and annoyed by the Cowboy's visiting him, but when Cowboy described the bear cub's problems his eyes lit with interest.

"He sounds like an exceptionally bright bear! Would he like to work with me?"

"I don't know. Do you want me to bring him over and you can find out?"

"Sure," Bill replied, shoving Cowboy out the door.

Two days later the Mexican Cowboy rode back to Bill's place with Ursula's cub on the saddle before him. The cub had been excited to meet a human for the first time, loved getting to know a horse, and was studying the world around him as Turco galloped smoothly down a winding mountain road toward Bill's place. Bill was standing out front when they got there. Silently, he studied the cub's attentiveness as the young bear was also studying Bill. Each was trying to make sense of the other, and pleased there was more there than either expected.

Cowboy lowered the genius cub to the ground. Bill turned his back on the bear and walked inside. After a moment's hesitation, the cub followed him inside.

Cowboy sat outdoors all afternoon waiting for Ursula's cub to return. Just before five Bill came out with the cub walking by his side. "We're going to become colleagues," Bill said to the Cowboy. "I'll teach him, learn from him, and we'll come up with projects to work on together. I'll take care of him as he grows up, of course, and he can leave whenever he wants to."

"Can I bring Ursula over to visit with him?"

"Anytime, of course."

Looking at the cub now, Cowboy asked, "Do you really want to stay here and work with Bill?"

The cub walked determinedly over to the Cowboy, stood on his back legs and stretched his paws up onto Cowboy's shoulders, licked his face, and nodded his head up and down. Cowboy was startled and enormously pleased. He'd never had a bear do this to him before.

"See," Bill said. "He has only been with humans for a day and already he's figured out how to work us."

Cowboy walked over to Turco and got a huge sausage out of one of his saddlebags. The cub raced over to him and Cowboy handed it over. "I know a thing or two about working bears also," Cowboy said back to Bill.

"The cub's helping you add to your knowledge of bears, and he is learning from you," Bill said. "So many think teaching is a one-way routine. Actually, we learn from our teachers, and at the same time they are learning from us."

"I can't imagine any of my teachers learning anything from me," Cowboy said. "I was a dumb student."

"You knew tons of stuff they didn't know," Bill said back. "And after picking up some of what you taught them, they probably remembered you better than good students who were only like them."

59. Mayor Howie And The Mexican Cowboy Come Up with A Deal

The Mexican Cowboy was growing older, and he was tiring each night after working very hard for long hours to feed so many wild animal visitors. "You've got to stop doing this entirely by yourself," his lady friend Cece insisted. "If you don't get some help, you are going to break down. Then your animals will have no one to feed them."

"You may be right," the tired Cowboy replied. "But I have no money. How can I pay anyone to help me?"

"Go talk this over with Mayor Howie," Cece said. "What you do brings lots of tourists to Cordoba. Merchants here in Cordoba are making more money than ever. Howie should be able to find a way to get some of it back to you."

"Howie already does that. Our tiny town pays for all this wild animal food I put out every night."

"So get him to help you feed more animals. That will put even more money into the merchants' coffers."

"He'll turn me down. He always does that."

"And you always figure out a way to make him change his mind," Cece replied.

Next afternoon the Mexican Cowboy was meeting with Mayor Howie in his office. His magnificent stallion Turco was outside, tied up to a horse railing the Mayor finally agreed to install—and which now was bringing other riders to the city's government offices. Horses tied to the railing attracted more tourists also.

"Why don't we try to find some volunteers to help you?" the Mayor said to Cowboy after hearing his problem explained.

"I asked Cece the same thing. She said volunteers don't show up as regularly as paid workers. And animals cannot be allowed to go hungry."

"Why not?" Howie said back. "Tons of humans everywhere don't get enough to eat."

"You politicians ought to be coming up with reliable ways to feed them!" the Mexican Cowboy said sternly. "Every person deserves not to starve."

"You always try to load me up with more work every time we meet!" Mayor Howie said angrily.

"And you, nasty sir, always load me up with more work every time you increase the animal foods you are supplying."

"I wouldn't keep doing that if it didn't earn me more votes."

"And I wouldn't work with you if it didn't help my animal friends."

"You don't like me, and you insult me every time we meet," the Mayor said frostily.

"You put me down and annoy me every time I see you. But I vote for you because you supply so much food."

"I wouldn't do that if it didn't keep getting me elected."

"You are selfish!"

"Selfishness is a politician's right."

"You can be vicious too."

"So? Aren't many of your animals more vicious than me?"

Furious and about to storm out of the Mayor's office, Cowboy asked, "So, are you going to hire someone to help me?"

"Yes, but I'll only be hiring someone to help me through you."

"We have a deal then?"

"More or less."

"Nice talking to you," Cowboy said rising to leave.

"Don't forget to vote for me," Mayor Howie said, pushing his chair back to the wall to keep his distance from the departing animal rights crusader.

60. A Badger Finds A New Way To Re-experience Joys

Beverly the badger was bored with her life. She didn't migrate, her territory was small and had been explored countless times, and nothing she experienced was ever new to her. "I wish I could lose most of my memories," Beverly said to herself one evening. "Then everything would be new and exiting to me."

But her memory was as solid as a cliff of sandstone. True, it eroded slowly, but all of her memory's main features were preserved.

As months and even years passed slowly by, Beverly became more depressed. "No one's life is as boring as mine," she said constantly to herself. To keep herself happier, Beverly kept looking for new foods she could try. For years she'd wanted to taste honey, but climbing up to the hive in one of the nearby trees would be very difficult for her. Aging now, one day she thought she really must give it a try.

Carefully clawing her way up the gnarly tree, her toes and legs ached and looking down, she was frightened what would happen if she let go and fell. Beverly wasn't even sure that she would be able to turn around and go down headfirst, the way most tree mammals do.

Reaching the bee hive at last, with workers humming around her, Beverly pried the hive open, put her wide head inside, and with her tongue reaching out as far as possible, got her first taste of honey. "Wonderful stuff," Beverly said to herself, sticking her head back in to get another swallow.

But workers inside their ripped-open hive were waiting for her. She couldn't see them, but she felt three bees land on her protruding tongue. And a moment later there were sharp bursts of intense pain as each bee stung her. Frightened into incoherence, she pushed herself away from the hive, stabbed a paw into her mouth to rub the tongue, and suddenly she was aware of falling.

Flailing and watching the ground racing up to her, she smacked onto a hard rock and passed out.

Hours later Beverly awoke, and with bees still hovering over her, she crawled onto her feet and stumbled away from the hive's nest.

All next week she had terrific pains in her mouth and head, and running a paw over her skull she could feel many bruises and cuts she'd suffered when she'd hit the ground. "I'll never do that again!" she assured herself. "And I can be sure I won't, because my memory is so perfect."

But just several months later, Beverly found she was having trouble remembering where to go to drink water. Sites she was seeing in her territory seemed new. And she was having trouble recalling the safe places she always slept in. Suddenly it struck her. "I'm losing some of my memories! I've always prayed for this but never thought this gift would be given to me. Soon everything will be new to me!"

Now, for many weeks, each day was wonderful, as she was having one 'new' experience after another.

Early in fall, enthralled with how exciting her life was going, Beverly was sitting under a tree looking up at a beehive. "I've always wanted to taste the stuff that's in there," Beverly said to herself. "But I wonder how I'll ever be able to climb that high in a tree. Should I do it? Of course I should," she said, starting a climb up the tree. "Tasting honey will be the crowning glory in my long life."

Bees began hovering over her as she worked her way up to their hive. Watching them, Beverly said, "I wonder what could happen if they sting me?"

61. **Good Advice Can Turn Out To Be Worthless**

In his upgraded ranch house, Cece had moved in with the Mexican Cowboy. Her room was upstairs and on the opposite side of the house from his, and except for meals together, keeping her life private from him was her desire.

"Cowboy's a windy talker," Cece complained to her friend Mirella Montagna, whom she used to live with. "He's always asking me what I did today, and when I tell him, he tells me I should have done these things differently. He's full of advice, but when it comes to my taking care of his house, he never offers me his assistance."

"Cowboy hasn't changed," Mirella said back. "That's exactly the way he was when we used to hang out together years ago."

Several nights later Coyote complained to his friend the Mexican Cowboy that he'd been offering him too much advice. "You've really got to cut back on this stuff," Coyote said, "because if you don't stop offering all this advice many of your friends are going to start avoiding you."

"Should I change the way I offer suggestions to others?" Cowboy asked.

"No. Just talk about yourself, and listen to what they have to say about themselves."

"But I never have much to say about *me,*" Cowboy replied. "My life is more boring than anyone's."

"That's not true," Coyote said back. "You do hundreds of fascinating things every month. Tell us about some of those. We won't feel so put down if you do."

"You've just offered me advice," Cowboy said.

"And it is better advice than you usually give," Coyote replied.

"I guess you get to be the judge of that," Cowboy said.

As days went by Cowboy worked at trying to become a silent listener, and it wasn't long before he got good at keeping suggestions to himself. A week later, he was outside picking up the plates and dishes he'd put food on for his wild animal friends, when he noticed his little, fuzzy, white puppy friend, Mazzie, going around and licking every plate clean before he got to it.

"Mazzie shouldn't be out by herself every night among so many wild animals. One of them might try to eat her," Cowboy thought.

He was about to shoo Mazzie back to the house when he realized that in essence he was imposing his worldview on her. "She may know more than I realize about taking care of herself out here at night," Cowboy said to himself. "I'll experiment by leaving Mazzie alone and letting her make up her own mind about what to do."

Two nights later Cowboy had collected and hosed off all the plates, and was relaxing in his green rocker on the porch. Suddenly he heard a dog fight going on out in the darkness. He heard Mazzie's tiny growls, her barks and snaps, and then his little dog whining in pain.

Grabbing his flashlight, Cowboy ran out to the edge of his property, pointed the flashlight where the noise was coming from, and saw a dark gray mongrel dog holding Mazzie by the neck and shaking her.

"Put her down!" Cowboy screamed. The mongrel saw the big human racing toward him and instantly realized that he could lose his freedom or even his life, if he didn't drop Mazzie and flee. He did both.

Watching to be sure the mongrel was not circling to attack him, Cowboy picked up the limp, moaning Mazzie and carried her back to his house. In the kitchen he treated her wounds then put her gently onto her dog bed for a night's rest.

Next afternoon, recovering Mazzie was sitting in the barn talking with Calli the cat. "You know that guy's always telling us what to do," Mazzie said. "But last night he rescued me when I was attacked by a mongrel where the animals eat."

"You shouldn't have been out there by yourself!" Calli insisted.

"And you are just telling me after the fact what I should do," Mazzie said back. "That's pointless advice."

"It's not pointless!" Calli said. "What I said may save your life if you want to do this again."

"Cowboy actually saved me, and that's something you didn't do."

"I heard you guys fighting," Callie said back, "but I thought this was just dog stuff. And I'd rather give you advice than get mixed up in a dog fight."

"Good point," Mazzie replied. "Each of us has to think of ourselves when we offer advice or intervene in a crisis."

"Interacting with others is far more complex than most of us realize," Calli said with a smile.

"And good advice can turn out to be worthless many times too,"Mazzie replied.

62. **Being With Others Is Good For Us**

Mayor Howie worked every night until six, and when important business needed doing, and city council persons needed to be made to change their votes, the Mayor could be in his office well past midnight. Normally Mayor Howie didn't mind these very long work hours. Getting things accomplished was his major goal. But in some months, when the council wasn't meeting, when just about everything that needed doing was finished, Mayor Howie sat in his office feeling very bored.

"Why don't you come and hang around with us," Police Chief Frank Corso asked.

"Thanks, but you guys bore me. All you talk about is crime, getting laws changed, catching people, and winning or losing at trials."

"This is pretty big and important stuff," the Chief said back.

"I know, but it bores me still."

On days he had little to do, Mayor Howie tried spending time in the little city's three bars. The Mayor was not a drinker, so he'd order only one beer or a glass of wine, and sit and wait for someone to interact with him. But customers kept away from the bars when the Mayor was there.

"Why?" a bartender later asked one of his missing customers.

"Because we talk about a lot of stuff that's illegal. We can't risk letting him overhear us."

Still trying to find something interesting to occupy his time, Mayor Howie began spending afternoons in the city's small park. He offered to push children's strollers around the park, and mothers refused, afraid this strange man meant to kidnap kids. Not far from an old man throwing tennis balls for his Australian sheepdog to fetch, Mayor Howie raced toward a bouncing ball, caught it in the air, spun around and threw it back to the old man. Rather than chase the ball, the sheepdog sat scowling about ten feet away from the Mayor. The old man was holding onto the ball with a stern look on his face too. Mayor Howie apologized to each of them and left the park.

The Mayor enjoyed hunting with his rifle buddies, but no hunting seasons were open yet.

"Maybe getting out of town would be my thing," Howie said to himself one afternoon. He climbed into his polished, black, 1953 Cadillac and went exploring some of the roads nearby he'd never driven on. Everything he saw bored him.

His secretary suggested he might like to do some dating. "No thanks!" Howie said back. "Dating can lead to marriage and I've got no time for a wife and children."

"Seems to me you have more time than you think," said the secretary, with a disappointed look on her pretty face.

One day Thelma, the caretaker of Chichimaya, the city's rundown church, dropped by his office to ask the Mayor some questions Father Gallapo, her priest, wanted him to answer. "So," she said, "the city won't help us pay to pave our rutty parking lot?"

"Sorry," the Mayor replied. "We are not authorized to do that."

"And you are not going to cancel the ticket your policeman gave to my priest for pulling a trailer behind his truck with a confessional on it?"

"Can't help you with that either. The law's the law. The patrolman discovered that your priest's confessional is also a two-door port-a-potty. He needs a license to tow it so often."

Thelma was disappointed in these turndowns, but looking at the Mayor closely, she realized something was going badly in his life. Sympathetically she reached across his desk, put her hand on his and said, "Mayor Howie, you look troubled to me. Is there anything I can do for you?"

Mayor Howie was shocked at this older woman's insight and offer of caring. For the first time in his life, and amazed at himself, he began to tell a woman visitor about things he was feeling. Thelma listened attentively, asked him questions, and when he'd said everything he dared, made him an offer.

"You won't believe this, Mayor Howie, but I think if you come with me to our church service tonight, you'll meet a lot of people who would like to be with you."

Howie shuddered, but Thelma would not take no for an answer. Reluctantly, he agreed to attend the service. "You'll be driving there, right?" Thelma asked.

The Mayor nodded yes.

"Well I'm going to write three names and addresses for persons who need rides," Thelma said, reaching across the desk to grab his writing pad. She could tell by the look on his face Mayor Howie regretted having been so frankly personal with her.

That evening Thelma was standing outside the church in the rough parking lot. When the ancient Cadillac drove into it she waved it to a special parking place near the church's entrance. Mayor Howie parked there and Thelma noticed he was talking attentively back and forth with the woman beside him and the older couple in the back seat. The four of them got out and, still talking earnestly, walked past Thelma, nodding to her as they went by.

Inside the church tens of people gathered around the Mayor, welcoming him, praising him, touching him gently. Father Gallapo came to the group and talked back and forth with the Mayor and the others for several minutes. Then the church doors closed and the ceremony began.

Two and a half hours later, Mayor Howie was sitting in his office again. His face was ruddy and smiling. He'd never had so many people reach out to him, express their appreciation to him, and appear to genuinely like him. The service had been brief, the coffee meeting afterward was warm and well attended, and the three people Howie had driven from their homes thanked him for picking them up and joining the service with them.

The young woman riding next to him in his Cadillac had said the most memorable thing to him on the way to her house after dropping off the couple. "Mayor Howie, you are a great person, and greatness carries its own penalties. Letting your hair down and being with others is good for you, and good for the people who are with you too."

She'd planted a small kiss on Mayor Howie's cheek before she exited his ancient Cadillac.

"I've found my empty time friends," Mayor Howie said, very pleased with how much would be added to his life now.

63. Humanology Saves Starving Pronghorns

Anka the pronghorn antelope was among the greatest athletes in her herd on the mesa east of the Manzano Mountains. She and her kin could outrun any animal in eastern New Mexico. She jumped over high fences with ease and loved soaring like a bird through the sky. But unlike most pronghorns in her herd, Anka was a fascinated learner. She enjoyed watching humans especially, because these were always doing novel things. Frequently she would race alongside slower moving vehicles to exchange looks with passengers and drivers, or study humans studying her from parked cars.

The pronghorn buck who was both her father and the herd's current leader kept trying to make her give up watching humans so much. "Thanks, Father," Anka would say, "but I'm trying to expand our knowledge of *humanistics*. When I start having fawns I want to make several of these into *humanologists* like me."

"That's unwise," her father insisted. "Learning about humans cannot help us in any way."

"One day you may be surprised about the value of what I'm learning," Anka said back.

All summer and fall Anka tried different ways to get her herd closer to humans. Her kin wanted only to get as far away as possible from humans. They were annoyed at the number of humans who would try to catch up with the herd, take pictures of its members, even reach out and try to touch does and growing fawns.

"They love us," Anka said to one of her friends.

"And some of them try to kill us," the friend said back.

Anka actually watched this happen to a distant relative of hers who was standing late one night against a roadside fence waiting for traffic to pass, so he could cross to the other side. A drunk driver saw the pronghorn and turned his steering wheel the wrong way to avoid him. The pronghorn was too close to the fence to leap back over it and he died upon impact.

"See," said Anka's dad, "we can never trust humans."

The memory of this terrible accident haunted her for weeks, but still Anka refused to quit studying humans. She'd already learned that humans would stop and park beside the road and study them if the pronghorn herd was stationary. Farmers however would come out with pitchforks and rakes to drive pronghorns away from their crop fields.

In the middle of Fall, the breeding season descended on the pronghorn herd. Bucks fought, does were docile and waited compliantly, and teenager Anka was learning the complexities of breeding in the pronghorn world.

Three weeks later, with winter speedily approaching, the herd returned to its usual ways. Temperatures dropped below zero as bitterly cold winds from the northwest bathed the herd night and day. In late December and early January, snowstorm after snowstorm filled the mesa with eight or more inches of snow. The pronghorns now could find nothing to eat.

"Some of us are going to starve if this doesn't end soon," her father said to Anka. And four days later, three pregnant does were so starved they were lying down and couldn't rise.

Anka couldn't bear looking at them. She leaped away from the herd and, soaring over the snow piles, made her way to the nearest highway. Standing next to the fence, staring at passing traffic, car after car slowed down. Anka noticed several humans reaching for their cell phones to make calls. She waited there all afternoon, and all night too.

Next morning, with another snowfall beginning, Anka was about to give up her plan, when a large truck with flashing lights parked near her. Humans wearing uniforms hurriedly climbed out of the cab, opened the truck's rear doors and put ramps up, went inside, started engines, and rode snowmobiles down to the snow-packed roadside. One of the humans used wire cutters to make a large opening in the fence. The humans loaded giant packages onto their idling snowmobiles, then drove through the hole and stopped, staring at Anka while their engines idled.

She looked back at them for over a minute before suddenly realizing what these humans were up to. Anka turned away and began leaping over the snow toward her herd. Every minute or two she stopped, turned around, and waited for humans to catch up with her.

Fifteen minutes later the humans approached Anka's herd. The frightened antelopes darted away, with Anka shouting at her father, "Don't go too far. Keep a safe distance, but turn around and watch."

The humans got off their snowmobiles, walked to the downed does, covered them with warming blankets, gave them injections and began trying to feed them. The humans scattered small mountains of good Pronghorn foods around the does, and when the sacks were emptied, got on their machines, waved goodbye to Anka, and drove back to the highway.

Anka followed them back and saw them put their machines away and get into their truck again. With her head sticking over the fence, she nodded up and down in thanks as the humans waved and departed.

Leaping back to her herd she found sick does back on their feet again, and herd members feasting on food the humans brought.

"Okay, Anka," her father said to her. "There's something worthwhile in humanology after all. You figured out how to get them to feed us."

"Figuring out new ways to help ourselves and others should be a constant objective for all species," Anka said, before beginning to fill her empty stomach with a wonderful meal.

64. Some Neighbors Are Better Than Others

For centuries prairie dogs had been living in a large 'city' on the plains east of Manzano Mountains. Indians and Spaniards had passed by, stopping to admire the village's well-kept mounds so sophisticatedly separated, and were fascinated with the attention the 'dogs always paid to passersby. Even with small ups and downs in its population, the community's durability continued year after year.

In the late 19th century, Anglos began moving into eastern New Mexico and soon there was a wagon road passing in front of the prairie dog village. Wagon trains would creak by every few days, but prairie dogs didn't mind. These visitors were interesting to them. In the 1920s, the road was widened, but it was still unpaved, and for the first time noisy gasoline powered vehicles began showing up. The 'dogs didn't mind these either. Novelty always affected the villagers' minds positively.

While the population of this prairie dog village had been more or less the same over centuries, populations of neighboring animals were always rising or falling. Constant climate change had much to do with this. Years of dryness reduced the number of neighboring mesa animals hugely. Not many years back, eastern New Mexico was enriched with heavy winter snows and drenching spring rains. The climate change didn't directly affect the prairie dog residents, but other species began to multiply rapidly.

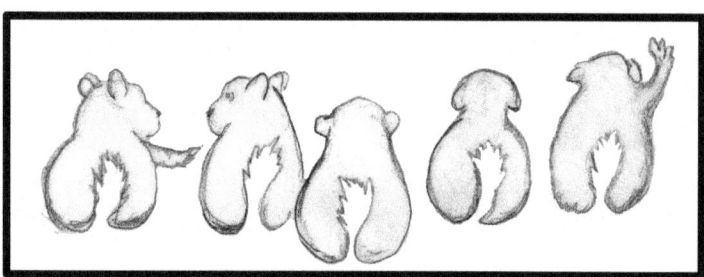

As the populations of each species increased, individuals' territories shrank and youngsters had to settle being nearer to each other. The prairie dogs wanted their village to be exclusively for them, but they could not prevent other animals from moving in with them. First it was a bunch of groundhogs who burrowed their way under the still unpaved road and began popping up and kicking soil away in holes they made on the prairie dog's property. "We can put up with this, I suppose," one 'dog shouted to its neighbor.

But then three badgers dug nest holes for themselves in the prairie dog village, then began going after groundhogs. The badgers would speedily dig up vast amounts of soil while trying to catch an escaping groundhog.

"How are we going to put up with this?" one 'dog asked another.

"I don't think we'll be able to," its neighbor replied.

"Are we going to have to move?" asked a third.

Two weeks later a fox dug a den for itself and actually connected with and took over underground 'rooms' the prairie dogs had enjoyed for centuries. The following morning the chief 'dog assembled his followers in a large underground 'room,' and opened a discussion of what the 'dogs could do to get rid of their unwanted neighbors.

"Some of us have bad odors. Maybe we could stink them out of here," a 'dog youth proposed.

"We could make a huge amount of noise when our unwanted neighbors are trying to sleep," an older 'dog said.

"We could steal food they leave in their dens when they go hunting," another 'dog suggested.

Next morning, musing over yesterday's discussion, guardian prairie dogs were upright beside their holes when they heard a string of loud, low rumbles coming from their right. With eyes narrowed to see in the bright sunlight, they watched a number of huge trucks coming toward them along the road. Trucks passed by every day, so this didn't bother the 'dog watchers. But this time the trucks parked along the road right in front of them.

Cars filled with workers followed the trucks. But late afternoon, bulldozers were flattening the ground on the other side of the road and workers were putting up frames for concrete pouring to make the foundation for a giant building.

"On no, humans are moving in on us now too," one of the worried dogs said to another.

"We've got to move away from all this," said the Chief. "Let's begin planning where to go."

Day after day while the prairie dog move planning was taking place, humans were constructing a giant warehouse. Trucks groaning with loads of concrete were arriving and driving away empty. Walls were speedily erected and a flat roof with solar glass panels was put on. Cars by the hundreds drove in and out of the tall wire fence every day.

All this was extremely frustrating for the prairie dogs.

Several days later a young prairie dog went to his chief and said, "I've looked everywhere and I haven't been able to find either the fox or the badgers. And even the gophers are burrowing away from us too."

"The humans must be driving them away," the chief said back. "That may be a good thing for us."

And it was. Soon traffic on the road in front of the prairie dog village was almost back to what it had been. Whatever was going on in the fenced warehouse, few humans were arriving or leaving each day.

"I guess we can get along better having humans for our neighbors," one of the prairie dogs said to her chief.

"I think you might be right," the chief said back. "They restored our property to us, and they didn't know they were doing this."

"Some neighbors can be better than others," said another prairie dog.

65. How Mayor Howie Wins His Races

Cece, Church Warden Thelma, and Father Gallapo, were sitting in the municipal building's waiting room, hoping Mayor Howie would agree to meet with them that afternoon.

"My bet is that he won't," the priest was saying. "He doesn't want to help us pave our church's parking lot."

"You think he'll just dodge us today then?" Cece asked.

"I don't think he will," Thelma said. "He's abrupt and good at getting his way, but he always meets people who are waiting to see him."

"After making them wait for hours," Cece said.

"He's slow and steady then," Father Gallapo said very loudly, with a grin. "And that's why he always wins each race."

Mayor Howie stuck his head out of the door and said, "You are good at getting my attention, Father Gallapo! Winning's my thing, but I need to help others get what they need if I'm going to win my races. Come in guys, and let's figure out what we can do to get your parking lot paved."

As they followed Mayor Howie into his office, Cece and Thelma hugged their Priest. "You are good at winning games too!" they whispered.

66. Did God Make His Creations Into Predators And Prey?

After climbing up the small hill behind the Mexican Cowboy's house, Father Gallapo sat on a rock and watched events taking place around him. Alert spiders, in the middle of their webs, waited patiently for the capture of their next insect. Grasshoppers were vigorously jumping around him in every direction. Pygmy blue butterflies fluttered from flower to flower paying no attention to buzzing bees doing the same. A hungry horned toad was sitting on the ground beside a small rock, expecting to snatch passing insects. Not far from the horned toad was a sinuous and alert four-legged whiptail lizard. The priest couldn't make out what the lizard was doing. Above him, a cactus wren was busily circling, trying to catch a meal for herself and her nestlings. Circling high over the cactus wren was an eagle, keeping an eye on the wren below.

Father Gallapo had been reading about the interactions of animals, birds, and insects, and he realized that each of these he was now watching were predators and prey simultaneously. This troubled him for many reasons. Lives should not be ended by being eaten, he believed. But he realized that he had to start thinking about himself as a predator now, because he wouldn't be alive if had not eaten the foods given to him filled with meat.

"Should I have been born a vegetarian? And should our Faith mandate vegetarianism?" the Priest asked himself.

When he brought this topic up with Cowboy, he friend had said, "You're going to be eaten by worms and lots of other tiny creatures when you die and get buried someday. So you are prey as well."

Hearing this made the priest shiver. "I don't want to be eaten, even after my death," he said to himself.

Now, on the rock, he was wondering whether Adam and Eve were vegetarians. Or was eating others and being eaten yourself part of the punishment God had mandated? But if it was humans who'd disobeyed Him, then why would God have picked on all living beings too?

Watching the busy life around him again, the priest saw a grasshopper jump over a spider web. Moments later the horned toad dived under a rock to avoid an attacking cactus wren. Flying away, the disappointed wren was attacked by a diving eagle. With its legs extended, the eagle made a snatching jerk while passing over the wren, just as she turned sharply aside and dodged being grabbed.

"Most of us are good at protecting ourselves!" the watching priest suddenly realized.

Then, instantly realizing that human's living meat stock of animals and birds were allowed no means of protecting themselves, the priest felt saddened even more.

"Should I work on changing that?" Father Gallapo asked himself. "No," he said, getting up and starting back to Cowboy's ranch after pondering on that question for several minutes. "This is a problem that's way bigger than I can deal with. I'll leave it in God's hands."

Six giant rocks away, a starving mountain lion peeked around the rock's edge and watched with disappointment as the priest limped away from her down the hill.

67. How To Earn A Stranger's Trust

Skano the young skunk lived in the Bosque by the Rio Grande River and loved how his life was going. Digging up grass he unearthed grubs. Insects were abundant. Humans dumped garbage there—which he loved eating. Birders spread birdseed about which tasted good to him. And in the spring there were baby ducks on shore, and thousands of mice and other small mammals. Further, he seldom had to turn around, lift his tail over his back, and defend himself. Life couldn't be better for a skunk.

Because there were no reasons to keep his territory in check, Skano kept expanding his feeding ground, stretching out in different directions on different days. Because humans he'd met in the Bosque were always wary of him, but oddly interested in him also, he'd never had any reason to fear them. Though sometimes active during the day, typically Skano did most of his searching for food at nights. Late one night, Skano made up his mind to cross the low bridge with no traffic on it that reached across the slow-flowing river.

Walking into Cordoba now, there was still enough traffic on the often-used downtown street to make the skunk decide to go behind buildings he was passing by. Huge garbage bins behind two adjacent stores attracted his attention. He could smell a variety of meats in one, and foods he'd never smelled before in the other. Skano clawed his way up one of the bins and was trying to figure how to get it open, when he heard a dog growling and barking inside one of the buildings.

This frightened him, because one furiously barking dog could speedily attract several others. And just a minute or two later there were two cocker spaniel-sized dogs jumping off the ground beside the bins trying to bite him.

Skano turned around, raised his tail, and sprayed the musky compound produced in his anal glands all over the dogs beneath him. Howling and screaming they ran away. The horrible smell he'd spilled even quieted the dog barking inside the building.

Skano clawed down from his bin and ambled away from the street he'd crossed the river on. In just a block he came upon a small park and, finding a thick bush, he crawled inside it and went to sleep until the next night.

Next morning the Mexican Cowboy got two phone calls, one from a butcher who gave him meat scraps to feed his wild animals, the other from a baker who owned the small store next to the butcher's. Both callers had fans running in their stores and were trying to clear out the skunk odor that was driving away all of their customers.

"We'll clean up this mess, Cowboy," the baker said to him, " but we need you to catch this skunk and get it out of here, or we'll kill it."

"I'll gladly take care of it for you," Cowboy said. "See you this evening."

That night Cowboy and his little, curly-haired, white dog Mazzie were sitting behind the buildings just a short distance from the two bins, while his beloved stallion Turco stood with dropped reins behind a third store. Mazzie and the Cowboy remained patient, even though it wasn't until almost eleven when sniffing Mazzie smelled a skunk coming toward them downwind.

Cowboy put Mazzie on top of one of the bins and stepped back a few yards. Lying down and breathing quietly, Mazzie waited silently for the skunk to crawl onto the bin.

And just a few minutes later brave young Skano did this! Topping the bin, Skano was astonished to see a dog sleeping there, but the dog was too small to hurt him, so he didn't immediately slide down and run away.

Skano heard footsteps approaching and turned around in bombarding position. Cowboy walked cautiously up to the bin, rested his hands on the top, and waited to see what Skano would do.

Skano had never sprayed a human before and wasn't sure this would be the best thing for a skunk to do.

Cowboy reached out and put a handful of tasty meat trimmings on the lid behind the arching Skano. Mazzie reached up and licked Skano's face. Very confused, and very hungry also, Skano turned around and began slowly sampling meats in the pile. They were delicious.

While the skunk was eating, Cowboy put out a handful of fruits and vegetables. Then he reached in his pocket and put out half a cinnamon roll he bought at the bakery store in front of him. Skano had never tasted a cinnamon roll before and wasn't sure whether he liked it. For twenty minutes the three different kinds of mammals were getting along well together on the garbage bin.

Now, with all the food eaten, Cowboy could tell the skunk wanted to get down and go its own way. Pretending to help it climb down, Cowboy gently lifted the skunk. But instead of releasing it onto the ground, Cowboy carried the skunk over to Turco, his fabulous pinto stallion. With the skunk zipped into his jacket in front of his belly, Cowboy mounted Turco and began riding out of town. Mazzie trotted happily behind them.

Cowboy wasn't nervous though he could feel the skunk squirming against him while crossing the bridge over the Rio Grande on the sidewalk. Turco came to a gentle bank leading down into the Bosque. Cowboy steered his stallion up the river for several hundred yards until the way ahead was blocked with thick brush. Dropping Turco's reins, Cowboy dismounted, got on his knees on the ground, unzipped his jacket, and lifted the dazed skunk to the ground.

Releasing Skano, Cowboy placed three more handfuls of delicious skunk foods as far away from him as he could reach and sat quietly, keeping his distance from the skunk. Skano wanted to flee, but first he wanted to eat the foods put out for him. They were filling and tasted wonderful.

With Mazzie sitting beside him, Cowboy watched the skunk eat, then move away stealthily into the underbrush. Lifting Mazzie up in front of him, Cowboy climbed onto his saddle and was about to ride back to the other side of the river and return to his ranch when he heard a mix of odd noises coming from the underbrush.

Chattering sounds, loud and very short low-pitched squeaks, and sounds like a house cleaner crumpling newspapers were coming from the skunk there.

"He's saying 'Thank You!' to us," Cowboy said, patting Mazzie and reaching over to rub Turco's neck.

Turco neighed, Mazzie barked warmly, and the Cowboy shouted, "Goooooodbyyyyyyeee" as he rode back toward the bridge.

"See, you only have to feed someone a meal to get him to trust you," Cowboy said to Mazzie, patting her neck as Turco trotted across the Rio Grande.

68. Cowboy Becomes A More Cautious Eater

Calli the cat, Mazzie the dog, and the Mexican Cowboy were sitting on the porch together, nibbling on snacks each preferred. Cowboy was eating a giant, thick pizza he'd picked up the night before in Cordoba. With a beer on the floor beside him, Cowboy was taking giant mouthfuls of the delicious pizza and gulping these down after a few chews. His way of eating pizza had always been to grab a large piece, get as much of into his mouth as possible, chomp, swallow, and take a big sip of his beer.

But now suddenly Mazzie heard a gulping sound out of Cowboy she'd never heard before. With a hand over his mouth, Cowboy reached down suddenly, grabbed his beer, tipped it up and tried to get the mass jammed in his throat to go down to his stomach with a mouthful of liquid. Calli and Mazzie watched as Cowboy coughed loudly, spewing partially chewed pizza all down his front. He tried to swallow again, took another big swig of beer and, making a croaking sound, began gasping for breath.

A paste of half chewed pizza and beer had gone down the wrong hatch. Choking, struggling to breathe, the Cowboy tried to get out of his rocker and go inside and phone for help. But breathing was so difficult for him he couldn't stand up. His face was turning faintly blue, he seemed faint, and Mazzie and Calli realized they must be the ones to save their beloved friend.

Mazzie ran through the dog door into the living room, Calli just behind him. Mazzie stood on her back legs and struggled to lift the phone off its base on the small table. She couldn't quite reach it. Realizing this, Calli jumped onto the armchair next to the little table, climbed onto it and, with a paw swipe, shoved the phone onto the floor.

Mazzie struggled to dial 911, but her paws were too big and clumsy to press the tiny phone buttons. She tried with her snout and that failed too. Watching what her friend was trying to do, Calli jumped down, put her small front paw onto the button that Mazzie had been trying to press, and looking up at her for approval, pressed the button.

It worked! With her nose Mazzie pointed the next two buttons Calli should press, and was delighted to hear the phone ring twice before it was answered. "What help do you need?" a deep male voice said.

"Save our friend!" Mazzie barked. "He's choking!" Calli mewed.

"I don't understand," the voice said back. "Can I speak with your owner?"

Mazzie barked and howled as loudly as she could for several seconds. Then Calli made a string of cat sounds that were far different from her usual soft mews.

"You can't get your owner, is that right?" the voice asked. Mazzie barked and howled even more insistently. Calli made a wavering noise that sounded like a siren.

"I've ordered a fire truck and an ambulance," the speaker said over the phone's earpiece. "They'll be there at the Mexican Cowboy's place in just a few minutes."

With Mazzie staying by the connected phone, Calli went outdoors to see how Cowboy was doing. He was still choking and struggling to breathe, his face bluer than ever. Calli paced furiously back and forth. Cowboy still was struggling to get out of his rocker and call for help. Then Calli and the Cowboy heard sirens in the distance. Mazzie ran out onto the porch. Two minutes later the ambulance followed by a fire truck raced into Cowboy's property and stopped in front of the house.

With Mazzie yipping and Calli mewing for attention, ambulance attendants and fire personnel ran up onto the porch and began working on Cowboy to save his life. Mazzie and Calli moved aside and lay down next to each other and watched what was happening. "This is critical, but I believe we can save him," one of the medical aides said over her shoulder.

Cowboy was lifted out of his chair, turned around, and given back blows, before trying the more controversial Heimlich maneuver. Cowboy coughed and coughed, and at last the thick mass came up enough from his breathing tube that more air could make its way into his lungs. Cowboy was carried down the steps, put on a stretcher, and lifted into the ambulance.

Looking through its side window from the porch, Calli and Mazzie could see medical attendants working on him more. A fireman turned around to the two animals and said, "The guy at 911 who ordered us here told us you guys were the callers. We've never before had pets summon us when their master needs immediate help."

Mazzie barked her thanks, Calli mewed hers, and the two emergency vehicles drove away. It was three days before the Mexican Cowboy was brought back to his house. Looking normal again, he sat in the rocker and Mazzie and Calli jumped onto his lap.

Petting them, Cowboy said, "You saved my life!"

"After earlier you saved each of our lives, and the lives of so many other animals," Mazzie yipped.

"No more pizza for you!" Calli mewed. "Gotcha," Cowboy said back. "I'll be a more cautious eater from now on."

69. **There Are Many Ways Of Learning**

On a Saturday afternoon, Celesto's mother, Mirella Montagna, was sitting on the Mexican Cowboy's porch complaining about her thirteen-year-old son. "He keeps running away from school," she said, "and refuses to agree to stop doing it."

"He likes to be outdoors learning," Cowboy replied. "In school you can't be outside often."

"Well, even if he is an outdoors kid, he's got to stay in school."

"Why?" Cowboy asked. "I dropped out after ninth grade and things started getting better for me then."

"Look at yourself. You've never made much money. You couldn't support a child. If kids don't go on to college now they'll never find good jobs."

"There are ways to live without having a good job," Cowboy said softly. "And there are different ways of learning too."

"Not in today's world," Celesto's mother replied. "Look, will you try to help him stop running away?"

"I'll try," Cowboy said, "but I'm not the best guy for this job."

"You saved his life once and he loves you for that. He'll pay attention to you."

"He won't if I try to turn him into a person he is not."

"Well, see what you can do."

After Celesto's mom left, Cowboy sat in his rocker for hours trying to come up with a way to get Celesto to want to stay in school. Some ideas occurred to him. Next morning his friend Cece stopped by Cowboy's ranch to drop off Celesto. Cowboy thanked her, invited Celesto to join him for a snack, and the two of them went inside. Celesto asked him why his mother had insisted on his coming to see Cowboy today.

"It's because I need your help," Cowboy said, sipping his coffee.

"Oh, that's different. I'll do anything I can to help you."

"Thanks. I hate to say this, but there are things you need to learn before you can be of much use."

"Things like what? I'm a good learner. Just teach me and I'll be ready to help you."

"Okay, let's go down to the barn. I need to teach you how to care for horses before I can teach you how to ride."

"Yippeee! I've always wanted to learn to ride," Celesto said, getting up to follow Cowboy down to the barn.

For the rest of the day, and after school each day for two weeks, Cowboy helped Celesto learn to care for his beloved pinto stallion, Turco. Celesto *was* a fast learner, and a responsible worker. He was eager to care for Turco, and Cowboy was eager to keep him learning. He gave him a book about horse care to read and learn from, and Celesto eagerly gobbled information out of it, always returning with more questions. Cowboy also began teaching Celesto how to ride. Turco wisely began gently, then advanced into difficult horse stuff as Celesto's skills rose swiftly. Turco and Cowboy were very pleased with how the thirteen-year-old was speedily learning.

Cowboy now gave Celesto a book on horse riding over different—and sometimes difficult—terrain. "Hmmm," Celesto said, skimming through it. "There's geology, forestry, horse and rider biology, and much more that's fascinating in this book. Thanks Cowboy! I'm eager to read it."

"If you come up while reading this with questions you can't answer, ask your school librarian to help you find them," Cowboy said. "We have to keep teaching ourselves if we want to get better at what we enjoy doing."

With Celesto eager to be with him, Cowboy began teaching him the various foods wild animals need. On Friday and Saturday nights, Celesto stayed with the Mexican Cowboy and helped him put out different foods in safe places for each species to enjoy. Cowboy handed over books on different animals' biology and Celesto eagerly learned about the biology behind their needs and behaviors.

Mayor Howie, who always kept half an eye on the Mexican Cowboy's unexpected doings, dropped by enough times to begin worrying about the thirteen-year-old spending so much time working there. "He needs to be in school, and needs time to do his homework," the Mayor said. "You're overworking him."

"Go talk to his mother and the school principal before you take him away from me," the Mexican Cowboy said with a sly look.

"I'll do that!" Mayor Howie said. "Then I'll yank him away from you."

"I won't try to stop you," Cowboy replied.

Two days later Mayor Howie came back and immediately apologized. "The school principal and Celesto's mother both told me they were very grateful for your getting this kid back into the learning game. He's a great student now. I guess you are a great teacher also."

"Nope," the Cowboy replied. "All I've done is to find things he's interested in learning, give him books and things in the real world to learn from, and help him become eager to know more."

"What you are saying is that there are different types of learning, and by getting the kid focused on learning outside of school he became eager to learn applicable things in school?"

"Pretty much true, don't you think?" Cowboy replied.

"Okay," the Mayor said. "Now you've got him working for you, you've got to start paying him something. But because he's just thirteen, you can't put him on your payroll."

"I haven't got a payroll," Cowboy said.

"Give me the dough and I'll pass it along to the school," Howie said. "They need it, and they'll respect Celesto for earning money for them."

"How do I know you won't cheat me and pocket the money yourself?"

"Trust me. Cheating is a difficult subject to learn, but I'm good at it. I don't cheat you in ways you can guess at."

"You are an oddball man," Cowboy said.

"But not as screwy as you," the Mayor said back.

"I make you think I'm screwy so you won't know how good I am at cheating you!" Cowboy replied with a huge grin.

70. **Wild Bull In The State Park Meadow**

Two ranches north of the Mexican Cowboy's, a rancher he knew only slightly raised beef cattle who were often on trucks passing by the Cowboy's place on their way to the slaughterhouse. For years Cowboy had hated what would be done to these mooing cattle, but he stopped himself from coming up with ways to rescue them, knowing he would be arrested and taken to jail if he succeeded.

Coyote offered to try to teach the cattle how to escape, but when he tried one night, two fierce guard dogs almost caught and killed him. He gave up this animal-liberating task.

One spring, however, a young male calf, Mooo-um, just before neutering and who had an uncomfortable relationship with his herd mates, decided to make a break for it. Speaking to nearby cattle he said, "It wasn't so long ago that our herds used to be free to wander wherever they liked. Now we are just slaves. If you won't go with me I'll go by myself to restore at least one bull's freedom." His herd mates ignored him.

Three nights later, while the guard dogs were sleeping, Mooo-um sneaked silently to the east side of the fenced ranch, pushed into the barbed wire, and with small wounds on his chest, knocked the not very sturdy fence down and vanished.

With only moonlight to guide him, Mooo-um rapidly walked east into the mountains. Following roadless canyons for three days, he eventually came to a grassy meadow, which he loved.

As weeks went by Mooo-um got to know lots of other animals. Deer grazed with him, a young mountain lion thought about eating him then decided with his growing horns this young bull might harm her, and he shared the meadow with badgers, a skunk, field mice, and occasionally, coyotes hunting at night. "Freedom is good for me!" Mooo-um said one night before curling up under a tree to fall asleep.

What Mooo-um couldn't realize was that he was 'trespassing' in a State park. Several weeks later a ranger spotted the young bull and went over to check him out. Used to humans already, Mooo-um didn't run away, which made the ranger certain that this was a domesticated bull. But the bull didn't have a brand, ear tags, or any other identifying markers that could make it easy for the ranger to call his owner to come and get him.

Before the rangers could figure out what to do with the young bull, a park visitor posted videos on-line of Mooo-um grazing with deer. Other visitors started showing up and photographing this odd combination of species, and it wasn't long until news media were in the park reporting on the wild bull living with his deer friends.

When rangers decided to remove the bull to keep the park inhabited only by wild life, mammalers got word of this and camped around the meadow to keep rangers from removing Mooo-um. Debates about this appeared on newscasts around the world. Hundreds of animal supporters poured into the park, determined to keep Mooo-um safe. Arguments about what to do raged in the New Mexico legislature and between the state's agencies.

After a week and a half of worsening battles, the state's governor signed an order prohibiting the rangers from removing the wild bull in the State Park. "Like Smokey the Bear, the wild bull's brought lots of attention to our state," the governor said afterwards to an aide, "and it is worth protecting him to keep that going."

Ignorant of all that was happening in the human world, one night before he fell asleep in the meadow, Mooo-um said to himself, "Freedom is good for me. I wonder if it is good for humans also? Do free people fight with one another over different things?"

That night, back at his ranch, the Mexican Cowboy was talking about the political battles with Mayor Howie. "This is really going to make a lot of people start working to let cattle roam freely," he said with excitement.

"This is really going to make me work closer with ranchers to stop all this noise and keep raising beef cattle their way," replied Mayor Howie.

"So, the war's going to grow?"

"Not if I can stop it," the Mayor said back.

71. Watching Special Ops Training

One afternoon in the early winter, Mayor Howie stopped by the Mexican Cowboy's ranch to warn him to be careful feeding the wild animals over the next three nights. "Don't tell anybody this, but I've been told that a Special Ops training program will be happening in the Manzano Mountains for at least three days. You don't want to mess with these guys. They are sneaky and very good at doing what they are told."

"I've heard about these warriors before. Will they be SEALS?"

"I don't know and I wouldn't tell you if I did."

"So, why are you telling me any of this?"

"Because I want you to keep that restless kid Celesto, who's been working with you for four years, from sneaking into the mountains while this training mission is taking place. There are huge ways he could get in trouble if he goes up there."

"Thanks, Mayor. I'll ground him."

"You do that," Mayor Howie said, before climbing into his ancient polished Cadillac and driving away,

Later that afternoon, when seventeen-year-old high school senior Celesto came to work with Cowboy, the two sat on the porch while Cowboy passed along what the Mayor had told him. "I think he's right. A lot could go wrong for you in your life if you sneak up there to watch the Special Ops guys doing their thing."

"I've told you several times that I want to be a Marine. But I don't think I ever said that I want to be selected for Special Ops training as well."

"I think you'd be great at that, you're good at so many things, but stick with me now please."

"Okay, I'll think about doing what you want," Celesto replied.

Late that evening, after the wild animals were fed," Celesto said goodnight, got into the older Toyota Cowboy had bought for him, and drove away.

"I hope he goes home," Cowboy said to himself, before getting ready to sleep.

Celesto in fact did go home, but only to change clothes, pack gear and camouflage materials, and head into the mountains. Earlier, while Coyote was eating his delicious meal, Celesto had sat beside him asking questions about where Special Ops training might be taking place in the Manzanos. Coyote, who knew the mountains well, offered several possibilities, and they had talked about these until Coyote was ready to leave. Now Celesto drove to a place on the mountains' edge he had visited only once previously. Putting on his gear, Celesto locked his car and disappeared into the mountains.

Late next morning as he searched for the Special Ops training team, he kept out of sight behind rocks and trees and avoided crossing open spaces, hiding as much as he could. He knew Special Ops forces used silent helicopters, and last night one had passed overhead, blanking out light from individual stars, and heading in the direction he was going.

Celesto also scanned the sky for drones using a good set of binoculars he'd been given. Around four that afternoon he heard a tiny whispering sound from the sky and, hiding in a bush, he looked up with his binoculars and spotted a drone. It was flying in large circles over a place two miles ahead. Remaining invisible, he sneaked in that direction.

Shortly after six, he was lying in a shallow ditch he'd dug, covered with brush, and happily watching uniformed Special Ops guys spying on soldiers dressed like Afghan Taliban leaders conducting a meeting in the mountains.

Late that night, the forces he was watching attacked the 'enemies' and subdued them in less than five minutes. Celesto watched a silent black helicopter descend, the bound 'enemies' put into it, and the 'copter lift off silently and disappear. The Special Ops forces melted back into the mountains moments later.

Celesto debated whether to follow them, then decided he'd seen enough and, gathering his gear, started back over the mountains to his car.

Seven years later Celesto had indeed become a Marine and had even survived Special Forces training. He was now with a team based in Hawaii, which called itself the 'Kukinis'—after historic Hawaii's most able athletes. One night drinking with several of his team at a bar in Kailua Kona on the big island, Celesto was telling the others about his successful spying mission on special ops forces in training in New Mexico.

"I watched everything they did, and they never spotted me."

"Actually, that wasn't so," the oldest team member said back. "I was there on that training mission. Some of our guys were conducting that operation, but the rest of us were watching anyone who was spying on them. When we wrote up our report we said, for a seventeen-year-old, you were good at what you did," his teammate continued.

"And more was going on than you ever found out. I was spying on you separated guys too!" Celesto said with a wry grin.

"No you weren't. We kept track of everyone around us."

"Did you happen to notice a coyote watching you?"

"Yes, there was one, but coyotes can't spy on humans and pass data on."

"This one could and did!" Celesto said, and proceeded to tell his teammates exactly where his force had been, how many they were, how they were dressed, how they spread out and observed, and how they left the site after the helicopter's departure. "That was a phony drone overhead. Even I knew that. And when I got back to my own base, actually a place where I fed wild animals, I downloaded all the information on you from the coyote. Back in those days you Kukinis were pretty special. But you made a better team for yourselves when you let me join you."

"You beat us, Celesto," his teammate said, "and you didn't let us discover what you'd done until now. I'm glad you are with us."

"Same here and, if I hadn't pulled that operation off in New Mexico when I was seventeen, I probably wouldn't have gotten to be a Kukini." Celesto said back, raising his hand for another filling of his team's glasses.

72. A Human Wants To Run With Wildlife

One evening, while the Mexican Cowboy was feeding him a delicious mix of raw meats, Coyote mentioned seeing something odd on the mesa east of Cowboy's ranch. "There was this human and dog running in many directions. It wasn't until I saw they were chasing a hare that I figured out why they weren't going in a straight line, as you guys usually do."

"Were they trying to catch the hare and eat it?" Cowboy asked.

"Perhaps, but I don't think so. This guy and his dog seemed to actually just enjoy running."

"Then why didn't they run up the road into the mountains?"

"Beats me," Coyote said. "You are better at figuring out humans than I will ever be."

That night what Coyote had told him didn't stick in the Cowboy's mind. But next afternoon, Mayor Howie drove up to his ranch house in his polished ancient Cadillac with a stranger beside him and a dog in the back seat."

Howie never lets animals get in his car," Cowboy said to himself. "What's this about?"

Stepping off his porch, Cowboy walked over to the Mayor to find out why'd he come this time.

"Cowboy, this is Cole Benesor, a long distance runner from back east, and his dog Romo."

"Pleased to meet you," Cowboy said, tipping his filthy yellow Stetson hat and offering a hand. "What brings you out here?"

"Pleased to meet you!" the runner said, smiling and shaking hands. "You are famous and I learned from many sources about all you are doing for wild animals," Cole said.

"He wants to run with them," Mayor Howie blurted.

"And I figured that you may be the guy who can help me do it," Cole continued.

"I don't know about that," Cowboy replied. "Wild animals are frightened of humans and only want to run away from them."

"I understand that," Cole said, "but I want to expand the activities of human runners, and get them to begin helping wild animals too. Runners always help their buddies."

"Well, come inside and let's talk," Cowboy said.

"I'll leave them with you," Mayor Howie said, starting back to his polished car. "They want to run back into town when they leave."

Indoors, with Romo nibbling rawhide on the floor next to Mazzie, the small curly-haired dog who was living with Cowboy, Cole told Cowboy about life in the running world and how so many runners were looking for exciting new ways to keep running.

"Why don't you just run with dogs?" Cowboy asked.

"Some of us do, and that's great, but I want to run with other animals too."

Cowboy mused on this for a minute or two, then said, "All right, I have a way to help you, but you are going to need to stay here with me for a month and do things I tell you."

"Most guys I wouldn't trust if they asked me to do that, but I'm yours for a month."

Starting next morning, Cowboy took Cole and Romo down to the barn to meet Turco, Gus and Calli. He warned Cole that Romo had to behave herself, and if she growled,

snapped at, or attacked any animals on his property she would have to leave permanently. But Romo, it turned out, actually enjoyed being with other animals. And she was good at figuring out their needs and responses.

In the mornings while staying at Cowboy's, Cole and Romo went for twelve- or fifteen-mile runs exploring the Bosque, the mesa, the edges of the Manzano Mountains. In the afternoon they helped Cowboy put together meals for wild animals. And in the evenings they were out feeding the mix of animals, getting to know them, becoming friends with them.

One bright evening, with an almost full moon, Cowboy gave Cole a new instruction. "Tonight I want you to go and keep up with the deer going back to the mountains. It will be bright enough out that you won't need a flashlight."

That evening Cole focused on the deer and fed them special flower treats, and when they abruptly left, Cole trotted along beside them. Worried, they turned away from him. He ran ahead of them, they turned back toward him, he slowed down, they stopped and stared at him, he trotted on toward their site in the mountains, they came behind him, he went off to one side to let them pass, and when the deer finally came to the edge of the mountains, Cole stopped, sat down, and let the deer go home. They passed by him with odd expressions on their faces.

"How'd it work?" Cowboy said when Cole and Romo ran back to his ranch.

"Wonderful! They let me go all the way to the mountains with them. Then Romo and I got to run back here in the terrific moonlight."

For the rest of their month together, Cole worked with the deer and with a visiting bear and a hungry mountain lion. "The bear was easy to keep company with going back to the mountains," Cole told Mayor Howie one evening, who'd stopped by to find out how

Cowboy's training was going, "But the mountain lion did everything she could to keep me from running with her."

"She attacked you?" Howie asked.

"No, but it was plain she was scared of me."

"For good reason," the Mexican Cowboy added. "But you stuck with her. If she'd grown up with you the two of you would get along just fine."

"You are right," Cole said. "Running with youngsters in the animal world should be my primary thing."

"It will help humans and other species learn to work together," Cowboy said.

"And if you do it out here I can get you lots of publicity."

"And win another election afterwards," Cowboy said with a wry smile.

73. **Act Twice Before You Think**

As he aged, Father Gallapo, the itinerant priest who lived with the Mexican Cowboy, spent more and more time sitting in Cowboy's armchair and thinking. The Cowboy was worried about his friend and asked him why he wasn't reading as often as he used to or spending as much time in Cordoba's run-down Chichimaya church.

"It's not complicated," the priest answered. "I have more things to do these days and therefore I need to spend more time planning. If you do twice as much as you used to, you'll need four times longer to plan."

"And you plan entirely by yourself and not with others' help?"

"That's right. Planning is a solitary thinking process. I have to be alone when I do it."

"So, you don't believe a group of church members could help you solve your problems?"

"I'm their priest and I want them to look up to me, not be my equal."

"This seems wrong to me," Cowboy said reflectively. "Your parishioners will always look up to you, but they want to help you get things done."

"Oh, I ask them to help once I have made plans," Father Gallapo said wearily. "But look, just as you are interrupting my planning now, many of them might do the same thing."

"I am not interrupting your planning, I am trying to help you get things done."

"Planning is getting something done."

"It isn't unless you do what you've planned."

"You are a nuisance, Cowboy."

"And you are turning into a lazy priest. I want you to get off your butt and go down to your church and get things done."

"I will get something done today, if you shut up and let me plan."

"You don't think twice before you act, you think a dozen times or more."

"And you do a lot of acting without planning."

"And I get a lot of things done!"

"I save a lot of souls."

"I save lots of animals' lives."

With the argument continuing, Mazzie began to woof, softly at first. Calli the cat jumped onto the priest's lap and began trying to lick his face. "Tell your animals to shut up," the cross priest said to Cowboy.

"They are trying to make us shut up," Cowboy said.

"We have a right to talk."

"But they can sense that our arguing is pushing us apart."

"What do you want me to do then?"

"Come out onto the porch with me and let's have a beer."

"I'll do it if you will give me a glass of wine instead."

"And let's get some great snacks for Calli and Mazzie."

"If that will make them keep still, I'll be glad to do it."

"You and I are never going to agree about much," Cowboy said.

"That's a good thing. One of us would have to stop being himself if we were trying to get along better," the calming priest said back. "Being one's self is righteous."

"So is having an afternoon drink on the porch. Suppose for a while we act twice before we think?" Cowboy said pouring beer down his throat.

"You swallowed and wiped your mouth. That's acting twice. Now I can go plan," Father Gallapo said, getting up and leaving.

74. **The Possum And The Goldfish**

When she first came to Cordoba, Cece stayed with Celesto's mother in an older house very close to the mountains. She liked living there and enjoyed being able to go hiking in the mountains without having to cross the mesa first. There was one thing though she didn't like about this well-kept home, and that was occasional pillage and thievery by a possum, which was somehow finding its way indoors.

Possums are omnivorous and this one was good at opening cupboard doors, pulling stored foods down, and munching away. The possum couldn't open cans, however, and tried throwing these onto the floor at night hoping they would break. They didn't. But when the possum began dropping glass jars, they often would break, and possum would gobble up olives, mustard, pickles, and anything else that was open on the counter or floor, before disappearing behind the stove.

If the possum were doing this every night Cece and Celesto's mother Mirella would have gotten the Mexican Cowboy to trap it and carry it far away. But this possum was shrewdly clever and only invaded the kitchen at unpredictable intervals. The women put up with it. But then an older couple, whose home Mirella was beautifully caring for, gave her a small present—a large goldfish in a huge bowl that was filled with fascinating underwater 'buildings' that would keep casual watchers' eyes fixed on the bowl for many seconds. Mirella loved the bowl and its inhabitant and put it on a table in the living room for all to see.

One night though, the possum discovered the goldfish and made up its mind to catch and eat it. The possum climbed up one of the small table's legs and began fishing with its front 'hand' while the goldfish darted in and out of the buildings in the bowl.

Next morning Cece noticed puddles of water on the little table and warned Mirella that the possum was back and going after the goldfish. Mirella moved the bowl onto the dining room table and then, when she found that sunlight was warming the water too much, moved it upstairs onto the reading table next to her bed.

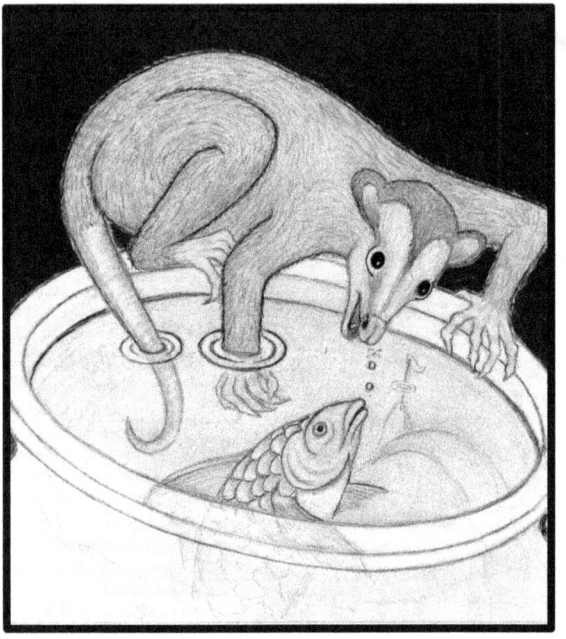

Three nights later she was awakened by something coarsely furry standing next to her and reaching into the fishbowl. She screamed, the possum stared at her for two or three long seconds and then, deciding not to play dead, disappeared. Cece was awakened by the scream and rushed into Mirella's room to see if she needed help. The two of them searched the house for the possum, but it had vanished.

Mirella started putting the goldfish bowl into her ancient rusty bathtub each night, even placing a thin board of plywood over it to keep the possum away. One night the possum worked several hours trying to pull the plywood off the tub, and almost succeeded when it heard Cece getting up to use the bathroom.

"I've had enough of this possum," Cece said to Mirella over breakfast next morning. "We need to figure where it is getting into the house and block it."

For the next several days they looked everywhere they could think of, but they couldn't discover how the possum was getting indoors. Then one day on a hike into the nearby mountains, Cece looked down on Mirella's house and spotted something odd. There was a pipe coming up through the roof out of the kitchen. She couldn't guess what this was for.

Next time Cece visited Cowboy, she asked if he had any ideas about the pipe. "Sure," Cowboy replied. "That's a very old house. If the kitchen used to have a wood stove, that was its exhaust pipe."

Back again with Mirella, the two of them struggled to pull the electric stove away from the wall—and behind it was a small hole, high up, that had to be the doorway the possum was using.

"What can we stuff into it?" Cece asked.

"How about a chunk of wood?" Mirella said. "We have lots of firewood in the back yard."

Cece held a piece of paper over the hole and traced the pipe's size. Then outdoors they found a chunk of wood just slightly larger. With several well-aimed hatchet whacks, Mirella shaped the piece nicely. Indoors again, they fitted the wood into the pipe hole and shoved the stove tight against it.

That night they listened to the possum banging at the obstacle it had encountered. "It won't be back again," Mirella said happily. "Tomorrow I'll put the goldfish back where it used to be."

"Don't bet on it," Cece said. "That possum is good at figuring out how to do things."

"But so are we!" Mirella replied.

"You are right. The possum learned from us, and we learned from it. But we won," Cece said.

"Bet you a nickel that we will learn it's in the kitchen again."

"Deal!" Cece said.

Three weeks later Cece had to hunt for a nickel to give to her friend Mirella.

75. **Is Safety Fatiguing?**

Gus, the well-muscled donkey, and Turco the pinto stallion were good friends. They enjoyed each other's company in the Mexican Cowboy's barn and pasture. But Gus was growing resentful of Cowboy always taking Turco out riding and leaving Gus alone in the barn. If this only happened once in a while Gus would not have minded, but spending hours by himself three or four times a week was growing painful.

He wrongly blamed Turco for abandoning him. And as hours mounted alone in the barn with no one paying attention to him, Gus began scheming on things he might do to get Turco's attention back. He loved Turco, but Gus was becoming so angry that he was now willing to put Turco's life at risk, if this would restore the time they spent together.

Out in the pasture the Cowboy was good at spotting plants that were dangerous for horses and removing these. The locoweed was especially easy to spot with the plants' blue-green stems and purplish flowers, and Cowboy yanked every one of these he spotted. But he did this only in the pasture. Locoweed grew happily in many other places on the ranch, but Cowboy didn't believe his well-fed horse and donkey would ever bother to eat any of it.

Cowboy didn't know this, but Gus was now trying to figure how to get Turco outside the pasture alone with him and persuade him to nibble some locoweed. One early fall day the Mexican Cowboy was away from his ranch and his young helper Celesto was taking care of Gus and Turco. Celesto led them into the pasture and closed the gate. The rusty gate latch Cowboy used was flimsy, but if his boss and teacher trusted the latch to hold Gus and Turco in the pasture, Celesto was willing to do the same thing.

His head hanging over the gate, Gus watched Celesto go back into the barn to begin putting together the night's meals for wild animal visitors. Then Gus turned around and with two well-aimed kicks with his back legs got the gate open again. Without paying attention to Turco, Gus then began grazing outside the pasture along the fence.

Turco watched him but stayed inside.

In half an hour Gus had worked halfway around the pasture and was moving away from it toward a thick bunch of plants ten or fifteen yards east of him. Watching Gus's head in the plants, envy rose in Turco and he decided to join Gus over there. As he approached, Gus had his head up and seemed to be chewing with delight some of the purplish flowers in front of him.

Turco had never tasted these, but he eagerly put his head down and began eating the plants. They tasted different to him, but their flavor wasn't bad. He began munching his way through these plants, taking his time.

About ten minutes later he looked up and saw Gus heading back into the pasture. Turco realized that Cowboy would be angry if he'd left without permission and, with a bit of disappointment, turned around and went back into the pasture himself. When Celesto returned in the early afternoon he was troubled that the gate was open, but pleased the horse and donkey were still in the pasture.

In the stable with Gus late that night, Turco's head began bobbing up and down, and he couldn't make it stop. Walking around his stall, his steps were exaggeratedly high, and he staggered. Frightened for his friend, Gus began braying as loudly as he could. Fifteen minutes later Cowboy came into the barn, turned on the lights, and seeing Gus looking anxiously at Turco, went into his stall to see what was wrong.

Watching Turco's atypical movements, Cowboy realized that he'd been eating locoweed. Cowboy left the barn immediately, phoned a local horse doctor, and stayed with Turco the rest of the night. Early in the morning, the doctor agreed with Cowboy's guess, treated the horse, and said if these symptoms continued Turco's brain cells might be unfixable.

Fortunately, next night the locoweed symptoms began disappearing, and soon Turco was back to being himself. However his doctor advised Cowboy to keep Turco in his stall for at least another week. Frightened over losing his stallion friend, and now enjoying his steady company, Gus was becoming very angry at himself for causing all of this. He was relieved though that Turco didn't seem to blame him for doing things that had caused these symptoms.

And now, Gus was being taken out of the barn for several hours each afternoon. Having to feed more and more wild animals every night, Celesto began loading Gus with their mix of foods and leading him out to the mesa to put pans down for the night's visitors. Gus was glad to be outdoors with someone again. And he stopped feeling isolated and angry when Turco returned to riding away with the Cowboy so often.

Coyote, who had been told by the Mexican Cowboy that there was no locoweed in the pasture and he couldn't figure out how Turco had eaten any, inspected the gate, saw dents where it had been kicked open and, sniffing, tracked the equine pair over the mesa to the locoweed he could tell had been eaten.

When he told his best friend about this, Cowboy was furious.

"Did Turco or Gus kick open the fence?" he asked.

"The hoof marks were Gus's," Coyote replied.

"Then I am going to get rid of Gus for kicking open the gate."

"They need each other," Coyote said back. "Most equines need company as much as you humans. I noticed that Gus was lonely when he had to spend so much time by himself in the barn."

"I don't get lonely whenever I'm not around other people," Cowboy said.

"You are an oddball when it comes to human ways, and Gus is a normal burro," Coyote replied.

"Then why did he lead Turco out to eat locoweed?"

"Maybe he'd come up with a way to change how you are treating him," Coyote said back.

"That way was dangerous as hell," Cowboy said.

"Well, it worked for him. What would you have had him do instead?"

"I'd have told him to start braying in the barn every time he's left alone there. Then I'd find something interesting for him to do."

"You are a genius," Coyote said. "You always come up with safer ways than others to solve important problems."

"Safety is my thing when it comes to changing how others' lives work," Cowboy replied.

"If that's so, then you should tear out the rest of the locoweed that's on your property," Coyote said.

"Safety is fatiguing," the Mexican Cowboy said with a groaning voice, nodding his head to accept Coyote's suggestion.

76. **Animals Manipulate Humans Too**

The Mexican Cowboy loved sitting in his rocker on his ranch house porch, watching every living creature that came into his view. He often spotted new visitors who might be staying for several minutes, or just passing through his property.

One day a golden-mantled ground squirrel, striped like a chipmunk, appeared and began digging its burrow just several feet from the porch. The squirrel then began raiding seeds, nuts, and berries put out in the late afternoon for several night feeders, and Cowboy watched it returning to its burrows with its cheek pouches bulging.

Cowboy had another welcome guest as well, a greater road runner, with its long, straight, black-and-white striped tail, head crest of brown feathers, and powerful bill, who began eyeing the ground squirrel with more than curiosity.

Cowboy knew that roadrunners kill and eat rodents, and he debated whether he should allow this to happen in front of him. When he brought the topic up with his best friend, Coyote said it was every species' right to eat its prey. Cowboy replied that he fed animals in part to keep them from killing one another.

"But you can't take killing prey away from any of them," Coyote replied. "Birds and animals are who they are."

"If I have to watch this, what will I see if the road runner nabs my little squirrel friend?"

"The bird will kill it with a fierce blow to the squirrel's neck. And if that doesn't work, he'll pick it up and bash it against a rock."

"I don't want to see this," Cowboy said with a pained look on his face. "I am going to see if I can help these two get along with one another."

"No way!" Coyote said with a predator's smirk.

Cowboy began feeding the roadrunner every day, but he was frustrated that the bird kept its eye on the squirrel every time it emerged from its burrow. Cowboy put food for the squirrel on the burrow's tiny mound and was annoyed when the roadrunner went and stood over the mound, hoping the squirrel would stick its head up and be grabbed. The squirrel simply tunneled to another exit and sat on the mound there watching the roadrunner. When it flew away, the squirrel ran over to the hole where Cowboy had put the food and began filling its cheek pockets.

One day Cowboy used a net on a long pole to grab the roadrunner. He dumped the large bird into a paper bag, stapled it shut, saddled his magnificent stallion Turco, and rode off toward the mountains. At the mountains' edge, Cowboy dismounted, ripped open the bag and released the roadrunner.

The dazed bird staggered several yards away, and turned and stared at Cowboy. Ignoring the roadrunner, Cowboy mounted Turco again and began trotting back to his ranch. He was halfway there when the roadrunner came racing past trotting Turco. Cowboy watched him disappear over the small hill in front of him, and guessed the bird was doing almost twenty miles an hour.

Back on his porch after caring for Turco and putting him back in his stall, Cowboy settled into his porch rocker again. He was amazed to see the roadrunner standing beside the long-poled net.

"The bird thought the race with Turco back to the ranch was fun," Coyote said that evening, when he asked why the roadrunner had returned. "He probably wants to do it again."

"I'm running out of ideas to stop him from killing the squirrel," Cowboy replied.

"You may have this wrong," Coyote said back. "The road runner may be working you, and not really going after the squirrel. The squirrel may be working you too."

"What makes you think that?"

"Because the road runner could easily run away and nab as many rodents as he wanted somewhere else. He's here because you feed him, you keep him safe, and he likes your company. And the squirrel is pleased with you too."

"And they make more work for me."

"All of your animals do," Coyote said. "You believe this animal feeding business is your idea alone. You've never realized that animals figure out how to manipulate humans too. You are not the bosses you think you are."

"Manipulating is a two-way street, you're saying," Cowboy replied.

"And you humans think it is one-way," Coyote said back.

77. Cowboy's Nature Picks What He Shall Read

Father Gallapo was having increased trouble walking. His knee joints were failing. He'd thought about having these replaced, but he didn't want major surgery, and couldn't pay for it anyway. The Mexican Cowboy noticed how badly his friend the priest was limping and, decided to have a talk with him over what to do about it.

"You spend too much time sitting," he said while they were sitting together on the porch one day.

"I'd be up and walking more if my joints were better," Father Gallapo replied.

"I believe if you tried to walk more you might actually make your joints better. Exercise keeps all parts of us healthier."

"I haven't heard that exercise fixes people with bad joints," the priest said.

"Well, try it, and let's see how it works for you."

"All right, I'll follow you around your property for the next week or two and we'll see if this works for me," the priest said with doubt on his face.

Every time Cowboy left his ranch house he tried to make the priest come with him. It was taxing, because his friend always offered excuses why he shouldn't go out now. "But I will certainly do it next time," the priest added.

"That's what you said to me last time. Come on. Get up. We're going outside," the Mexican Cowboy demanded, yanking the priest off his chair.

Cowboy was frustrated every time he walked with the priest. The old man was tipsy, walked slowly and carefully, and almost fell several times. It took Cowboy three times as long to get things done when his friend was with him. When he stopped to work somewhere, the priest would hunt for a place to sit, and Cowboy would have to strain and pull him up before they could walk further.

"This isn't working for either of us," Cowboy said.

"True. And you know what Aesop said, 'You may change your habits, but not your nature,' " the priest replied.

"Who is Aesop? One of your fellow priests?"

"He is a famous fable writer," the priest replied. "And your ignorance proves we need to get you to read more."

"I'll read more if you like, but only about wild animals. My nature always gets to pick what I'm going to read."

78. Making Flower Beds Look The Same Year Around

Last spring the Mexican Cowboy's lady friend Cece had planted flowers around the Cowboy's ranch house. Cece loved and planted asters, lilacs, chrysanthemum, roses, lupine, hollyhock, columbine, nasturtiums and petunias and tended these carefully so the flowers she collected were abundant and beautiful.

But alas, when a hard winter arrived in New Mexico, the flowerbeds were scraggly, stripped and ugly. Cowboy hated how these looked.

"Dig 'em all out," he ordered. "You can replant the beds again next spring.

"No. We need to leave the flower beds alone now," Cece responded. "Some will return nicely and be even more beautiful."

"I want my ranch house to look the same all year round," Cowboy said. "I hate how it looks now."

"The flowers were beautiful."

"Maybe, but the flower beds are ugly now."

"You ought to admire the beds for what they were and what they will be next spring."

"And you ought to stop making my ranch house look so awful in the winter."

"Why don't you enjoy the seasons of flowers?"

I hate putting up with changes others make to my life."

"Each of us is different than you, and we want different things."

"Are you saying what I want doesn't matter?"

"Tell you what I can do," Cece said, and began explaining the idea that had just popped into her head.

Ten days later, Cece's flower beds were filled with loaded bird feeders every eight or ten feet, and two birdbaths. Wearing his heavy coat and gloves, the Mexican Cowboy sat on his porch watching goldfinches, cactus wrens, canyon towhees, Steller's jays, chipping sparrows, and many species of migrating birds gobbling seeds and other bird food from Cece's feeders.

"You love watching them, don't you?" Cece said, with her hand on Cowboy's shoulder.

"I do indeed," Cowboy said with a smile. "Now your ugly flower beds work for me."

"And they will work even better for you when the beds are filled with flowers."

"I don't know about that," Cowboy said with a hard-to-read expression on his face.

"I do," Cece said back, giving the Cowboy's shoulder a hard squeeze with her resting hand.

79. I May Save My Life Many Times In The Future

Young Celesto was growing up and learning a great deal by observing others. He was also a cautious and kind youth and he committed himself to warning others of dangers he perceived in their paths.

He warned Coyote when a wild dog pack he'd watched was figuring out how to kill him. He warned his mother when she forgot to shut off a stove burner. He warned Calli the cat when he spotted her walking across a loose beam overhead in the barn. He warned Mazzi the dog when the small, friendly guy began wandering between the hooves of the restless stallion Turco. He warned the priest, Father Gallapo, when he spotted him leaving for Sunday Mass unshaven and in dirty clothes. He warned the Mexican Cowboy when he noticed him heavily overloading the donkey Gus. And he even warned Gus when he saw him outdoors in the fenced pasture one night peering through the barbed wire at a nearby mountain lion Cowboy was feeding.

Celesto was a cautious youth, but he also had a wild streak inside him. Most days he lived safely, but this necessity slipped away from him when he was occasionally struck by an idea of something new he wanted to do. There was that hole in the roof of the barn for instance. The hole wasn't big and little rain or dust came through it. Cowboy insisted that they could live with the hole for years to come. But the tiny burst of slowly moving sunlight coming through the roof hole vexed Celesto more and more each day he worked in the barn.

One morning, when his employer, the Mexican Cowboy, was inside the ranch house making breakfast, Celesto decided to go up onto the roof and fix it. He put a ladder against the barn wall, a piece of cloth and scissors in his pocket, and carrying a small can of tar with a spatula sticking out of it, began climbing up.

The top of the ladder was almost three feet beneath the roof. Celesto reached up and put the tar, tools, and cloth up there, then struggled to get himself onto the steep shingled roof. With his hands searching for something to hold onto and pull himself up from, he had one foot on the ladder and one knee on the roof, when his searching hand knocked over the tar can and rolled it off the roof. Reaching out to grab it, he accidentally pushed the ladder sideways. Very frightened and grabbing the roof's gutter, he edged the ladder straight again with his foot. Catching his breath, Celesto realized there was no point in getting on the roof without tar. Cautiously and trembling, he put the tools in his pocket and climbed safely down to the ground.

"I could have lost my life up there," he said to himself, staring up at the roof thirty feet over his head. "I'm smart enough to warn others, but too stupid to warn myself when I do something life-threatening. If I pay attention to what happened today I may save my life many times in the future."

80. Give Garbage Away To Win An Election?

An election was four months away and Mayor Howie was feeling almost certain he would lose when voters' ballots were counted in Cordoba. He needed to come up with an idea to turn around the many voters who mistrusted and were angry with him. And because his little city was deep in financial peril, he had almost no money to spend on sneaky ways to get himself reelected. City Council members disliked Mayor Howie too and several of them were hoping to be reelected also.

To make matters worse, the pushy Mexican Cowboy was harassing Cordoba's tiny city government to come up with a way of providing him with more help feeding wild animals. Mayor Howie had one other major problem to deal with too. The eight-acre garbage pit two miles east of tiny Cordoba was filling up, and the city lacked the money to either buy more land or pay the town's two garbage trucks to take the waste elsewhere.

Pondering this mess of things to deal with, the Mayor was close to deciding not to run again. "I'd rather retire than lose an election," he said to himself.

Next afternoon his friend Frank Corsa, who was the town's police chief, one of its few police officers, and who also ran the garbage dump, was sitting in the Mayor's office, asking support for an idea he wanted to implement.

"Is this about police or garbage?" Mayor Howie asked.

"Garbage, this time," Corsa said. "I want to start giving the city's garbage away."

"Who would take it?" Howie asked.

"The Mexican Cowboy. He needs more food every month for the rising number of wild animals he's feeding. People in Cordoba are poor and thrifty, but they still throw away lots of eatable foods."

"Why should we do this?" Howie asked.

"The reason I came up with this suggestion is that our garbage pit is almost filled and we can't afford to buy new land. If we sort and give away a lot of the garbage that would go into it, we'll have years more until we have to come up with another answer. "

"But we can't afford to hire more people to sort the garbage," Howie said.

"We won't need more workers. My wife's a birder and I am a mammaler. We'll do the sorting ourselves and see if birders in the region are willing to volunteer to help us out."

"It's a crazy scheme," Mayor Howie replied.

"True, but if it works out it might attract more visitors to the town to see the expanding bird and wild animal population the Cowboy feeds, and they'll spend money here. And when local voters hear about this tax free idea, they may change their minds and vote for you after all."

"I don't think any of this will happen, but let's give it a try," Mayor Howie replied, after thinking for several moments.

Several weeks later the Mayor visited the garbage dump and was surprised to see fifteen workers, mostly women, raking and sorting garbage, and shoveling edible foods back into an empty garbage truck. A reporter and a photographer from the nearby Socorro newspaper were covering the event, and they followed the garbage truck when it drove away.

In the newspaper that came across his desk next day, Mayor Howie read a front-page story, with pictures, showing how Cordoba's surplus garbage was being used to feel wild animals and birds. And Frank Corsa and Mayor Howie were given credit for coming up with the idea.

As weeks went by many people in Cordoba began separating garbage before putting it out in different bags, so it would be less work for volunteers at the garbage pit to load a truck to take to Cowboy's ranch. Many junior high and high school students began stopping by to help out. One day Mayor Howie put on work clothes and shoveled for hours with photographers and reporters watching him, and next day his picture was on the front page of the Socorro paper, with a praise-filled story.

In the week before the election Mayor Howie joined the garbage workers in picking up sacks throughout Cordoba. Word quickly spread through town that their current mayor was good at both coming up with ideas to solve critical problems, and willing to do whatever work was needed to make these ideas do the job.

On Election night, votes were speedily counted and Mayor Howie was told he'd won the election with more votes than he'd ever received before. That night, driving home in his polished ancient Cadillac, Mayor Howie said to himself, "Who else but me could win an election by deciding to give garbage away?"

It's a good thing Frank Corso didn't decide to run against me, thought the Mayor, pulling into the gravel driveway in front of his house.

81. **A School Band Gives More Than It Gets**

Hilda Thompson was the music director—and assistant principal and gym coach—at Cordoba's tiny elementary school. She felt she worked at least three times harder than most elementary school grownups and was proud of herself for all she accomplished each day. With Christmas nearing, she was helping the school's band put together a Christmas concert for school staff, student and parents.

Mayor Howie, whom she dated occasionally, had made an unexpected request of her in mid-October. "Could you please play also outdoors while my friend the Mexican Cowboy's wild animals are feeding?"

"Why ever would you ask me to do such an odd thing?" Hilda had asked, and Mayor Howie said back, "It is because we want to get reporters there to get the story on TV and in the papers."

"For your sake, not for my kids'?" Hilda asked.

"For theirs too! Their performance might even make the national news," the Mayor answered.

Hilda had cleared the idea with her principal, with students in the band and their parents, and so she began working very hard to come up with music associated with animals. With a little bit of online research she'd put together a lengthy list of songs about animals, including: *How Much Is That Doggie in the Window? A Horse With No Name, Bird On The Wing, Dragonfly, Eyes of the Squirrel, Hound Dog, Land of the Snakes, Lions, Tigers & Bears, Playing Possum, Prairie Dog Town, Rabbit, Rocky Raccoon, Running Bear, Sly Fox, The Bear With the Maiden Fair, The Chipmunk Song, The Lion Sleeps Tonight, True Men Don't Kill Coyotes, White Rabbit, Yertle the Turtle...* by loved, famous, and even little-known bands. But when she tried to find orchestrated copies of most of these songs to look over she quickly became frustrated.

"This isn't working for me," she said. "And I couldn't get my young musicians to perform most of these in the time we've got to prepare," she added.

Hilda then searched for children's animal songs, and quickly found a number of well-known ones, *Bear Went Over the Mountain, Crocodile Song, Farmer In The Dell, Mary Had A Little Lamb, Three Blind Mice, Turkey in the Straw...* But these pieces bored her. For her school concert she had already put together a list of classic and one or two less familiar works for her band to perform. But none of these were about animals.

Then an oddball idea crept into her head. Hilda went online and began searching for sounds wild animals make, and minutes later she was sitting down next to the piano trying note combinations she had never come up with before, and transcribing these into music scores.

It was a clear, chilly night when Hilda, her student musicians and their parents showed up at the Mexican Cowboy's ranch. Hilda's students carried instruments, folded chairs, and music stands off their school bus, and put these up in three rows creating a partial circle in front of Cowboy's porch. The city's firemen had lit bonfires behind them, which provided light and some warmth. About twenty-five yards away, a mix of wild animals enjoyed their lavish Christmas meals. Several crews with TV cameras were taping the setup and a dozen reporters were watching attentively. With parents sitting around the band, and the Mexican Cowboy, Mayor Howie, and many of their city's leaders sitting on the porch, the concert began.

After the first song was performed and the audience applauded, Hilda said—turning her head and body back and forth to face the parents and the filled porch, "And now we are going to perform a song for coyotes." She raised her baton, swirled her left hand in the air, and the saxophones, clarinets and flutes began making howling songs, just like those coyotes make to one another.

Baffled, the audience and people on the porch tried to make sense of what was going on and could not, until suddenly they heard coyotes from all directions joining in. When the 'song' ended, there was unexpected silence from the audience, and then a roar of applause with shouts of delight. The band members were thrilled.

And now, after every Christmas song for humans, the band played one for a different species of animals. Next came bear music. A tuba and a French horn produced rising growls, a tenor saxophone played without its reed was making sharp coughing noises, and a drummer ended each few notes with a muffled beat. The song lasted over three minutes, and just when the band was coming to its last notes everyone made out the return calls of two bears.

And so the concert went. Clarinets and flutes put together the fast, birdlike, high-pitched chattering sounds of raccoons. Cellos with tape over their strings produced mountain lion sounds. Flutes and clarinets together again produced the sounds of whining deer. And for the last animal number, all of these pieces were repeated in mixes, filling the audience's ears with 'music' that would be impossible for them to imitate, much less describe.

At concert's end, there was a mix of applause and curious looks on people's faces. "This is something they've never experienced before," the Mexican Cowboy said with giddy happiness to Mayor Howie.

"And it is something they'll never forget either," Howie replied.

"I bet the animal parts of tonight's performance will attract listeners from all over the world. It's going to be on YouTube," Cowboy said.

"It is going to make Hilda Thompson famous as a composer, and her young musicians famous for playing music no one's ever heard before in a concert," the Mayor said a couple of minutes later during his short thank you speech to the band and parents.

"These kids are all geniuses," Cowboy said when he spoke to the audience. "Their performance was far more memorable than any of us expected."

From all around the humans there came a mix of extended animal sounds, which everyone took as applause from the listening wild beasts.

"Way to go!" Cowboy said, before getting off the porch and passing out Christmas stockings filled with tasty nibbles and sweets to the band members. "You guys gave us a lot more than you'll ever get from me."

82. **Why Do Humans Praise One Another?**

The Mexican Cowboy was feeling depressed. Over a meal at his dinner table one evening his friends were applauding and admiring each other. But when no one congratulated and praised him, he felt ignored because he was unworthy. It had all started when Cowboy praised Mayor Howie for finding ways to make impoverished Cordoba expand and become prosperous. "And you found ways to help me feed so many wild animals too!" the Cowboy said warmly.

The group applauded. Then Mayor Howie, and the Cowboy's friends Cece and Thelma, each said how proud they were of their priest, Father Gallapo, for finding funds to rebuild their crummy little church and attract more believers. "You are the best priest this town's ever had," Mayor Howie said to Father Gallapo.

Feeling proud, Father Gallapo nodded while he was being applauded and then responded by praising his friend Thelma, the church's manager, who did most of the work of maintaining the church, finding funds for it, and coming up workable ideas to attract more members. Thelma was vigorously applauded.

In turn, Thelma praised her close friend Cece. "You come up with so many wonderful ideas, and show us how to make these work," she said. "When I think of everything you've accomplished I know you are an amazing human being!"

With everyone applauding, Cece smiled, stood up, and hugged Thelma. Then she said to the dinner party, "I may be good as you say, but you know the person here who is best doing things is Coyote. Coyote is terrific at doing things coyotes do. But he has also helped humans and hundreds of animals in so many ways. He's our real champion."

Everyone stood up and applauded Coyote, who shyly put his head down into his rich bowl of food and began eating without looking up.

Then the people around the table changed subjects and began talking about things they might like to do together in the future. Being the only person at the table who wasn't praised, Cowboy tried to paste a happy look onto his face, but he mostly kept head down and kept nibbling. Thelma kept her eye on him and decided he was upset because no one had praised the Mexican Cowboy. When she and Cece cleared the table and went into the kitchen to bring out dessert, Thelma hunted through the wine cupboard and found to her delight a cheap bottle of champagne. She carried glasses and the champagne out to the table and Cece brought delicious deserts. Everyone at the table looked at the champagne and wondered why it had been brought to them.

"Open it for me please, Mr. Mayor," Thelma said, handing him a corkscrew. The bottle was warm and there was an enormous bang when the cork was pulled out of it. Champagne fountained onto the floor. Promising to clean it up, Thelma filled glasses and passed them around the table. Then she stood and said, "All get ready to rise please, we have a toast to make. It is to the Mexican Cowboy, the best person at this table. I'm going to say a word or two and then I want each of you to add a few words in honor of our host." Looking at him and raising her glass, Thelma said, "Cowboy I adore you. Before I got to know you my relationship with Father Gallapo was uncomfortable and perhaps even hateful. Since you became our close friend, everything you've done has made us more comfortable working together. I'm so grateful to you!" Smiling, the others applauded.

Mayor Howie rose, raised his glass and, facing the Cowboy said, "If you hadn't started feeding so many wild animals and working with Coyote, all that I was able to do for Cordoba would have been impossible. You are the real champion at this table." People around the table applauded, cheered, and thumped the table with their fists.

Father Gallapo didn't rise when the Mayor sat down, but he raised his glass, stared at the Cowboy for ten or fifteen seconds, then said in his preaching voice, "You are a better person than you will ever believe, Cowboy. You are unlike the rest of us in so many ways, but even though you are not a Believer, you are a better Christian than I am. God did a superb job when he created you."

Puzzling over this, there were raised eyebrows and light applause around the table. Then Cece rose, raised her glass to her friend the Cowboy and said, "You saved my life once. I'll never forget your doing that for me. But you also helped me to become such a much better person. No one here could do for me everything you've done." People shouted, applauded, banged on the table even harder.

Then everyone looked at Coyote, sitting on a chair with his head down in his pan. They waited. And waited.

Finally Coyote looked up and said, "Okay. You humans are good at praising one another and one of you even praised me. But look, coyotes don't praise each other. We believe that each of us is better than others in some ways, worse in others. Let me say that this is true of you humans too." Coyote stopped speaking and put his head back into the food bowl.

The Mexican Cowboy stood, raised his glass, and now genuinely smiling said, "I agree with Coyote. Even though we've praised each other, each of us is better in different ways. What makes humans so effective is that we think well of each other and we work together. Coyotes, alas, cannot work together. I'm raising my glass to every human on this planet!"

People sitting around the table nodded, applauded perfunctorily, sipped their champagne, and heard Mayor Howie say, "Do you guys agree with what the Coyote and Cowboy just said?"

"Nah," said Father Gallapo. "He's got a lot wrong with him."

"You all do," Coyote said, raising his head and holding it high. "But he's still better than each of you."

83. Can Grape Growing Be A Good Personality Test?

Cece, the Mexican Cowboy's friend, woke one morning with an urge to plant grape vines and make wine. "It's a nice thought," the Cowboy told her, "but wine grapes won't grow on the clay mesas here. Why don't you just buy grapes to make wine with?"

"Because I really want to try raising them."

"Okay," Cowboy said back. "Let's go outside and pick out the land you want to farm on."

Cece and Cowboy explored much of his property until she decided which spot might be best for her grape growing experiment. "It is yours," Cowboy said, "and you can use all the tools in the barn. Feel free also to help yourself to the garbage that Frank Corsa's people deliver three times a week. If you mix some of it with the clay you might make it fertile enough to make grape vines you plant hardy."

Cece worked for seventeen days to clear the mesa clay, turn it over, fertilize it, and plant young wine-grape vines. Watering these became her first problem. The deep well Cowboy's water system drew from was too limited to supply all the water she would need. A nearby farmer on the edge of the Rio Grande Bosque offered to water the half-acre she'd planted with his tractor and water sprayer, providing she'd pay him for the water she'd need. "How much?" Cece asked him.

"About seven hundred dollars, by harvest season. Water for agriculture is hard to come by out here. We're not allowed to draw from the river, so unless we have terrific wells, we have to buy water to put on crops we're growing."

Cece paid him, and he took care of the watering problem for her. Weeding was continuous and painful work for her, because as the vines began growing, every kind of mesa plant wanted a share of the fertilized soil and water. Windstorms pasted the young vines with tumbleweeds, which were painful to pull away gently. Large animals that Cowboy fed every night were cutting through the field of vines, ripping these up. Deer tried to eat them and had to be chased away on many days and nights.

Cece was a dedicated worker, and she dealt more or less successfully with problem after problem threatening her crop. In late September, she did have good looking grapes on most of the vines, but many were showing insect damage because she had forgotten to come up with approved ways to keep bugs off them. Picking grapes turned out to be exhausting work, which Cowboy declined to help her with. But at last she had about a hundred and ten buckets of grapes dumped into cardboard boxes in the back of Father Gallapo's Ford pickup. When she was ready, he drove her into Albuquerque to hand over her crop to an amateur wine producer, who was eager to make wine for her.

In late November, they drove back to Albuquerque to pick up the bottles, he'd been able to produce about sixty for her, and with labels she had designed on each of them, she took these back to Cowboy's ranch and stored the bottles in an empty stall. A few evenings later Thelma Whitenose made a nice dinner for her priest Father Gallapo, Cece and the Mexican Cowboy. Cece took two bottles of her wine to share. When she opened both and sniffed, the wine smelt okay. But when she tasted it, the wine was so bitter and sludgy that she was almost afraid to swallow it.

Thelma got out a pitcher and poured the wine through a meshed strainer to get some of the sludge out of it. They opened a bottle of wine Thelma had bought to serve with the meal first. "We want to get some wine into them before they try yours," Thelma had suggested. And now, with the main course coming onto the table, Cece brought out the pitcher and poured some into everyone's empty glass.

"Let me know what you think of this," she asked as she sat down.

Cowboy raised his glass and offered a toast, "To Cece, our great wine maker," he said.

"Amen," the others replied, lifting their glasses and sipping. Cece, watching their faces intently, saw a mix of suppressed coughs, and waves of dislike passing over each person's face. "It is pretty good stuff," Thelma said, trying to get a happy look on her face.

"I've had worse," Father Gallapo said, struggling to hold back an explosive cough.

"I think it is so wonderful, we ought to give a number of bottles you made to Mayor Howie," the Mexican Cowboy said.

"You still want to kill him," Cece said. "This stuff of mine is awful. Give me your glasses. I'll dump this crap down the sink and bring out another bottle of good wine."

"You are a blessed soul," the priest said to Cece. "You are the only one here who told the truth when we tasted your wine."

"You are a terrific wine grape farmer," Cowboy said to Cece. "Maybe it was the wine maker who screwed up your grapes."

"No, it was me who didn't listen when you told me grapes won't do well on the mesa," Cece said. "I may be a good grower and a good soul, but I'm also good at doing things which should not be done."

"And you are a truth teller too," Father Gallapo answered, a genuine smile on his face as he tasted the new wine.

Listening to what the others had been saying, Thelma lifted her glass, tasted the new wine, and with a smile on her face said to Cece, "Raising grapes and serving your terrible wine proved to be a good personality test for you and the rest of us."

"And you, Thelma, came up with a bright remark," Father Gallapo said, taking another drink from his glass.

"See," Cowboy said to Cece, "all your hard work's made a great evening for us. Thank you," and he reached over and kissed her.

"I'd hoped for more than your brief kiss for my wine-making efforts," Cece said with a sarcastic grin on her face.

84. Help Others And You Get Helped Back

When he was a youngster Coyote noticed several crows overhead making aerial attacks on a soaring eagle. "Why are they doing that?" he asked his mother.

"Probably to keep that eagle from trying to snatch baby crows from their nests to feed her own young eaglets," she answered back.

"Eating other's babies doesn't sound right to me," young Coyote said to his mom.

"The time will probably come when you enjoy them," his mother replied with a light laugh.

Coyote was much older now and so far he had never caught and eaten anyone's babies. He was tempted though, and one day he was hiding in a bush watching crow youngsters get ready to leave their nest. While its parents were away, one of the crow chicks stood on the edge of its nest, flapping its wings, and then suddenly leaped into the sky. Coyote watched it falling through the branches, getting thumped and turned, until it hit the ground lightly and seemed to pass out.

Coyote was struggling with himself over whether to pounce on the young crow when an eagle dived out of the sky, landed beside it, and pecked it to see if the youngster was still alive. The youngster peeped loudly, calling for help.

Without a thought Coyote raced out of the bush toward the eagle. Startled, the eagle leaped into the air before Coyote landed where it had been.

Staring at Coyote, the baby crow was even more frightened now, and peeped loudly for help. Up in the nest, its family looked down, certain that Coyote was going to kill the youngster before they could do anything to help save it.

They were stunned when Coyote oddly lay down and wrapped his body around the young crow. The youngster peeped more softly, and seemed to be comforted by its protector.

Several minutes later its parents landed close to Coyote and stared at him silently. Coyote uncurled from the youngster and got up and backed away. When he was back under his bush again, both parents flew over and landed near him. One was carrying in her bill a lizard she'd just caught. Walking over to Coyote, she opened her bill and dumped the flailing lizard down in front of him. Coyote tried to caw a thank-you, as the crows flew back to their grounded youngster.

"They'll look after it now," Coyote said to himself.

Three days later, around sundown, Coyote was ambling along one of his well-known routes when two crows dived at him one after the other and raked his back with their bills. Snarling, Coyote stopped, sat and threatened to snap the crows if they did this again. But they didn't.

So Coyote got up and started trotting along his forest path again. A moment later the two crows attacked him once more. Coyote snapped at them, but they both got away safely.

Now he sat and tried to figure out what all this was about. Low in a tree across from him, the pair of crows was staring intently at a bush twenty yards along his route in front of him. Seeing him watching them, both of the crows leaped into the air and made two low passes over the bush.

"They are trying to tell me something's in there," Coyote guessed.

As the crows each made a third pass over the bush a paw with sharp nails and yellow fur suddenly reached up and tried to grab one of them.

"It's a puma there!" Coyote said to himself. "And it was hiding to pounce on me when I trotted by."

Back up in the tree again, the crows understood that Coyote had at last figured out their warning. They flew down and landed before him, cawed pleasantly, and departed. Coyote tried to caw back his thanks for saving his life.

"Because I saved their baby they protected me," Coyote though with gratitude. "If you help crows, they'll help you back. For my own sake I should do more of this in the future."

85. Mayor Howie Doesn't Take Credit For What He's Really Done

Mayor Howie's election was nearing and he was spending long hours in his office deciding upon everything he needed to do to win again. Hardest for him was whether he should boast about himself as the great provider of food for wild animals, or whether he should boast to hunter voters that he was helping to increase supplies of their game. Being an effective conniver, Mayor Howie decided he should do both. So he had meeting after meeting with farmers, hunters, and gun-favoring conservatives who relished his defense of their positions—and liked to hunt with them also. And he had meeting after meeting with birders, mammalers, wildlife experts, and the general liberal public who didn't want to see animal species being destroyed by humans. These people loved Mayor Howie for his manifested support of providing food and funds for wild animal feeding. Two weeks before the election Mayor Howie was far ahead in polls and certain he was going to win for the fifth time.

Then the local newspaper interviewed the Mexican Cowboy, who was feeding so many birds and animals, and put his picture and story on the front page of their widely read Sunday paper. "I would prefer to read only the comics," Cowboy was quoted as saying. Asked if he supported Mayor Howie, Cowboy answered truthfully, "He gives me things to win my vote. I'll keep my promise to vote for him, but I will be pleased if someone else wins."

City Council president Julia Garcia, the candidate who was trailing Mayor Howie in the polls by twenty percent, seized on the Mexican Cowboy's opinions in her next interview with the press. "If I'm elected, we're going to stop paying the Mexican Cowboy to feed animals and birds at his ranch. He needs to get private funding for this venture, not our city's money.

Well, Mexican Cowboy read that story when it appeared in his newspaper. And he wasn't surprised when a reporter knocked on his door to get his reaction. What Cowboy said made the front page of the paper's next edition. "Helping wild animals is my thing, true. But Mayor Howie's helped me in many ways, and I've brought tons of money to merchants in our small city by attracting tens of thousands of tourists who want to meet the animals who eat here every night. If she wins, candidate Julia Garcia will chase all these tourists away and the city's merchants will suffer, though not more than the animals I'm feeding."

Next evening the press took photographs of Mayor Howie personally feeding wild animals. These made the paper's newest front page. Several pages back there was a story about Julia Garcia saying she could come up with many new ways to keep tourists visiting in the same numbers. "Our Bosque is wonderful. Let's make it into a park," she said.

Next day there was a major demonstration in the small park in Cordoba of protesters who wanted to keep 'their' Bosque 'wild.' A major speaker said: "Garcia's going to take the Bosque away from us and the animals living there. We can't let her turn nature's Bosque into a city park." This story made the front page of the newspaper's next edition.

Mayor Howie then held a 'Save the Bosque!' rally in the Bosque itself. Hundreds of supporters showed up, along with tens of opponents.

Next day an editorial in the town's newspaper made it clear that public opinion was becoming divided in so many ways that no voter could decide confidently now which candidate to vote for. "Many voters will stay home on election day," the writer suggested.

Three days later the election was held and, when the ballots were counted, Mayor Howie won by over two thousand votes. He gave a gracious acceptance speech, which appeared in the newspaper. But a week later, when a reporter asked the Mexican Cowboy how he though the Mayor had gotten himself reelected, the Cowboy said, "He probably came up with ways to pay many voters to go to the polls and choose him. Also he may have bribed the persons who counted the ballots." The paper's editors refused to publish these comments.

"I'm far craftier than that!" Mayor Howie told a reporter who asked for his response after being told what Cowboy said. "I won this election by starting a divisive public fuss over feeding wild animals. What I made the Cowboy say won me many votes. And I know he hates me. But don't publish any of this! I never take credit for things I really do."

"You don't want to be credited for what you really did to win the election?" the reporter asked.

"If I tried to get credit for things I really do, that would destroy my reputation and get me kicked out of office."

Next Sunday Cowboy sat in his green rocker on the porch, skimming through the local paper. "Good, no more political crap," he said aloud, while turning to the comics. "Comics interest me more than politics."

In his office, skimming through the same edition of the tiny city's newspaper, Mayor Howie said to himself, "I should figure out how to get them to dump the comics and print more politics. I've glanced over these comics for years, and not one has ever been about me." Mayor Howie spent the next fifteen minutes trying to figure out how to get himself put into a comic strip.

86. **Never Eat A Fish The Way Cranes Do**

Coyote was annoyed because it was springtime and 'his' Bosque had many humans lining banks on both sides of the Rio Grande trying to catch fish. "Why do so many of you humans spend time catching these odd-looking things?" Coyote asked his friend the Mexican Cowboy.

"We eat them," Cowboy answered.

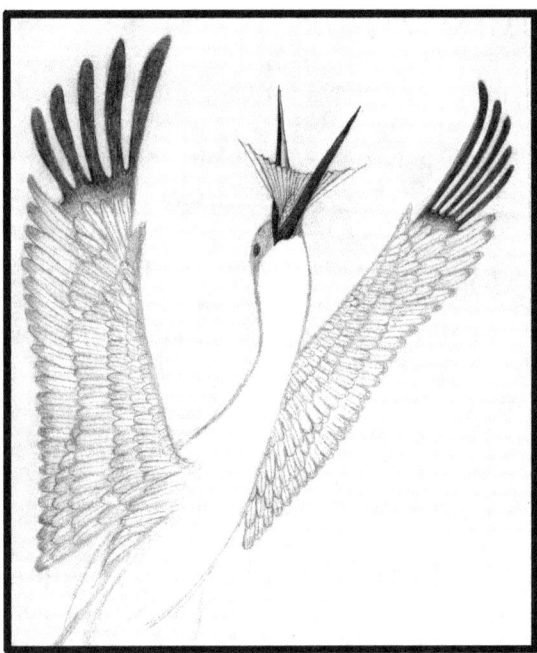

"Are they tasty?" Coyote asked back.

"Many humans and animals think so," Cowboy replied.

"How can I catch and try one?"

"That's hard question to answer. Why don't you wade into the river, learn to swim underwater, and see if you can catch one yourself?"

"That sounds scary to me."

"Well, how about trying to steal a fish from one of the buckets fishermen put their catch into?"

"Are the buckets filled with water? If so I don't want to stick me head into one."

"Usually they are," Cowboy replied.

Every day for the next week, Coyote hid in thick bushes near the shore and watched fishermen catching and unhooking fish. He couldn't understand why many of these fish were tossed back into the river.

"For several reasons," the Mexican Cowboy told him that night. "Laws govern which fish you get to keep. Some species have to be thrown back, and little ones often are as well. And many fishermen don't want to eat their catches and so they throw them back in the river."

"They wouldn't throw one at me, would they?" Coyote asked with a hopeful expression.

"I've never heard of any fisherman throwing part of his catch at coyotes," the Mexican Cowboy replied.

Next night the Coyote didn't show up at the Cowboy's ranch for his usual tasty feeding. Waiting by the river until all humans left, Coyote waded from a low bank into the muddy river. Holding his head up high, he sniffed and sniffed, but could not smell an underwater fish. Putting his head under water, Coyote sniffed again... and jerked his head out, coughing with water sucked into his lungs.

Trying to learn how to move around in the water again, Coyote stepped over a submerged log and found himself in deep water. He had no choice but to paddle hard, and was surprised that he could stay afloat and actually swim. He then tried to swim underwater. He could do it for a moment or two, but holding his breath he wasn't able to smell anything down there, and the water was so muddy he couldn't see much around him.

Swimming back to the low bank, he was standing ankle deep and shaking himself violently to get his fur drier, when a beaver stuck its head out of the water behind him. "What are you doing in my pond? I've never seen a coyote swim here before. If you come after me or my children, I'll swat you in the face with my powerful tail and swim under you biting your belly and feet."

"Please don't!" Coyote answered. "I'm trying to learn how to catch fish. I've never tasted one."

"I can get one for you, if you'd like to try it."

"Thank you. I would, very much."

As the Coyote got onto the riverbank and shook furiously to get more water off his fur, the beaver vanished under water. Less than a minute later, beaver surfaced again, swam over to the low bank, and waddled over to Coyote, carrying a big catfish in her mouth. She dropped it beside Coyote and went back into the river.

Coyote looked at the flopping fish's big head, gasping gills, and jerking tail, and wondered how he was going to eat it. He put his front paw on the struggling fish and debated whether he should chew it into pieces. Then he recalled watching crane with a fish in its bill bend its head straight up and let the fish slide down into the crane's throat. "That's the right way to eat a fish," Coyote said confidently.

Holding the fish sideways in his mouth, Coyote sat on his fanny, bent his head back, and struggled to swallow the catfish. Using his tongue and teeth he turned the fish around until its head was lowest and, with a swipe of his paw against the fish's tail, shoved it into his throat. It stuck there.

Coyote began coughing, trying to get the fish out of him. Sticking out of his mouth the fish's tail was bobbing furiously in many directions. Coyote stood up and bent over, coughing even harder. The fish was wedged in there. Nothing he tried got the fish out of his throat. Wondering if this mistake was going to kill him, the beaver was suddenly in front of him saying, "That's the wrong way for a mammal to eat a fish. You can choke yourself to death. Want me to help you get that fish out of you?"

The choking coyote nodded his head furiously up and down. "Can you stand up on your back legs?" the beaver asked. Coyote nodded and stood on his two back legs, swaying back and forth with each mighty cough. An instant later there was a terrific blow to his upper chest. Coyote fell over backwards, his chest hurting horribly. But when he rolled onto his side and struggled to get up he realized the fish was gone from him.

"Sorry. I had to give your chest a hard smack with my powerful tail. But it pushed the fish back up and out of you."

"Thank you," Coyote said. "I owe you a lifetime of favors."

"If you willing, I'll ask some of you. Now, do you want to keep the fish?"

"No!" said Coyote, picking the flopping fish up gently with his mouth. He carried it to the high bank, bent his head back, and hurled the catfish into the river. A moment later the fish stuck its head out of the water near Coyote, bobbed its head back and forth in what may have been thanks, and disappeared.

Next evening Coyote told the Mexican Cowboy everything that had happened when he'd try to eat a fish. "You went about it the wrong way, but beaver saved you and you saved the fish. I owe you both a bunch of rewards," Cowboy replied.

"So how about fish bites for me tomorrow and food the beaver can feed her youngsters."

"Shall do," Cowboy replied. "But first promise me you'll never try to eat like a crane again!"

"I do promise that," Coyote said putting his right front paw on his chest, "but is it alright if I try to eat a crane my own way?"

"Sure, but I bet you can't catch one, unless you learn to fly."

"I've always wanted to fly," Coyote said back. "It would give me a lot more game to snatch for my kids."

87. **Who Won The Bet?**

The badger god and prairie dog god were long-time friends, and one day they decided to have a contest to see who could get the Mexican Cowboy to take off his faded yellow cowboy hat. "This is going to be hard for us," the prairie dog admitted. "It may take a long while before one of us wins."

Badgers, under their god's orders, began throwing up beneath the Cowboy's rotting porch. The stink was pronounced, and the badger god hoped Cowboy would take off and wave his hat to blow away the stench. He didn't. Instead he turned on his hose and sprayed water under the porch for several minutes. That took away the smell.

The prairie dog god had a hard time coming up with an idea. At last he decided to have one of his followers dig a hole in the small patch of grass beside the porch, hoping the Cowboy would step into it, fall, and have his hat knocked off when he hit the ground. Cowboy spotted the hole from his porch one morning and filled it in.

The badger god tried to persuade the eagle god to make one of his followers knock Cowboy's hat off. The prairie dog god insisted that using other creatures was outside the game's rules, and the badger god reluctantly agreed.

As months went by, attempt after attempt to make Cowboy take off his hat failed. The badger god was ready to quit, but the prairie dog god had one last idea to try. Fifteen miles away, one of his followers had spotted a capped bottle of Mexican beer standing upright in front of one of the prairie dogs' underground villages. The god ordered his followers to deliver the beer as a gift to the Cowboy.

For week after week, tired prairie dogs rolled the bottle across the mesa, up the hills and down, over sand dunes, around rocky patches and over car bridges, until one evening they were finally near enough to see Cowboy rocking on his porch. Struggling to keep the bottle going the right way, they slowly rolled it nearer. Coyote was with Cowboy on the porch and was the first to spot the prairie dogs coming their way. He told his beloved friend about approaching prairie dogs. Cowboy stared into the darkness until he finally located the bunch of little guys taking turns rolling a bottle towards him.

Near the foot of the porch now, the dogs wrestled for ten minutes getting the bottle upright, then backed away, and sat upright to see what Cowboy would do.

Curious, he came down the porch stairs, picked up the bottle to make out the label in moonlight, then turned around to ask Coyote what this was about. "It must be a gift they've brought for you," Coyote said. "Get some food to thank them." Cowboy agreed and went down to the barn to search for things the prairie dogs might like to eat. He brought back and scattered roots, green leafy plants, and garbage coated with insects around them. The prairie dogs watched, sniffed, and he could see they were eager to eat, but they still wouldn't budge from their places.

"That didn't work," Cowboy said to Coyote. "What else should I try?"

All of this was annoying Coyote. He couldn't figure out what was going on and wanted it to stop. "Wave your hat and chase them away," Coyote replied. "They are being just nuisances."

Feeling much the same, Cowboy opened the bottle of beer, took a few sips enjoying the taste, then turned to the prairie dogs, bowed deeply, and waved his hat in a sweeping salute gently before them. The prairie dogs leaped up, ran to the food Cowboy had scattered, and chattering with each other began feasting.

"I bet that I'll never figure this out," Cowboy said to Coyote, sipping his beer with his hat back on.

"You got a deal," Coyote said back.

Three nights later, sitting together on the porch again, Coyote told his beloved human friend about the bet the prairie dog and badger gods had made. "My coyote god told me," Coyote said. "I win our bet."

"And I won the previous one, and got a terrific bottle of beer from it," Cowboy replied.

88. Celebrating An Anniversary

One snowing February evening the Mexican Cowboy and Coyote were sitting on the porch with a powerful electric heater next to them. Coyote was looking down at food in the bowl the Cowboy had brought out for him. It was heaped with fresh meat and smelled wonderfully to Coyote when he put his nose down to sniff it. "This is unbelievably good. It may be the best food you've ever put out for me," Coyote said. "Is there a reason why you've given me this?"

"Indeed there is. It's our anniversary, and we've never celebrated one before."

"What anniversary are you talking about?" Coyote asked.

"The date when you found me and saved my life."

"That was a terrible day for me," Coyote replied. "You were trying to rescue that boy who'd crawled into a cave in the mountains and was being held by the hibernating bear who thought he was her newborn cub. You fell down the snowy mountain and broke several bones when you were going to get help to save him."

"Actually I fell when I was going down to get a rope to pull him away from Ursula, the bear who thought she was his mother. They wound up loving each other."

"I had to be the one to get rescuers for you."

"You figured out how to make a party of hunters follow you back to me when one of the guys took a shot at you and hit your ear."

"It still hurts some nights," Coyote replied, gently scratching his left ear with his back leg.

"But then after I was hospitalized and fixed up, you came here to see me."

"I never figured out why I did that," Coyote said. "My mother warned me to keep far away from all humans."

"You did it because I'd reached out to you and asked you to save me. By saving me we formed our lifetime friendship."

"I'll never know why I spoke back to you and let a human find out I could speak his language."

"Because you are a heroic soul, that's why."

"I don't know about that. You are the guy who takes care of so many of us. You've saved my life several times."

"So, this relationship has been good for both of us?" the Mexican Cowboy asked.

"Of course it has, and good for other animals too. You helped many species work together better with each other."

"I wouldn't have been able to do any of this without you!" the Mexican Cowboy said, rubbing his dear friend's neck. "Eat up."

"I will, in a moment," Coyote said then breaking into a short howl.

"Why'd you do that?"

"Because I knew also that today was our anniversary. I've put together something for you!" Coyote said.

A moment later just about every one of the Cowboy's friends walked around from behind the house, where they had been waiting and shivering. Each was carrying a present for either Coyote or the Mexican Cowboy. Handing Cowboy a large decorated cake in an open box, Cece said, "Let's go inside guys. It's freezing out here. We have so many ways we want to thank the two of you for making our lives better. Your meet up matters to us too. Let's celebrate your anniversary together."

With tears of gratefulness streaming from his eyes, Cowboy rose, hugged Cece, opened the house door, and motioned his friends to lead the way.

"It's hot in there," Coyote said standing beside Cowboy. "If this goes on long take me into your bathroom and give me a cold shower. That's what I'll want for my anniversary present."

"Love to! And I'll put your bowl of delicious food in the shower with you," the Mexican Cowboy said, rubbing the top of Coyote's head before the two of them went inside.

89. Evil Stirs Up Good

It was a bad year in the very small city of Cordoba. The economy was dropping and many persons were suffering. Merchants' sales dropped. A much warmer, drier agriculture season left farmers with fewer crops to sell. The tourist trade was worse than ever. Teachers' salaries were cut back to keep schools open. And students were given more homework so school hours could be cut back.

All this was differently affecting persons in Cordoba. Celesto, the student the Mexican Cowboy had rescued years before from the bear Ursula's hug, was suffering as much as any one. Celesto's soccer team was disbanded and he was let go from his part time job. He wasn't a very good student, and being given more homework to do was devastating. Lunching with his friends, everyone agreed with him when Celesto said, "Evils are taking over Cordoba." Several buddies talked back and forth about whether to quit school and run away from their homes. That suggestion appealed to Celesto! He spent the night thinking about how he might do it.

Next day he was lugging his homework bag walking back to school when a bicyclist pedaled by him swiftly. He recognized her. Mandy Diggins was a cheerleader as well as a star in several women's sports. "She going to go far in life," Celesto said, watching her pedal away from him.

A block ahead he watched a car passing Mandy when a dog suddenly ran out before it. Not realizing how near she was to the bicycle, the driver swerved to the right to avoid killing the dog. To save herself, Mandy swerved to the right also, but smacked into the curb, got tossed over the bike's handlebars, and smashed onto the sidewalk.

The driver parked and called for an ambulance. Celesto ran to her, threw his school bags down, knelt and began to help Mandy. For reasons he could never explain, Celesto enjoyed his First Aid classes and knew exactly what to do. He checked her breathing, noticed her unconsciousness, found several places she was bleeding—though not seriously. Worse, he guessed that her right arm was broken in at least two places. Sitting beside her, stroking her gently, using his clean handkerchief to mop blood from two minor face wounds, he waited for the ambulance to arrive.

Next afternoon he went to visit Mandy in Cordoba's small hospital. "She won't know me, or why I'm here," he thought as he walked down the corridor to Mandy's room. She was awake in bed, with her arm in a cast beside her.

"Hello, Celesto," Mandy shouted gladly when he walked in. "Come sit beside me! I'm so grateful for everything you did for me after that terrible accident."

"I thought you were unconscious. And I didn't think you knew me. You are a high school super star and I'm just a soccer player."

"You are a great soccer player. I couldn't take my eyes off you while several of us cheerleaders were watching one of your games. You scored the two winning goals. I wanted to get to know you, but this was a terrible way for us to meet. And, while you were on the sidewalk caring for me, I was more aware than you think."

"I took your bicycle home and my friends and I are fixing it up. It will be like new when you are able to ride it again."

"Thanks, Celesto. I didn't know you were such a thoughtful person."

"I didn't know I was either. This is the first time in my life I've been able to help someone so badly hurt."

"Do you think we might like to have a few dates after I leave the hospital?"

"I'd like that very much. Meanwhile I will do everything I can to help you. Can I carry your homework back and forth?"

"Yes, but you'll also have to write it for me. I'm right-handed and my arm's in a cast. I will tell you what to put down. And we can cuddle on this hospital bed too."

Next day having lunch with his guy friends in the school's cafeteria, Celesto told them everything Mandy had felt and said about him. "You are the luckiest guy in our school! We all wanted to hook up with her," a friend across the table said.

"A good thing happened to you!" another friend said.

"And this good thing sprang out of so many evil things going on around us," Celesto said.

"Evil stirs up good," a physics student said.

"And good takes our minds off evil," a psychology student replied.

"And Mandy's going take my mind off you guys," Celesto said with a wry look on his face.

90. **Humans Attack Those Who Accomplish Much**

One fall, the New Mexico Wildlife Division published an astonishing report. Every year small changes occur in the population of animals throughout the state. But for fifteen years wild animal numbers had been steadily growing in just one part of New Mexico. Every species studied in the Bosque, mesa and mountains near Cordoba was larger each year. Workers at the agency suspected this was happening because the Mexican Cowboy, supported by the mayor of Cordoba, was feeding wildlife every night. The agency's workers debated if they should stop the Cowboy from doing that. Soon many on-line posters were asking the same question. A heated controversy sprang up.

The Mexican Cowboy's close friend Cece, who always kept an eye on fights on-line, began following battles over whether Cowboy should quit feeding wild animals. She wrote notes to pass on to the Cowboy:

—*Some hunters are praising Cowboy online for making it easier for them to find game. Here's one post :* "These days I don't have to work so hard to find an animal I want to shoot. If the Mexican Cowboy's done this for me, I'm grateful to him."

—*Other hunters are posting that Cowboy must quit feeding wildlife, because he is turning them into domesticated animals. Here's an example:* "I don't want to shoot an animal that a guy who lives near me has been feeding every night. They are his pets."

—*Many wildlife lovers are upset too because they believe Cowboy is domesticating wild animals. They want him to stop doing that. But here's a contradictory remark posted by a bird lover:* "I feed wild birds every day, and they remain wild."

—[Four hours later] *This conflict over you is expanding explosively. Here's another post. A concerned mammaler wrote:* "If it is going to be illegal to feed wild animals then it also should be illegal to feed wild birds!"

—*This made many birders worry about their existing rights. One wrote:* "We don't want the state to make us stop feeding wild birds!"

—*An out of state tourist posted this:* "One night I got to watch deer, foxes, badgers, and even a bear eat together. It was the best thing I ever saw."

—[Two hours later] *A poultry farmer posted this:* "We've got way too many coyotes around here. I need someone to come and kill them." *A mammaler wrote back:* "Raise your chickens in a barn." *And another contributor rebutted:* "Chickens deserve to be outdoors as much as coyotes do!"

With pages of notes in front of her, Cece phoned her close friend the Mexican Cowboy, told him about what was going on, and asked what he wanted Cece to post under his name.

"Nothing!" Cowboy answered. "I only care about feeding wild animals. I never go online."

At the same time, a local judge phoned Mayor Howie and warned him she was going to order the Mexican Cowboy to quit feeding wild animals, or pay a hefty fine.

"Do that and you'll lose the next election," Mayor Howie said.

"If I don't do it, you will lose the next election too," the judge replied.

Late that evening Cowboy sat on his porch talking with Coyote about the mess he'd stirred up by feeding so many wild animals.

"Don't worry," Coyote said. "Whatever a human does well will generate some controversy, and much more if their achievements are widely known, as yours is. You humans can't ever agree about much."

"So I'm not the only guy on the planet who's being attacked," Cowboy said.

"You are famous and that means you'll be attacked online far more than unknown humans will."

"It was attacks on me that made me famous. Why do you think this happens?" Cowboy asked.

"Because you humans are so different from one another, you disagree more than you agree with one another. This doesn't happen between coyotes because we are all pretty much the same person."

"Should I stop feeding wild animals then?" Cowboy asked.

"No. Please don't. In a day or two this will all blow over. You humans can't keep your minds together on the same thing for more than a day or two."

"You coyotes ignore each other."

"And you humans get pleasure out of disagreeing with one another. This works for humans. Disagreement actually helps humans advance, so don't mess with it. Keep feeding wild animals. They'll love you and not attack you for doing it."

"And I will ask Cece to quit telling me all the bad things people online say about me. That's my way to peace."

91. **Savings Others' Lives May Save Our Own**

Ursula, the mother bear, and Anada the mother doe, had gotten to know each other while eating at the Mexican Cowboy's ranch. Late one spring, each brought their new daughters to the ranch to feed. Eda, the fawn, and Oohla, the bear cub, reacted differently when they saw one another.

Eda was frightened, frozen, and hated not being in the mountain high grass where she could hide, when she first saw two bears.

Oohla, a playful cub, was trying to go over to the fawn when her mom hauled her back.

"Thanks for stopping her," Anada said to Ursula. "We deer are frightened by you predators."

"I understand," Ursula replied. "I don't kill deer, but I'll eat one I find lying dead in the forest."

"We need to keep our distance," Anada said, backing away.

"That's fine with me," Ursula replied, going back to eating.

It was a hot dry year in New Mexico, and as weeks went by both Ursula and Anada needed to come back to the ranch for nourishment. Seeing each other evening after evening, the fawn and the cub became accustomed to each other's company.

"Why don't bears try to eat me here?" Eda asked her mom.

"Because the Mexican Cowboy would never feed them again if they tried. He feeds all of us, and we aren't allowed to harm each other here."

The friendship between the bear cub and deer fawn kept growing, though as winter neared, Oohla stayed away, fattening herself with fall season's goodies. Now, it was a freezing winter, and Eda struggled to stay alive as the snow came and melted. Fortunately, most days were sunny and warmish.

Oohla hibernated in a cave not far from her young deer friend. When spring came again, the cub and the fawn, nearly grown-ups now, crossed paths often in the forest, saying hello to each other. Grazing in many places, Eda spotted the remains of several animals each day, as well as food and garbage human visitors had left behind. One day when she was grazing where Oohla was eating roots, she told her friend about all the bear foods she'd spotted. Oohla thanked her and left immediately to eat what the deer had found.

Now the bear was determined to intercept the doe several times each week, always expressing gratitude for being told where she could find food. "But what can I do for her?" the nearly grown bear asked herself. She couldn't think of an answer.

Then, in the fall, when open deer hunting season began, Oohla watched two hunters kill a deer, gut him, and carry the carcass away. After eating remains the hunters left behind, the bear had her answer. "I need to protect her from being shot!"

Oohla began warning her friend Eda with the whereabouts of every hunter in her vicinity. She even tried to persuade Eda to hide during daylight in her cave. Because deer hate being enclosed, Eda couldn't abide doing this.

The young deer was devastated two weeks later when a hunter took down her mother, who was grazing beside her. Next day when her bear friend Oohla found her, Eda was curled up inside tall grass, crying and shivering with fear. The bear lay down next to her, curled around her, and cuddled and licked her as her mother had when she was born. This was enormously comforting for crying Eda.

When bear hunting season began, Eda kept an eye out for human hunters and passed along their whereabouts to her close friend Oohla. The young bear was never shot at.

Now, with winter approaching and just before hibernating, the young bear and doe were eating side by side at the Mexican Cowboy's ranch. "It is good to be here with you again, the young deer said."

"Yes, we saved each other's lives. Let's keep doing that. And I will always love you."

"And I will always love you back. Working together has been the best thing our two species have ever done."

"I agree," Oohla replied. "Next year shall we see if we can get more deer and bears to help each other?"

"Yes! And perhaps get other species doing this too!" Eda said back. "Yes," Oohla said. "All animals will live longer if we help one another!"

92. **How To Help Fire Do Its Thing**

Cece was born in Ohio and grew up enjoying flowers planted by her mother and neighbors. When she married and moved to New Mexico, Cece was disappointed over how hard it was here to keep a flower garden free of weeds and thriving. Years later, when she moved from Corrales to live near the Mexican Cowboy east of Cordoba, Cece began exploring wild flowers on the mesa and in the nearby mountains. She grew to like these very much and decided to try making a garden of wildflowers outside the house she was living in.

For starters she dug up and replanted blue-eyed megs, thimbleberries, fire wheels, arrowleafs, and hairy bittercress plants. She was angry when these failed to thrive and jimson and laguna dirt weeds took over her garden.

Reading up on the gardening of wild flowers, next year she tried planting the same flowers again, making the soil, fertilizer, distance apart, and watering suited to each wild flower. Once again only the invading weeds spread happily and her wild flowers struggled to survive.

Realizing how difficult wild flower gardening was, Cece decided it wasn't worth her time and efforts. She abandoned the garden and spent her free time instead exploring wild flowers on the mountains and mesa.

Surprisingly, her garden didn't exactly die. Her wild flowers failed to reproduce and spread, and each year the jimson and laguna dirt weeds took over more empty spaces. But if Cece looked closely when she walked through her garden she could still see many of the wildflowers she had planted.

The following summer was the hottest and driest any person in Cordoba could remember. Cece thought about watering her former garden, but decided she wouldn't help the weeds survive. Then in early August, when the mesa was as dry as it had ever been, a lightning strike touched off a rare mesa fire.

Hot wind drove the fire in the direction of Cece's house.

It was the only home in the fire's way and the Cordoba fire department sent out a truck to soak Cece's wooden house and hopefully prevent it from burning.

With the wildfire nearing, Cece got into the fire truck and went down the road to a safe parking place. Standing on top of the fire truck, Cece watched a wave of fire sweep through her former garden and brush against the house. The garden burst into flames, but the wet house smoldered for a few minutes, then quit burning.

With the garden fire dying out, firemen returned to the house, sprayed the outside and appraised whether the dying garden fire could spread. Deciding it would not, they drove away, carrying Cece's thanks with them.

Next day the Mexican Cowboy came to see the damage the fire had done. After looking the house over carefully and finding little to fix, Cece took him out to see her former garden.

Huge patches of jimson and laguna dirt weeds were burned, but somehow all the wildflowers had escaped that.

"I don't see how its possible my wildflowers survived that fire," Cece said.

"Oh, that's easy to explain," Cowboy said. "Fire is choosey. It doesn't like isolated plants. Fire does get larger, hotter, and happier when it lands on large patches of dry plants. The more burnables you've got bunched together, the better fire can do its thing."

"I'll add 'wild fire burning' to my list of how to deal with New Mexico weeds," Cece said back, with a happy face.

93. Helping Sufferers Can Lead To Good Friendships

One fall day the Mexican Cowboy's farmer neighbor plowed a three acre patch next to the pasture where the prized mustang Turco, and Turco's friend Gus the donkey, were grazing. Then the farmer put a bull he called Mooko into the soon-to-be finished pasture. Turco didn't pay attention to Mooko, but Gus was surprised there was a bull now in what used to be one of the farmer's major crop fields.

"Maybe he's just being fattened before the farmer sends him to the slaughterhouse," Gus said to Turco.

"I don't want that," Turco replied. "He seems like a nice bull, and humans slaughter too many cattle."

"Do you want us to try and save him then?"

"Yes, but first let's get to know him. If I don't like him I won't try to save that bull."

Next morning Gus grazed along the fence separating the two properties. An hour later the farmer led Mooko into the pasture, checked him over, rubbed his neck, hugged him and left the bull to graze. Gus and Turco locked their eyes on this while it was going on. With the farmer out of the pasture now, Gus raised his head and brayed a gentle hello.

The bull studied the donkey intensely, but did not say anything back. Turco came over to the fence, put his head over, and neighed his own greeting. The bull ignored him too, and moved away to the other side of his new pasture to graze. There he hung his head over the fence on the other side and seemed to be looking for the farmer.

"I don't get what going on here," Turco said.

"The bull and the farmer seem to be good friends," Gus replied.

"I think we ought to just ignore him," Turco said back. And they did.

Two months later a young woman starting bringing the bull into the pasture, unbridling and turning him loose without any show of affection.

"Where's Mooko's farmer's guy?" Turco asked Gus.

"I don't know," Gus said. "Perhaps he sold the farm."

"Or he might be sick," Turco said back.

"I'll try again to reach out to Mooko," Gus said. That morning Gus grazed near the fence, keeping an eye on the bull. Mooko seemed to be despairing, and Gus's sympathy for him rose rapidly.

Late that afternoon Coyote was passing outside the fence hunting for rabbit prey, when Gus brayed to attract his attention. Coyote understood a bit of donkey talk and he agreed to do what Gus asked him. That evening Coyote explained what Gus had said to him to his dear friend the Mexican Cowboy.

Next morning when the Mexican Cowboy led the horse and burro from their stalls to the pasture, he carried a bucket of fragrant plants. Gus eyed him sharply and Cowboy explained, "This is for Mooko, the bull next door. His owner is very sick and his daughter told me the one thing he misses most is being able to spend time with Mooko."

"Why?" Gus brayed.

Guessing what the donkey asked, Cowboy said: "This farmer has always liked bulls. He grew up with several and was miserable when his father had them slaughtered. Until the farmer gets better, his daughter wants me to care for the bull." With that Cowboy put down the bucket, got wire cutters out of his back pocket, removed a section of fence wire, and walked onto the farmer's property toward the gate on the other side.

Twenty minutes later Cowboy returned, pulling the wimping bull. Leading Mooko through the hole in the fence, Cowboy dropped the halter rope, reached down into the bucket, and began feeding the sad bull handfuls of wonderful food.

That night Mooko stayed in a stall across from Turco and Gus in Cowboy's barn. As weeks went by Mooko returned to happiness and looked forward to seeing the Cowboy every day.

Then, one day after Thanksgiving, the farmer walked onto his field carrying a bucket, crossed the pasture, went through the fence's hole, and began offering apples and carrots to the delighted mustang and donkey. When each had all he wanted, the farmer spent an hour with Mooko. Cowboy joined them, bringing a bucket of delicious food for Mooko. At day's end the five of them were happier than they had ever been.

That night Coyote asked Cowboy what he had gotten out of all this.

"It's the first time I've gotten to know a bull and had one love me," Cowboy said with a happy face. "Helping suffering others can lead to good friendships."

"It's something coyotes never do," Coyote said back.

"You might want to start practicing helping strangers," Cowboy said. "Connecting genuinely with others increases happiness all around."

"We just eat them," Coyote responded.

"Because you do that, coyotes are the most alone, least helped animals on the planet. Finding ways to build ties with us humans is the best thing coyotes can learn to do."

"I'd rather you'd teach us how to take down a bull," Coyote said with a wry smile on his face.

94. Coyote Hunts A Mallard

Coyote had always wanted to learn how to fly. "I know I don't have wings and feathers and I weigh too much, but is there any way you humans can get me into the air?" Coyote asked his dear friend, the Mexican Cowboy.

"Sure. I can get you a plane ride, but tell me what you want to do up there."

"I want to soar like an eagle, change positions as fast as a humming bird, and dive like a mallard."

"You want to catch birds in the air too?"

"I'd love to be able to do that, but first I've got to learn to fly."

"All right, I'll see if I can find a ride for you," Cowboy replied.

Next morning Cowboy saddled his beloved mustang Turco and rode across the mesa to a tiny airstrip where a few people in Cordoba kept their aircraft. Buck Swinton was there repairing his glider. Cowboy rode his mustang into Buck's hangar only to hear Buck shout: "Get that horse outta here. I'm putting on dope to stretch the fabric I'm replacing. The stuff can kill your horse if he licks it."

"Sorry," the Cowboy said, leading Turco outside and tying him to a hangar door hook.

"Thanks," Buck said when Cowboy came back in. "What can I do for you?"

"This will sound crazy, but how would you feel about giving my coyote friend a ride?"

"I might like to take him up in my glider. He won't freak out or bite me from the back seat?"

"No, he's very well-behaved."

"If you'll let my friends take pictures, we got a deal."

For several days the next week, Cowboy rode over to Buck's hangar and helped him finish glider repairs. The two men liked each other and talked back and forth about many things. Together they designed a leather harness for Coyote, and Cowboy's friend Thelma helped him cut and stitch the harness together. With the glider ready to fly, now they had only to wait for the right weather.

When Coyote visited several evenings later, Cowboy told him Buck had phoned and said next afternoon looked like a good day to have his first flight. Coyote was thrilled.

Early next afternoon Cowboy rode over to Buck's hangar with Coyote on the saddle in front of him. Riding into a steady eastern wind, Cowboy was surprised to see tens of cars parked behind Buck's hangar. The glider was outside, resting on its left wing, Buck was checking it over, and a large crowd was snapping pictures. Cowboy was almost blinded by flashes going off as he rode up and dismounted. He left Coyote on Turco so the poor animal might feel just a tiny bit safer among all these humans.

When Buck was ready, Cowboy lifted his coyote friend off the horse and carried him to the glider. With the canopy open he put Coyote in the back seat and began fastening the harness around him. Worried, Coyote said, "Birds don't have to be harnessed when they fly."

"Coyotes and humans have to be," said the Cowboy, pointing at Buck strapping himself tightly into the pilot's seat. "Behave yourself, and have a nice ride," Cowboy said, pulling the plexiglass canopy over the pilot and his passenger and backing away.

With watchers feverishly taking pictures, a friend fastened a tow rope connecting the glider to the twenty-five-year old Super Cub in front of it, its engine idling. More friends lifted the glider's wings so only the main and rear wheels touched the ground. Buck raised his left fist with thumb up, then jerked his hand forward with the signal to take off. The Cub pilot taxied forward slowly to tighten the rope, then with full throttle began accelerating down the rough dirt glider strip.

The glider was airborne almost immediately and soon the Super Cub was climbing also. Climbing in great circles around the airport, and always higher than the tow plane, the towed glider climbed to 8,500 feet. Then Buck reached forward and released the tow rope. The tow pilot lowered his nose and dived away to the left. Silence descended upon the Coyote's glider.

With his nose sticking outside through the three inch window on his left, Coyote sniffed and sniffed, smelling a new universe. Buck began gently maneuvering the glider so Coyote could experience what flying is about. Coyote couldn't see the rudders or stick Buck was pushing, but the stick in front of him was moving at the same time. And on top of the stick was a plastic songbird! Looking out, sniffing, watching the stick move, Coyote's sense of how to fly grew rapidly.

"Would you like to try flying?" Buck leaned around and asked.

"Yes!" said Coyote, and leaned forward and put his mouth around the bird on top of the stick. Bill held up his hands to show Coyote the glider was his and Coyote began gently maneuvering the aircraft. Left bank, right bank. Climbing and approaching a stall, descending until he sensed the glider was going too fast, the coyote was learning to fly.

"You are a terrific beginner," Buck said over his shoulder.

Passing over the Bosque now, Coyote saw a flock of ducks descending for a landing on one of the ponds. Instantly Coyote rolled the glider more than ninety degrees on its left wing and began a dive approaching the landing ducks from behind. With the airspeed just beneath the red line, and Buck studying what was going on and getting ready to grab back the stick, Coyote put his snout out the tiny window to grab a duck's head as he swooped by the flock.

"Okay, that's it friend," Buck said taking the stick back, pulling the nose up and turning back toward the landing strip.

On the ground again Buck sat in the cockpit telling his friends about Coyote's flight. "He's the best first-flight stick guy I've ever flown with," Buck said, with cameras going off all around him.

As Cowboy was unharnessing the Coyote his friend whispered, "I almost caught a duck on a dive I was making."

"Did you think about how you'd make it back to strip if you lost most of your altitude?" Cowboy asked.

"No. Thank you. When I spotted those ducks I forgot all about conserving glider altitude. I realize now next time I go hunting in the sky I'd better be in a powered aircraft."

"Hunting birds with an aircraft is unsafe business," Buck said.

"Coyote life is generally unsafe," said Coyote back, smiling at all the picture takers.

95. **Turtle Mating Is Coming To Depend On Humans**

Booa, the box tortoise, lived on the desert-like mesa east of the Mexican Cowboy's ranch. He was almost fifty years old, his hardened yellow shell had defended him many times from being eaten, and life was going well for him. Or had been going well until, about eight years ago, the Mexican Cowboy started feeding wild animals every night.

With scores of hungry animals passing by him each evening, many of whom would enjoy eating him, Booa had to keep more alert than any box tortoise he knew. Complaining to Towah, a box turtle who was hatched the same week he'd been, Booa asked for suggestions to keep the hungry wild animals away from him.

"It... can't... be... done," Towah replied slowly. "Mammals... came... onto... our... planet... millions... of years... after... us. They... move... and... think... faster. No... tortoise... has... ever... been... able... to... control... one... of... them."

"You.. are.. right.. but.. I.. am.. a.. little.. faster.. than.. you. Perhaps.. I.. can.. do.. it."

"You'll... be... safer... if... you... move.... away... from... them," Towah said, before inching back slowly to his part of the mesa.

That evening Booa moved under a large rock, retreated into his shell, and spent the night thinking and listening to animals passing near him. Next morning he had only one answer. Booa came out from under his protecting rock and began walking s*l*o*w*l*y toward the nearby highway.

It took him three days to reach it. Spotting a large, flat, almost black rock near the road, he climbed on top of it and retreated into his bright yellow shell. As the day went by Booa heard cars slowing as they passed by and guessed humans were looking at him. Next afternoon, a car stopped and parked near him. He heard the driver's door open and close, and footsteps approaching him.

Peering out from inside his shell, he saw a human woman looking down on him. She picked him up gently, turned him upside down looking for cracks in his shell, and carried him to her car. She opened the trunk and put him inside before driving away. Ten minutes later she reached her house on the edge of the mesa a mile east of Cordoba. She opened the trunk, lifted Booa out, carried him for a minute, and put him down on the edge of a garden next to the mesa.

"You are free to leave," she said. "But if you will stay for a few minutes I will bring you some desert grass, desert dandelions, pear cactus and other foods you'll enjoy eating."

Booa didn't understand her, but wasn't feeling threatened either. Twenty minutes later the woman brought a handful of mesa foods he loved eating. She put half of it in front of Booa and walked ten yards away and put the rest down. "It is for another box tortoise," the woman said before going inside her house. While Booa slowly ate he saw her keeping an eye on him from a house window.

Early that evening the woman and a man came out to the tortoise carrying several large rocks. In the mesa next to their garden, they constructed a shelter for him, and departed for the night. For the next several days she brought out snacks for him and the other tortoise he had yet to see.

Then one day the woman and her husband got in their car and drove away. At snack time a hungry tortoise appeared, going slowly into the garden to find her own foods. Booa went to meet her.

In the years that followed Booa and the female tortoise hatched many box tortoises together. As their children grew up Booa explained to each how they had come into existence. "Some... humans... are... feeding... desert... tortoises... now. We... wouldn't... have... gotten... together... and... bred... you... if... the... woman... here... hadn't... found... each... of... us... and... brought... us... together."

"So... humans... are... our... friends?" one of his children asked.

"Very... few... of... them, ... but... these... humans... are... doing... everything... they... can... to... help... turtles... live... and... multiply."

96. **The Mexican Cowboy Gets Married**

Sleeping in his porch rocker one evening late in September, Cowboy was having a marvelous dream. In it, he had proposed to his close friend Cece, and she had accepted. Thelma and Coyote were now putting together the couple's wedding plans, and Father Gallapo had agreed to perform the ceremony. Mayor Howie had gotten the license for the pair.

And now, the **DAY** had come! It was a warm, moonlit evening, after ten o'clock. Cowboy and his best man, Coyote stood under the only tree on his ranch next to the arroyo. Cowboy was wearing the mariachi costume he wore when he led the animal parade in Socorro on his marvelous mustang Turco. Father Gallapo was standing behind him, studying the marriage ceremony he would conduct. The priest felt nervous because he didn't marry people often.

The precious moment had arrived! Thelma and Mayor Howie escorted Cece down a nearly imaginary aisle. She was wearing a Mexican wedding dress Cowboy would love. On Cece's right were fifty folding chairs filled with Cece's and Cowboy's friends, each trying to see over the others' heads as the bride passed by. On Cece's left side there were more than a hundred wild animals, from many species, who adored Cowboy for taking care of them.

The ceremony began. It was brief and speedy—at Cowboy's request. When the wedding band was placed on Cece's finger and each partner said, "I do," Father Gallapo pronounced them man and wife and backed away. Cowboy and Cece kissed passionately as the human audience applauded and cheered loudly.

Teary-eyed and holding hands with her husband, Cece turned around, curtsied, and began applauding back. Sweeping her eyes over her human friends, she wore the biggest smile they'd ever seen on her face.

The huge volume of noise humans were making frightened animals on the other side of the aisle. Many started to slip away.

Beside his new wife, facing his adored wild animals, Cowboy waved and bowed with a huge smile on his face.

Realizing they *are* safe, the wild animals began calling out their best wishes for the human couple.

The mesa rattled with the thunder of applause and the barks, yowls, pitch-changing mews, grunts, howls and other happy sounds from Cowboy's audience of animal friends.

Overhead, the stars moved into words in the sky.

Cowboy and Cece looked up. The moon had turned into a smiling face and around it was written, "**Happy Lifetime Together, Dear Kaiti and Rob!**"

"They got our names wrong up there," Cece said to her husband.

"Someone else must be getting married today," Cowboy said to his wife, turning to kiss Cece again.

"We should meet this pair!" Cece said.

Beside them Mayor Howie said, "I can find them and introduce you."

Back on the porch, sitting next to Cowboy, Coyote watched his dreaming friend smile and actually say, "I want to meet Kaiti and Rob. They must be doing wonderful things or I would not have seen their names in the sky. I bet I will love them!"

Coyote stood and whispered in the dreamer's ear, "Tell them I will love them too!"

Sleeping, with a giant smile on his face, Cowboy nodded his head, and reached out to pat and scratch his beloved friend Coyote.

97. **Buddies Defend Us**

Twenty-nine-year old Mergen Mapleleaf was a psychopath, a burglar, and a social misfit who could not get along even with his cellmates in prison. Free again, Mergen went back to house burgling in Albuquerque, Socorro, and even in tiny Cordoba. In his jumbled mind he kept struggling to decide what he might do for humanity. One day, watching a program on television about the Mexican Cowboy's feeding and saving wild animals, an answer occurred to him.

"This rat puts animals above humans, and he is trying to make all of us into mammalers. He needs to be punished for that."

Two evenings later, Mergen joined the small evening crowd watching and helping Cowboy feed several dozen wild animals. With nobody paying attention to him, Mergen walked around Cowboy's house, noticed the famous green rocker on the front porch, and even went into the barn to see how it was set up. The animals inside were startled by the stranger's appearance, but assumed he had permission from Cowboy to be there.

For the next several days Mergen parked on the road a mile from the ranch, lay down in a hiding spot where he could see Cowboy's routine movements, and began to plan the Mexican Cowboy's murder. A week later, in the middle of the afternoon, Mergen sneaked into the barn and hid in the room where riding gear were kept. He had a loaded pistol in his pocket.

An hour later Cowboy came into the barn carrying a giant bucket filled with human food scraps, which he began sorting into dishes for different animals. Several things happening in the barn troubled him. Turco and the donkey Guy were more restless than he had ever seen them. Calli the cat was on the rafter overhead, looking down intently at the door where the riding gear was kept. The little white dog with ragged fur was sitting in front of the door, sniffing.

Hearing a rattle behind him, Cowboy turned around and watched a four-foot rattlesnake crawling out of a hole in the wall. Two nervous squirrels came in through the open barn door. Sure now that something was very wrong, Cowboy opened the stall doors of Turco and Gus, then knocked on the closed riding gear door.

The door was thrown open and a man carrying a gun pointed at him came out.

"This is your last day Cowboy. Say goodbye to your animal friends."

"Why me?" Cowboy asked, glancing up and seeing Calli creep across the rafter.

"Because you are trying to make all of us animal lovers. Humans need to take care of one another."

"Has any one taken care of you?" Cowboy asked.

"No! And this is mostly your fault. Say your prayers."

Sure he was going to die, Cowboy got down on his knees, put his hands together and tried to think of a prayer. Mergen walked over to him and began to lower his gun to the side of Cowboy's head.

With perfect aim, Calli leaped off the rafter over Mergen, and landed on the gunman's weapon, knocking it from his hand. As Mergen bent over to pick up his pistol, Mazzie snarled and bit the killer's reaching hand. Trying with his other hand to pull Mazzie off him, two squirrels ran up his leg and began biting Mergen's cheeks and nose. Slapping the squirrels off his face, Mergen turned and saw a coiled rattler about to strike him in the leg.

Backing away and wanting to flee, he bumped into the magnificent stallion Turco, crosswise in the aisle blocking the barn door. Turning around once more, Mergen bent over to pick up his gun. Gus the donkey kicked him hard and sent him flying through the air. Banging his head into the wall, Mergen slumped and passed out.

Turco put his two front hooves on the disabled killer. Shaking, Cowboy stood up, picked up the gun and threw it into Gus's stall. Gus stood in front of the stall's open door, ready to kick Mergen if he tried to get his pistol again.

Groaning and crying, Mergen began pleading with Cowboy to let him go. He shut up when Turco put more weight on the killer he was holding down.

Ten minutes later, police were handcuffing Mergen and lifting him off the floor. "You did a great job of keeping this madman from killing you," one of the officers said.

"Not me," Cowboy replied. "It was my animal friends who saved my life."

Looking at the animals surrounding and still guarding their beloved human the second officer said, "Wish my buddies were as good at defending me as yours are."

"If we save others, they will protect us too," Cowboy said, beginning to sort garbage again.

98. Are Animals Self-Centered?

Early one day in February there were snow showers and temperatures below zero on the mesa east of the Mexican Cowboy's ranch. Midday, Cece put on her lightweight coat, got into her well-maintained car, and left the building where she worked to drive to her friend Cowboy's house. With snow tires, and Cece's careful driving, the car moved safely along the snow-packed road. Cece drove very cautiously down a steep hill, and crossed a dry arroyo. Starting up the hill on the other side, Cece pressed too hard on the gas pedal. The car's front wheels spun on the snow, it twisted sideways, and began sliding down into the arroyo again. Cece struggled to keep the car on the road, but this was impossible. The front of the car slid off the road into the arroyo. Cece knew it was stuck but tried several times to back out, without success.

Cece took her cell phone from her purse and called AAA for help. The phone wouldn't send the call because it couldn't pick up a wireless signal in the arroyo gulch. Shivering, Cece got out of her car and with her smooth sandals slipping, tried to walk up the icy road. Twice she almost fell down. She thought about taking off her sandals and walking uphill barefoot, but she was afraid her feet would freeze. Back in her car, she turned on the engine and, with warm heat flowing over her, rested and tried to think what to do. She couldn't come up with an answer. Tears filled her eyes.

A hawk circling in the sky overhead looked down at the Mexican Cowboy's stuck friend. The hawk had seen her many times helping Cowboy feed animals and birds. Making wide circles in the sky, the hawk began looking for a coyote. Spotting one hunting rabbits, the hawk landed yards away from his potential predator and began making odd hawk sounds the coyote had never heard before.

The coyote couldn't understand what this was about, but suspected it was something very important the hawk wanted her to know. The coyote stood, nodded her head in an accepting gesture, and watched the hawk take off. Flying low and slow, the hawk led the coyote to the top of the hill above the stuck car. Diving over the stuck car three times, the hawk watched the coyote puzzle out what was going on. Coyote still wasn't sure what this was about however. As the hawk flew away the coyote sat on her haunches and began to howl with sounds humans never heard before.

Staying warm, Cece watched the circling hawk dive on her car and was surprised when the unfamiliar coyote on top of the hill began howling strangely. "Something's going on," she thought. "If they are trying to rescue me, I'll ask Cowboy how this came about."

Twenty minutes later Coyote, wearing a pink collar, appeared on the hilltop with the sitting coyote who was watching her. "It's Coyote," she blurted. He is going to get me rescued." The two coyotes put their heads together several moments, then her friend Coyote vanished.

Racing over the rough mesa, Coyote followed his usual route to the Mexican Cowboy's ranch. Arriving there in fifteen minutes, Coyote darted over to the ranch house and began to howl for his human friend. Coyote was surprised when the ragged, little white dog Mazzie stuck her head out of the dog door and barked, "Sorry, Cowboy's gone to a meeting with Mayor Howie. Can I help you?"

Coyote yipped thanks and darted away toward the barn. Pushing the door open with his head, Coyote ran in and began barking and howling in front of Turco, who was in his stall wearing a horse blanket. Turco could not understand what Coyote wanted, but he realized his help was critically needed.

Turco tried to push open his locked stall door, but could not do it. Following this closely, Gus the donkey spun in his stall and kicked the stall door open. Then, standing next to Coyote, Gus turned, kicked again and again, and broke Turco's stall door open. Turco rushed from his stall and followed Coyote out the barn door. Racing up the slick road toward the mountains, the four-legged pair hurried to rescue Cece.

Sitting in her car, Cece had turned off the engine to save fuel when she saw Coyote and Turco coming carefully down the slippery road toward her. "I am saved!" Cece said with a tears welling in her eyes.

"Get out of the car," Coyote ordered her.

With Cece standing next to Turco now, Coyote said: "Take off his blanket and hang it on his neck."

Cece unbuckled the blanket, folded it, and put it over the horse's neck.

"Good," Coyote said. "Now, climb onto your car's hood."

Cece crawled onto her car's hood as Turco moved beside her.

"Now stand up and take hold of his mane, then swing your left leg over his back and climb on." Cece did that perfectly.

"Now wrap the horse blanket around you. It will keep you warm," Coyote ordered.

As soon as Cece was covered, Coyote barked gently and Turco turned and began walking gingerly up the slippery hill.

Cece was warm and humming a song as Turco trotted toward Cowboy's ranch house. About halfway there she saw the priest's ancient Ford truck coming toward them, with the anxious Mexican Cowboy sitting in the right seat. The truck stopped on one side as Turco trotted by.

"A hawk and a coyote saved my life!" Cece shouted.

Turning his truck around to follow them back to the ranch house, Father Gallapo said to Cowboy, "I didn't realize that animals we help would help us in return."

"Animals are not as self-centered as most people think!" Cowboy replied, with a happy smile on his face.

99. **Women Always Take More Sides Than Men Do**

Late one evening Cowboy and his housemate the priest, Father Gallapo, were sitting in the kitchen drinking wine and talking. Cece, Cowboy's friend, had cooked their meal and now was in the kitchen doing dishes. Normally self-reserved, the Mexican Cowboy was turning boastful. He had just praised the priest, saying, "Father, I know you take excellent care of your parishioners, but won't you agree I'm even better at taking care of my animals?"

"That well may be so," the priest replied. "You put food into many more mouths than I do. But my job is to look after my parishioners' souls, and not merely feed them."

"Ah, Father, have you forgotten that I cooperate with every one of the animals' gods? I take care of their parishioners on earth, many, many more than you look after. I feed them every night and look after them in other ways too."

"I pray for my parishioners every night," Father Gallapo said, "and with my help they will all go to Heaven."

"Well I negotiate with their gods, and do everything I can to make my animals' lives enjoyable on earth!" Cowboy said back.

"They still eat each other," the priest replied, " which my parishioners never do."

"But you eat my parishioners, while I only try to help yours!" the Cowboy said back.

"But your 'parishioners' are easier to help than mine are," Father Gallapo replied.

"Nonsense! You only spend a few hours in your church every week. My whole life is devoted to helping my animals!"

"Your animals would do just fine if you quit doing this, my parishioners wouldn't."

"Lots of humans don't go to church and we do just fine!"

"But you won't do so fine after you die!"

"Your parishioners pay you. Mine can't!"

"They don't pay me enough to have my own house!"

"That's still more than I get!"

"I'm an itinerant priest. I get to travel."

"And there is no place on the planet I want to be but here! And you only get to Texas anyway."

"I take care of a suffering former president there."

"But when you confess him he has to sit in your two door porta-potty, which you've turned into a porta-confessional."

"He's had worse."

"But he's had nothing so horrible as many of my animals!"

"Why are you attacking me?"

"Why are you putting animals beneath humans?"

"Because animals don't have souls," the priest said smugly.

"That's the biggest insult you've delivered all evening!"

"It's the truth, not an insult!"

"Guys! Guys!! Guys!!! Stop this please," Cece said coming out of the kitchen. "This argument is ridiculous because you are only insulting each other."

"We're both telling our truths," Father Gallapo said to her sternly.

"And if you keep on doing that I'm going to bring out the rolling pin and pound some mutual respect into both of you."

"You see, Father, Cece wants to take both our sides," Cowboy said, calming down.

"She's a woman," Father Gallapo said softly back. "Women can always take more sides than men do."

"That isn't all we can do better than you," said Cece going back into the kitchen to bring out the lovely dessert she'd made for them.

100. **The Way a Priest Writes Affects His Parishioners**

One Monday afternoon Father Gallapo drove to his church to begin writing his sermons for the week. In the tiny cramped space behind the altar he used for an office, he noticed the ancient green Olympus typewriter he'd been using for thirty-five years was missing. "A thief?" he asked himself. "Surely a normal thief could have picked something better to steal from me."

Frustrated, he took a pencil from the jar that Thelma, his church's maintenance officer, kept sharpened, picked up a blank page of paper, and begin trying to compose. The priest wasn't used to writing with a pencil, and with one in hand now he found himself struggling to come up with thoughts for his Sunday sermon. "This is going to be a hard week for me," he thought. "And perhaps better for my parishioners if I don't get much written."

Over the next several hours he kept calling Thelma at her house, but she never answered. "Maybe she decided to pawn my classic typewriter," he said to himself angrily. That evening he tried to find a replacement typewriter. His friend the Mexican Cowboy of course didn't have one. Mayor Howie told him the city might have several very old and worn IBM electrics in a storage building, but he doubted any of those would still work.

"They have little balls in them instead of the bars connected to the keyboard most electrics used," Howie said. "If you swipe and clean the little balls and find a new ribbon, one of these machines might work for you."

"Thanks, Mayor, but all that is beyond me," the priest said back.

Now, at Cowboy's kitchen table, Father Gallapo tried writing with his ballpoint pen. His text was legible, but very empty-minded. Frustrated, the Priest went to bed, praying on his creaking knees for God's help, before he crawled in and went to sleep.

Next morning after a hurried breakfast, Father Gallapo got into his truck and drove to nearby Socorro. Not one of the stores he visited had a typewriter for sale. A pawnshop did have several, but after trying each one he was more frustrated than ever. There was only one typewriter he knew he could write with.

Thinking about where to go now to locate a replacement Olympus, he drove back to his little church and went into the office space.

And, Bingo! There, sitting on his desk, was a beautiful 'new' Olympus typewriter, just like the one he'd owned. Next to it was a small note.

It was from Thelma. In it she apologized, explaining to him that on Sunday while she was cleaning the church after services, she bumped into his beloved typewriter and knocked it onto the floor. Thelma had picked it up and tried typing with it, but it wouldn't work. The keys jammed with every push. "So," she went on, "I drove to Albuquerque Sunday night, hunted for a typewriter repair store, found one, stayed in a motel, and Monday morning persuaded the owner to immediately fix your broken machine. It took him until Tuesday morning. I paid him out of my own pocket, with a little extra, and raced back to put the great Olympus on your desk. I'm so sorry I had to take it away from you. But it is better than ever now."

With joy filling his heart, Father Gallapo sat down, rolled a page of paper into his beloved typewriter, typed several sentences, and suddenly found his mind filling with ideas for this week's sermons.

On Sunday morning, now almost finished with reading his sermon aloud, Father Gallapo concluded with several unexpected points. Bored throughout most of it, his parishioners began straining to understand the spiritual meanings behind what their priest was saying. His final sentences were the most difficult for them.

"After getting my missing typewriter back, I'd written most of today's sermon when a new and unusual idea swept into me. Each of us needs to understand that watching what we are saying is not the only important thing we must do in our communications. We also must pay attention to how we write."

Several of his parishioners nodded agreement after hearing that point. But a few seconds later there were puzzled looks on everyone's face after Father Gallapo said:

"Words that we put onto paper are not the only vital thing here. The tool we use to put words onto paper makes more difference than we suppose. For example, I discovered on Tuesday that I could never have become a priest if I only used a pencil."

Talking in the parking lot afterwards, parishioners were saying they couldn't make much sense of this sermon.

"I think he was telling us that pencils are evil," one woman said to another.

"I think he was warning us that our right hand is good and our left one is evil," said a man near her.

"Is he saying everything we write will be evil if we don't use his typewriter?" a teenager asked.

"I think he should have said that what he writes is not what we understand," another woman added.

"I believe this topic has little to do with religion," a different man added.

Looking out the door at his discussing parishioners, Father Gallapo felt a wave of pride pass through him. "That fixed-up typewriter helped me engage everyone today," he said to himself.

Behind him Thelma was praying to God, apologizing for the mess in sacred understanding she had stirred among parishioners by bumping into her priest's typewriter. "I'm the evil one here," she said despondently.

Late that afternoon, after cleaning the church, Thelma returned to her home. On the dining table was a huge bouquet of beautiful flowers. Thelma loved them and was very grateful, but there was no card with the flowers.

"Was it Father Gallapo who got these for me?" she wondered. "I hope instead it was God."

101. **Sometimes Honesty Is Not the Best Strategy**

The more animals Cowboy fed every night, the more his desire to feed animals grew. Getting food for them had become much easier for him because Mayor Howie had begun publicizing the hundreds of wild animals showing up outside Cowboy's cabin every night to attract tourists. Many visitors were coming to tiny Cordoba for that reason alone and their visits were putting money into Cordoba's merchants' pockets. Winning more support for future elections, Mayor Howie was gladly willing to deliver extra garbage each day to the Mexican Cowboy.

Cowboy was feeling overworked however. This didn't bother him, but the growing presence of visitors who were walking around his mesa each night with flashlights, talking and bothering all of the eating animals, was something he couldn't stand. He began to think about ways he might persuade night tourists to leave him and his animal friends alone. It wasn't long before a plan occurred to him, and his woman friend Cece agreed to help him pull it off.

Several nights later, with TV reporters following the crowds around the eating animals, Cowboy summoned them, saying a woman had been attacked and injured by the animals. With bandages soaked with ketchup on her legs and arms, Cece—crying while being videoed—said she had been carrying pans of food to the animals when she was attacked by both a badger and a mountain lion, who were feeding side by side. Cece continued, saying to the reporters something that became widely reported all over America, "Hungry night-feeding animals will attack annoying humans to make them beat it, so they can finish their meals in peace." This story may headlines everywhere.

Cece's lies cut back the influx of night tourists for several months, pleasing Cowboy enormously.

But then the tourist flow returned, thanks to Mayor Howie's renewed publicizing.

To fight back, Cowboy came up with a new scheme. Coyote agreed to try to persuade a number of animals to help carry out the plan. It didn't take long to put it in place.

After ten o'clock on a warm summer night, Cowboy's yard with filled with parked cars. Flashlights were bobbing up and down everywhere toward the mountains and Cowboy heard annoying chatter as voluminous as he heard once in the bleachers of a baseball game.

Suddenly the chatter increased in intensity. Cowboy heard warning cries and shouts to run away. The flashlights were jerking about as people ran, several tripping and falling and down. And the wind from the east was blowing a horrible smell Cowboy's way. He went indoors and closed every open window. When he came out, over a hundred tourists—some carrying or holding onto crying children—were hurrying into the parking area. The smell in the air was worsening behind them. Several minutes later, every car had disappeared.

With the smell fading, Cowboy sat in his green rocker, waiting for his friend Coyote to appear. "It worked!" Cowboy said, when Coyote sat down beside him.

"You are going to have to feed a lot more skunks for the next few days," Coyote replied.

"I know," Cowboy said. "Nothing will make me happier than having them here."

"They were all eager to come, though many of my coyote friends had to carry skunks on their backs for eight or ten miles to get them all here."

"You promised they would be safe?"

"Of course," Coyote said.

"And you told the dining animals what the skunks were planning?"

"No," Coyote said. "I kept this to myself. If the animals knew what we were planning they wouldn't have stayed, and the tourists would have gone away before the skunks could let them have it."

"You were dishonest," Cowboy said with a grin.

"Dishonesty can often be in the interests of many," Coyote replied.

102. Everybody Saves Everybody

The tiny city of Cordoba was experiencing its first period of economic growth in decades. Mayor Howie, and the city council members he'd appointed, were meeting to figure out which parts of the surrounding countryside should be built on, and which ought to be protected.

"Expanding eastward on the mesa as Albuquerque did, is what I believe we should do," the Mayor said.

"Well I believe we will attract more people and sell more property if we take over and sell land along the Rio Grande River," a council member said.

"I agree, Bosque land is much more beautiful. And it is warmer in winter, cooler in summer," a second council member said.

"But beavers live there, and many species of birds. If we preserve it, our beautiful Bosque will attract even more property buyers to Cordoba," another council member said.

"Protecting animals and birds is not my thing. Let's buy and clear the Bosque," Mayor Howie demanded.

Afraid of losing their jobs by voting against him, council members agreed to buy, clear, and sell the gorgeous, animal- and bird-rich Bosque near Cordoba.

When Cowboy learned about this he was horribly frustrated and angry. "We have to find a way to stop Mayor Howie from doing this," he told Coyote.

Coyote came up with a suggestion.

A week later on a Saturday morning, animals and birds from all around Cordoba gathered in huge numbers in the part of the Bosque the Mayor wanted to buy and clear. Deer, pronghorns, raccoons, skunks and even several beavers, black bears, and two mountain lions, stood along the edge of the busy freeway closest to the Bosque slowing and blocking traffic, while every species of bird living there flocked and flew back and forth over cars.

The freeway jammed and impatient drivers blasted their horns. The Highway Patrol set up animal protecting barriers and began trying to drive the animals away.

They wouldn't budge. Birds flew close to patrol officers' faces when they shouted and waved their arms at the animals blocking traffic. Soon television news helicopters were circling overhead, with animals moving into the most visible positions.

"These masses of animals and birds are protesting the proposed clearing of the Bosque," one of the television station's best-known newscasters said in a broadcast.

Soon groups supporting animals and birds began appearing on the scene in growing numbers. Traffic kept crawling by. Citizens of Cordoba were in the Bosque watching this happening, and some were petting and feeding animals too. Bird watchers were angry with the Mayor and strongly against his plan. "Let's kick him out!" many protestors were saying, in front of TV cameras.

Watching this happening on television, Mayor Howie realized that he would be out of office in days if he didn't back down. He ordered his city workers to join him in feeding and patting the courageous birds and animals protecting the Bosque.

Cameras on him, the Mayor said, "We were just exploring the idea of allowing people to build new homes in the Bosque. It is plain now we shouldn't allow this."

That evening, happy drivers got their freeway back. Happy and well-fed birds and animals went back to their own territories. Happy bird and animal lovers congratulated themselves for what they had done so speedily. Happy Mayor Howie was better known and better liked by the voting public. And Cowboy and Coyote sat on the Mexican Cowboy's porch with a deep current of pleasure flowing between them.

"You saved them," Cowboy said to Coyote, who had put together the animal and bird invasion.

"No, you saved them, protecting animals and birds was your idea in the first place."

"Perhaps then we ought to say everybody saved everybody," Cowboy said.

"That's a good way of putting it," Coyote answered.

103. **Hen Names Her Chick Little Miss Furry**

Floria the hen was a wild chicken, a great egg layer, and a terrific mother. Floria was proud of herself for adding so many wild chickens to the mesa she lived on. Most of these were her chicks, raised with her rooster partner Doodledoo.

Unfortunately, one day her reproductive tract became filled with pain. "You may have an egg stuck in your oviduct," Doodledoo told his crying partner.

"Can you help me get it out dear?" Floria asked her partner.

"Bend over and I'll peck at it," Doodledoo said. She did, he tried, and she had even more pain.

"This isn't working," she shouted.

Doodledoo stopped and said, "A stuck egg can be fatal for you, as well as our next chick."

"I don't want to die!" Floria said.

"Then I need to find help," her partner said, and started walking around their nest, clucking with thoughts.

That evening the wild rooster left his suffering partner and ran over to the Cowboy's wild animal feed, flapping his wings for maximum speed. "I can ask for help there," he'd said to her. "And the Cowboy will protect me from predators who will prefer to have a rooster for their dinner."

"Keep safe," Floria said.

"I want to keep you safe," her rooster said back.

Cece was helping The Mexican Cowboy feed wild animals when she spotted the wild rooster. "Lead it over to the porch steps," Cowboy said. "I don't want him to get eaten here."

Cece filled a plate with tomatoes, grapes, watermelon, added a dead spider and some grass, and put the plate down on the porch steps, shouting to Cowboy, "We'll see what wild roosters like to eat." The rooster pecked at his plate food, but looked around anxiously for someone he could talk to.

Several minutes later Cece brought out a plate filled with meat scraps, including some chicken, and put these down a few yards away from the worrying rooster. "I don't know what's wrong for you, Honey, but if Coyote shows up he may be able to help you."

Twenty minutes later she saw Coyote sneaking up to the pan of meat scraps she'd set down for him. "When you are done, please see if you can find out what's troubling that rooster on the steps," Cece said.

Coyote looked up at the worried rooster and gobbled down his meal. Cece watched him then crawl on his belly over to the rooster, stopping several times to let the wild chicken escape if he wished to.

At the bottom of the steps Coyote made some rooster sounds she'd never heard from him before. The rooster began making sounds back that Cece had also never heard. These sounded almost like words. Coyote listened attentively, made some rooster noises back, then turned to Cece and said, "Get Cowboy over here."

Five minutes later Coyote was explaining to the humans the reason why the rooster wanted help. "His mate has an egg stuck up her. Can you dig it out?" he asked Cowboy.

"No," Cowboy said. "But I bet Cece can help her." Ten minutes later Cowboy rode out from the barn on his superb mustang Turco, and trotted after the wing-flapping racing rooster. Half an hour later he rode back, holding an attractive chicken in his right arm. Cece put the chicken in her car and drove home.

In the back yard there was an empty doghouse, and Cece made a nest out of towels for the suffering hen, and put a fireplace screen in front of the doorway to keep out predators.

Next day Cece tried everything she could find online to remove the stuck egg. She was wearing a fake fur coat outside because the day was so cold. Floria thought she must be a rare furry human. Getting nowhere herself, Cece put agonized Floria in the back seat of her car, drove to Albuquerque where she'd found a veterinarian who specialized in birds, carried her into the office, and waited for forty minutes.

With a big smile on her face the vet's nurse came out to the waiting room carrying the happier looking hen. "We got it out! Here's your chicken back, and here is the hen's stuck egg," the nurse said handing both to Cece.

That night Cowboy rode back to Floria's nest and gently put Floria on top of the egg he'd brought with him. The rooster appeared, checked out his mate, clucked his gratitude, and Cowboy rode away.

Twenty-one days later there was a happy new chick in the nest. "This turned out wonderfully," Floria said to her mate.

"What shall we name her?" Doodledee asked back.

"The human who saved us was furry. Let's call our new chick Little Miss Furry."

"Love that!" the rooster father said with a cackle of rooster laughter, and bent over to gently peck her on the side of her head.

"Furry humans are the best!" the grateful hen said back.

104. **Bruce Visits Turco**

The Mexican Cowboy was annoyed. He had received a request from an old guy in the state of Washington he had never met or heard of. But the request had an interesting proposal in it, one that had never occurred to him before. This guy—named Bruce—said he wanted to come to Cowboy's ranch and have his picture taken with Turco and Cowboy, and explained why. Cowboy agreed to let him visit Turco. Anybody could of course, though usually only wild animals did.

On a lovely day in early June, with the purple mountains and cloud-traced sky beautiful to see, a little white Focus drove slowly onto the Cowboy's property and parked in front of the ranch house. Cowboy was sitting on the porch in his green rocker, watching a crippled man hesitantly climbing out of the driver's seat. The visitor waved at hand at Cowboy, though he was obviously having trouble lifting his arms. He said something also, but it was unintelligible to the Cowboy. But Cowboy could see that he had a warm smile on his face. He was a nice man, Cowboy could tell. Getting a walker out of the back seat of the Focus with great effort, Bruce walked with tiny steps in the direction of the Cowboy.

Cowboy realized there was no way this visitor could make it up the rail-less steps onto his porch, so he went down to meet him. "I see your car has a license plate from Washington. You must be Bruce," the Mexican Cowboy said, reaching out to shake his hand. His visitor tried to shake hands but he became tipsy when he let go of the walker's right handrail. "Let's get back into your car," Cowboy said. "I'll drive you down to my stable." Bruce nodded and Cowboy helped him get into the passenger side of the car, then folded and put his walker onto the back seat.

Cowboy hated cars usually, but for a reason he couldn't understand he liked the interior of the Focus. He did though want to slam his fist through the giant screen on the dash when a mechanical woman's voice kept insisting, "Tell me your name, new driver. Tell me your name new driver." His passenger tapped a hard-to-find 'button' on the screen and the bossy woman shut up. "Thank you," Cowboy said. "She was making this short drive miserable."

"She makes my drives miserable too," Bruce said almost clearly enough to be understood.

At the barn the Mexican Cowboy offered to help his new friend sit onto a bench across from Turco's stall. But before he sat, his visitor limped across the aisle to Turco and, with his hands by his side and wobbling, he waited for the magnificent wild mustang with the odd white stripe on his left side to decide whether he wanted to spend time with this stranger. Surprisingly, Turco reached out, looked the visitor up and down, and then put his head down so the stranger could pat him. Realizing that the man needed to hold on to the stall door separating them, Turco slowly backed away from his visitor. Holding on to the stall door, Bruce stood there for several minutes, saying things that Cowboy couldn't

understand. Oddly though, Turco was frequently nodding, and seemed to be making sense of what the mumbling visitor was saying.

At the other end of the barn there was a wall plastered with pictures of Cowboy and Turco, some of the two of them in the famous Parade the Cowboy led riding Turco. Cowboy opened the stall, Turco came out and, with no bit in his mouth, the stallion led the slow moving man to the wall and turned around in front of the pictures. Bruce put his walker aside, limped over to Turco, and stood beside him, trying to brace himself with an arm over the tall stallion's back. Turco invisibly moved his front hooves apart and bent his front knees, to lower himself and be better for the broken man's reach. Steady now, Bruce reached into his pocket and handed Cowboy a small camera to take pictures with. "Looks simple enough," Cowboy said. "Hold on. I'll be back in a moment."

With both legs trembling, Bruce waited anxiously for Cowboy to return. The wait was long for him, but actually in less than two minutes Cowboy returned with a little, white, fuzzy dog behind him, and an orange cat leading the way. Cowboy picked up Mazzie the dog and put her onto Turco's back. Turco was smiling. Mazzie licked Bruce's hand to greet him. Then Cowboy picked up Calli the orange cat, and gently put her onto Bruce's shoulder against Turco. Then Cowboy stepped back and began saying things in sounds Bruce didn't grasp, but which he gathered were instructions for picture taking. Mazzie bent toward Bruce. Calli opened her mouth and tried to put a human-like smile on her face. Bruce stood up as straight as he could, gripped Turco tighter and smiled, while Cowboy snapped picture after picture.

Then Cowboy helped Bruce back to the bench he needed to rest on. Breathing heavily, the barn's visitor sat down. Calli jumped into his lap and began purring. Cowboy lifted Mazzie from Turco and put her on the bench next to his visitor. With Turco's head in reach, Bruce patted each of the animals, while thanking Cowboy and Turco for the appreciative warmth they had shown him. "Turco, you are magnificent!" Cowboy said. "And you two are wonderful also!" Bruce said gratefully to Mazzie and Calli.

Several minutes later Cowboy and his visitor drove away from the barn.

"Now, tell me what was all that about?" Calli asked Mazzie.

"I think our nice visitor wanted a picture of all of us together to send to his daughter Kaiti for her birthday," Mazzie answered.

"She loves horses," Turco said, stretching over his stall door.

"I hope she will love all of us," Calli said.

"At least we all will still love each other," Mazzie said.

Turco whinnied and nodded. Mazzie barked softly and joyfully.

And Calli added, "Each one of us wants Kaiti to have a joy-filled birthday!" Turco whinnied long and loudly, Calli mewed, and Mazzie barked her birthday wishes for Kaiti.

In his cabin, on his Verizon smartphone, the Mexican Cowboy was texting Kaiti "Happy Birthday" too.

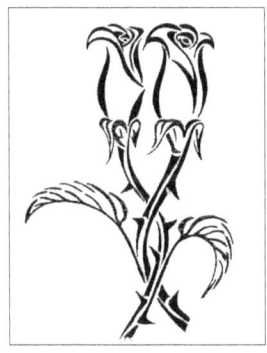

About the Author

Bruce Saunders is a retired, world-linked sociologist, born in and loving the American Southwest. A citizen of the earth by first grade he had lived in five major American cities. At sixteen he was a world traveler; flying in a small plane from Austin to Peru, living for a summer in Guatemala, and traveling to England and Ireland before he hit junior high. From Reed College in Portland where he received his BA in philosophy, he entered UC Berkeley at a critical time in the counterculture revolution. He acquired a PhD in Sociology, and focused his research on alternative lifestyles. He later taught at Penn State and the University of Washington. As a clinical sociologist like his father, who helped slow world population  growth, Bruce helped form the Clinical Sociology Association and, with two others, established a world-based corporation applying sociology to business problems.

About the Book

Bruce then developed a worldwide study of the different contributions of secular and religious rural schools to rural development and economic uplifting. In early spring of 2013, Mr. Saunders was diagnosed with fast-moving Amyotrophic Lateral Sclerosis. *Bruce's Fables* is a companion volume to *The Mexican Cowboy, Coyote, and The Thing in the Sky*. The Fables are set in the Rio Grande valley and Manzano mountains south of Albuquerque. The characters are numerous and include The Mexican Cowboy, his beloved friend Coyote, Father Gallapo and the woman who looks after his church. Bruce's Fables are set in the Rio Grande valley and Manzano Mountains south of Albuquerque. Also running rampant in these tales are a local mayor, a city council and police chief, Cowboy's lady friends, and a boy who may be the Cowboy's son. No set of fables detailing the American character would be complete without a drunk driver, an assassin, a glider pilot, teachers and high school students. This book of fables samples the minds of a variety of animals: a mustang and burro, a cat, a dog, and a mouse, green shell turtles, badger, raccoon, beaver, pronghorn antelopes, does and fawns, bear and her cub, mountain lion, fish, queen bees. Unexpectedly terrific individuals, including a music composer, a very ill person, the best bio engineer in the world, and even a battalion of United States Marines, deliver equally unexpected pieces of wisdom.

About the Artist—Thom Laz

I was born in Chicago on October 4, 1944—before the bomb—and came to the countryside on the foothills of Mt. Pilchuck after the war. Art, nature, and daydreaming are favorite escapes. We are all artists and hopefully are allowed to play in our media, whatever they may be. As artists, our responsibility is to do justice by honing our tools and skills, then using them. Joy in the act of creation is the first reward—sharing it is the best. This shared joy I offer to you to enrich this delicious tale.

I have dabbled in wood carving, jewelry, block prints, photography, poetry, writing, hot glass, stained glass, fabric design, and printing, followed by clothing design and construction. I have yet to meet a medium that couldn't excite me, so, in 1984 when good fortune landed me in Bali (where art is part of the religion), I became zealous in my craft. I returned to my floating home (purchased in 1968 – a very good year) three years later, where I live with my wife, daughter and three cats. It has been a year since my two dogs, with whom I shared life for almost 15 years, passed, so Coyote re-warmed my Canid connection.

Jack brought me in to this project by introducing me to Bruce, a kindred spirit, who with one paragraph sucked me into this story. I could sketch scores of illustrations for this rich adventure, but Bruce brought up a convincing deadline. I hope I do the story justice with these characters I offer here. Travel is the best teacher and the class room the best stone to sharpen the tools discovered. So enjoy as you are schooled on this imaginative journey.

I thank, Jack, Bruce, and Dana, for feedback, encouragement, and keeping me focused and on track. Truly, thom

About the Editor – Dana Gaskin Wenig

My love of words and their meanings, reading, and writing, led me to editing. In high school I worked in book publishing, in my thirties, as a new mother in Seattle, I edited a quarterly parenting 'zine, Kangaroo Kids. I earned my editing certificate from the University of Washington Professional & Continuing Education program and studied Developmental Editing with Barbara Sjoholm.

I'm so glad I found Louisa's Writers, hosted by Louisa's Café, facilitated by Robert Ray and Jack Remick. I am deeply grateful to Jack for recommending me to his friend of thirty-five years, Bruce Saunders, I'm humbled that Bruce trusted me with his story, and I'm in awe of Thom for his ability to make Bruce's characters visible. Thanks to the gods for this slice of time and learning with this small group of creative collaborators.

I live in Shoreline, Washington, with my husband of 21 years, our 19-year-old daughter, two dogs, and two cats.

Index

www.ingramcontent.com/pod-product-compliance
Lightning Source LLC
Chambersburg PA
CBHW080755120626
46557CB00006B/1281